# THE HORSE
# THIEVES

Center Point
Large Print

**This Large Print Book carries the
Seal of Approval of N.A.V.H.**

# THE
# HORSE
# THIEVES

## Giles Tippette

CENTER POINT LARGE PRINT
THORNDIKE, MAINE

This Center Point Large Print edition
is published in the year 2017 by arrangement with
Betsyanne Tippette.

The text of this Large Print edition is unabridged.
In other aspects, this book may vary
from the original edition.
Printed in the United States of America
on permanent paper.
Set in 16-point Times New Roman type.

ISBN: 978-1-68324-282-6

Library of Congress Cataloging-in-Publication Data

Names: Tippette, Giles, author.
Title: The horse thieves / Giles Tippette.
Description: Center Point Large Print edition. | Thorndike, Maine :
Center Point Large Print, 2017.
Identifiers: LCCN 2016049578 | ISBN 9781683242826
    (hardcover : alk. paper)
Subjects: LCSH: Grayson, Warner (Fictitious character)—Fiction. |
Large type books. | GSAFD: Western stories.
Classification: LCC PS3570.I6 H67 2017 | DDC 813/.54—dc23
LC record available at https://lccn.loc.gov/2016049578

To Owen Laster
12-24-68
Approx. 2:25 P.M. C.S.T.

# THE HORSE
# THIEVES

# 1

He saw the horse just as he was beginning to be afraid that he wasn't going to make it. He'd dropped to his knees the instant he was sure it was a horse he was seeing and then remained there, motionless in the sand and rocks and cactus, for fear he might spook the horse. The horse was his last chance. By the sun it was sometime in the early afternoon. He'd been hobbling along on his burned and bloody feet ever since dawn, ever since the *bandidos* had ridden away and left him to die.

Now he watched the horse at what he reckoned was a distance of about two hundred yards. The horse was gnawing at the bark of a little mesquite tree. The tree, and a few others like it, were the only things that appeared alive in the harsh and barren south Texas prairie. Except for a few rises and, here and there, a thin and shallow gully, the prairie was flat and nearly empty of any cover that would help him to stalk the horse and get close enough to have any chance of catching the animal. The whole country, at least as far as he could see, was just a big alkali flat growing nothing but rocks and cactus and a few mesquite trees and huisache and some greasewood brush and the dried stubble of last year's buffalo grass.

He was motionless, watching the horse and slowly working the pebble around in his mouth. He'd been sucking on the stone for the last couple of hours. Some fool had started the rumor that you could start the saliva flowing by sucking on a pebble. He was here to give the lie to that rumor. He spit out the pebble, but very carefully so as not to make any motion or movement that would draw the horse's attention.

His name was Warner Grayson. He was twenty-eight years old and he was closer to dying than he'd ever been in his wild young life. The only thing in his favor was that he knew more about horses than most people who'd ever lived. He was a horseman; it was his business and his calling and his pleasure. In a little while it might also be decided if it was his salvation.

He studied the horse through the clear air, watching its every move, calculating on just what kind of a horse it was; whether it was wild or a runaway using horse, what it was doing in such a godforsaken place and how spooky or nervous it was. It was the last days of winter, late February, but it wasn't cold. It was almost never cold in that country down near the border. What it mainly was was hot and dry and merciless.

For the time being he was content to just study the horse. But he knew he was going to have to make some sort of move pretty soon. He was already very weak and he knew he wasn't going to get stronger sucking on pebbles and kneeling in the sand. But he figured he was going to have one chance at the horse and he knew he had better make it work. So, as fuzzy as his mind was from the bad treatment his body had received, he tried to carefully think out an approach to the horse.

One thing he'd decided—the horse must be as lost and desperate as he was if it was gnawing at the bark of a winter dead mesquite. In the spring and summer the mesquite tree put out pods of mesquite beans that horses and cattle both liked, but this mesquite tree had nothing to offer the horse except the illusion he was getting something to eat. The animal would have been just as well off trying to crop at the stubble of dried-up buffalo grass. At least he'd have gotten a little sand to swallow for his troubles.

The horse had worked his way around the gnarled tree until his back was to Warner. What little breeze there was, was in Warner's favor, blowing into his face from the horse.

He decided to try and cover most of the distance on his hands and knees. It would at least give a little rest to his blistered and bloody feet. The Mexican desperadoes had held them to the fire the night before just to see the expression on his face when he tried not to give them the satisfaction of hearing him scream. But they'd laughed just as hard as he'd writhed and jerked and clenched his teeth. They'd gotten one hell of a good time out of searing the soles of his bare feet.

He started forward, crawling slowly and carefully yet still cutting his hands on the jagged rocks that hid in the sand. There was a danger in crawling on all fours. The horse might look around and take him for a wolf or a coyote and spook. But there was also a drawback to walking upright. He couldn't walk properly. He had to hobble and the horse, with a horse's poor eyesight, would not see a man but some strange and scary beast hobbling and weaving toward him. Warner knew from long experience that horses could get some strange ideas into their heads and do just about everything you hadn't figured on.

He kept his head down as he crawled, afraid to look up, afraid if he did the horse would have vanished. Occasionally his knees found sharp-thorned cockleburs or rocks or spiney cactus just hidden under the sand. He took the pain without a murmur, afraid to make the least sound. All the *bandidos* had left him were his jeans and the torn flannel shirt he was wearing. That and his hat. It was a good hat and the only reason they hadn't taken it was because they'd sailed it up in the air for meanness and for target practice and then had lost interest after a while and forgotten about it.

Now, after only about a hundred yards of crawling he could feel the knees wearing out of his jeans. They'd been worn before, but worn in the places a horseman's britches got worn, on the inside of the legs. Not much on the seat because he rode as befitted a horseman, with most of the weight on his feet in the stirrups. Only a green-horn plopped his weight right down on a horse's back.

The shirt was just ragged where the *bandidos* had ripped it jerking him around. There was a cut in the right waist where one of them had taken a swipe at Warner with his knife. He'd cut Warner, but the cut hadn't been very deep and it had bled enough that Warner could hope it wouldn't get infected.

Now, when he'd come what he figured was half the distance to the horse, he very cautiously raised his head. The animal was still there only now he'd left off gnawing at the tree and was smelling around on the ground looking for anything that might act like fodder. It worried Warner. If the horse started ground hunting he'd begin to wander. So long as he kept after the mesquite tree he'd stay in one place.

And that was important because Warner knew he didn't have the strength for an extended stalk of the horse.

He stayed still for a moment, resting and studying the horse. He could see, now that he was closer, that the horse was slipping his hair, losing his winter coat. That was something Warner, with all his years around horses, could

13

never understand. What did a horse who lived in a climate where it never got much below fifty degrees and might be ninety degrees in December, need with a winter coat? But they all did it. He'd seen horses shipped up from South America arrive with a winter coat and not slip it until the first signs of spring. And this horse looked to be losing enough horsehair to stuff a fair-size mattress ticking.

There was something else about the horse Warner couldn't figure. The horse had now turned in silhouette to him and Warner was damned if he'd ever seen a horse with just such a conformation. He was a beautifully lined horse with a high hindquarter and a big, arched neck. He wasn't quarter horse and he wasn't American saddlebred or thoroughbred, and he sure as hell wasn't mustang or range horse. The horse was blooded stock; Warner could see that in his lines. But he was damned if he knew what breed. He'd seen an Arabian stallion once and the horse came closer to looking like the Arabian than anything else he could think of. But then, he thought to himself, what would a high-priced animal like an Arabian be doing in one of the worst patches of country in the world?

He gave up wondering what breed the horse was. There'd be time enough to think about that if and when he had the horse in hand. He put his head back down and began to crawl again, slower this time, toward the horse. Every movement was painful. His hands, his knees, his side, his face, and especially the soles of his feet throbbed and ached. But he tried not to think about the pain just as he tried not to think about the Mexican bandits who'd robbed him and tortured him and killed his partner. The first thing was to catch the horse and somehow find food and water, especially water. After that, after he was sure he was going to survive, would come the proper time to think of the bandits.

His thirst was beyond torture. It was weakening him the most. That morning, just before they had ridden out, the Mexicans had made him drink water until he could swallow no more. Then two had held him while others took turns punching him in the stomach until he'd thrown up all the water he'd drunk plus everything else that had been in his stomach. It had been a cruel trick, one calculated to make him even more dehydrated than if he'd never had any water at all. They had emptied him out as cleanly as if he'd been a barrel and they'd turned him upside down.

After he calculated he'd gone another fifty yards he carefully lifted his head. The horse was looking straight at him, switching his ears back and forth and twitching his nose. Warner froze. He stayed just as he was, with his head not quite all the way up and his right hand on a sharp rock that was digging into his palm.

The horse was even closer than he'd thought, maybe only thirty yards away. Warner couldn't see a brand because the horse was facing him, but he could see that the horse was wearing a halter. The horse definitely belonged to someone though how he'd managed to stray into such a piece of country was more than Warner could guess. The nearest town was Del Rio, on the border, about thirty-five miles away. The nearest water that could be counted on was the Rio Grande which was easily twenty miles away. He and the horse were in the big middle of an alkali flat that was some fifteen miles across. It was a badlands area you crossed with plenty of water and provisions, getting across it as fast as you could. It wasn't a piece of country for a highbred horse to be wandering around in even if he was as dumb as most horses were. And no man entered it crippled and afoot unless he was unwillingly put down in its midst by *bandidos* who thought it would be more of a pleasure to let him slowly die of thirst and hunger than to give him an easy out with a bullet. He reckoned he was paying for his partner's grit and courage and fight. They'd had no choice but to shoot Red because Red hadn't believed they just wanted to come into their camp to rest and smoke and drink a little tequila and then be on their way. So Red had gone for his revolver the first time he saw one of them flash iron and they'd had to shoot him. At least

Red had got one of them and that one had died.

But it had made them mad as hell at Warner, and they'd spent most of the night showing him just how angry they were. He reckoned if they hadn't been more interested in drinking tequila and examining the little herd of trading horses that he and Red had put together to start the season with, they'd have probably killed him before, one by one, they'd either passed out or given in to sleep.

Now he and the horse stared at each other. The horse flicked his ears back and forth and switched his tail, obviously confused by this strange looking thing that had come upon him but not sure if he should be frightened or just curious.

After a moment or two of the staring the horse took a tentative step toward Warner. Warner held his breath. Wouldn't it be wonderful if this horse was so lonesome and in need of a guiding hand that he'd just walk up and let Warner take him by the halter?

But it was not to be that easy. After only a few steps the horse stopped and stood there, switching his tail. The switching was a sign of nervousness, uncertainty. Warner didn't like to see it. An uncertain horse, a nervous horse, could spook at any second and run off to such a distance that Warner would never again have the strength to come up to him.

It had to be now. He stared at the horse, trying

to think of the best way to get his hand on the horse's halter. The palm of his hand was almost itching for the feel of that halter. The horse was still looking at him, but now his tail was twitching harder and harder. Warner knew he didn't have much time.

And then he had a thought. This was a blooded horse, this was a horse that was most likely used to barn care. If that was the case this horse knew what a feed bucket was, knew what grain sounded like when it was swished around in a feed bucket. Warner, through the years, had called up many a horse out of a big pasture with nothing more than the sound of oats being swished around in a feed bucket. Maybe this horse was domesticated enough and hungry enough and curious enough to respond to such a sound. Right then it didn't make much difference because this was a horse that was about to bolt and this horse represented the difference between life and death for him. With this horse he could make it to the Rio Grande. With this horse he could make it out of the alkali flat. Without this horse he was dead.

Moving very slowly, very carefully, he put his hand up and gently took off his light tan, wide-brimmed, high-crowned Stetson ten X beaver hat that had cost him $20.50, the most money he'd ever paid for a hat in his life. The hat was still whole, though a little battered from being run over by the *bandidos'* horses, but they'd been such bad shots that none of them had been able to hole it when they'd sailed it up in the air and then tried to hit it with revolver shots.

Keeping his eyes on the horse, trying to physically will the horse to hold still, he held his hat, crown down, with his right hand while he gingerly groped around on the ground for small pebbles and what little of the buffalo grass he could pull up. Still looking at the horse he put the pebbles and the grass and what sand came with them in the head hole of his hat. He kept doing that until he thought he had enough trash material in his hat to make the sound he wanted. When he was satisfied he had enough "grain" for the proper effect he slowly began to stand up. The horse had slowed the switching of his tail, which was a good sign, but his ears were still rotating around the way a horse's did when he was nervous or sensed a danger he couldn't quite identify.

Finally, Warner was on his feet. For a second his head swam so that he thought he was going to drop over in a faint. But he clenched his jaw and bit his lip and, gradually, the dizzy spell passed.

When he was sure he was fairly solid on his feet he took a tentative step or two forward, just to see how the horse would react. The horse just stared at him. Warner took another couple of steps and began to whistle lowly and steadily, not trying to whistle any tune, just trying to catch the horse's attention and hold it, get him used to his, Warner's, presence. He took a couple more steps forward. The horse lifted his head and his nostrils began to twitch. His tail started swishing harder. Warner stopped dead in his tracks. He said, in a low voice, "'At's a boy. Good horse. Good horse. Hold right still, now. Got some oats for you. Got some good grain." Very slowly he began shaking his hat back and forth. He didn't want to scare the horse with the motion of the hat before the sound of the "grain" being swished back and forth could reach the horse's ears.

It really didn't sound much like grain in a tin bucket. The hat deadened the sand. Warner swished harder. The horse suddenly pricked his ears forward, listening for the sound coming from Warner's hat. Warner said softly, "Come on, you barn baby. Come on, come on here. Got some oats for you. This is a big bucket of oats. Reckon you've come to this sound before."

He swished the hat harder. Now, finally, it sounded a little like oats. But he should have put in more sand and been more patient about grubbing up some of the dried grass or finding some twigs or something.

But the horse was reacting. He'd quit switching his tail back and forth and had taken a step toward Warner. Warner very carefully closed the gap with two steps of his own. The horse took another step toward him, obviously now very interested.

It was taking too long. Warner could feel his strength going fast. To keep from swaying or stumbling or making any kind of move that would frighten the horse he was having to keep rigid control over his body and that was rapidly using up all his strength. He was breathing as hard as if he'd just run ten miles or swum a river. The hand holding the hat was beginning to shake, his knees were beginning to tremble. He thought, *Not now, son, you got to hold on. You got to hold on!*

The horse took another step. Only a few yards separated the two of them now. Warner could see the big, liquid eyes in the Arabian-looking face of the animal. Now he could plainly see that the horse was pretty badly worn down himself. The loose winter hair had covered up the horse's thinness, but now Warner could see that the horse was nearly in as much need of a meal and some water as he was. It was, he thought, probably what was making the horse less cautious, less suspicious. Hunger, Warner knew, would do that. You could about catch wild mustangs with a little bit of hay if you kept them on the run and didn't give them a chance to stop and eat. Warner had done it plenty of times, just set out with a saddlebag full of fragrant hay and a string of good saddle horses. Switch off horses and run the mustangs until they'd almost come up and take the hay out of your hand—while you were putting a loop around their neck with the other.

He said, his voice faint, "Come on here, you old fool. Come on, horse. Please God, come on, you dumb ol' horse. Come here an' get these here oats . . ."

The horse was now only a step away, leaning forward, his neck arched and outstretched, his big nostrils flared and snuffling toward the hat. He was achingly close. Warner had to resist the urge to drop the hat and make a grab for the horse's halter. If he did the horse would react and jerk back and Warner knew he wouldn't have the strength to hold him. He had to will himself to continue creeping slowly forward, talking softly to the horse and keeping the hat in his right hand back enough so that he could slowly extend his left hand toward the halter.

The horse suddenly snorted and Warner's heart almost stopped. He stayed frozen, not even daring to blink. But the horse wasn't spooked, he'd just snorted, maybe from blowing sand or something. Warner rattled the hat again and said, softly, "Com'on, boy, it's oats. I swear it's oats. Been a long time since you've had any oats by the look of you. Or a good grooming or a night in a barn. Or maybe even some water. But I know where the water is and we'll both go and get us some if you'll just stay right steady."

The horse was not particularly big; Warner judged him to be about sixteen-and-a-half hands high and something short of a thousand pounds. But he could see that what was there was all muscle and quality conformation.

The horse's muzzle was only two feet from the hat. By turning his body to his left Warner was able to bring his left hand within a foot of the side strap of the halter. He knew, once the horse got his muzzle inside his hat, he was going to have one mighty disappointed horse on his hands. For that reason he wanted to have touched the horse and soothed him before they got to the fact that there wasn't anything inside his hat but what could be found on the ground.

Warner was close enough now he could see his reflection in the horse's intelligent-looking brown eyes. He stretched out the fingers of his left hand and very gently stroked the horse above the nose, working his fingers around toward the side of the horse's head to where the halter strap was. He kept talking to the horse, gentling him, reassuring him.

The horse stepped forward and plunged his nose into Warner's hat. At that instant Warner gently grasped the side strap of the halter. For a second he continued to hold the hat so the horse could nose around in it. Finally the horse lifted his head and looked at Warner. Warner said softly, "That's right. Ain't no oats. But I promise you, if you can get us out of this I'll buy you some oats and a barn and a ranch if you want it."

Then he dropped the hat and took hold of the halter with both hands. The horse just stood there, not moving, acting very gentle. Warner let out a long, slow breath. And then he began trembling. For a second he sagged down, letting some of his weight drag on the horse's halter. He stayed like that for a long moment, a tall, slim young man of just over six feet with light brownish hair and clear hazel eyes that were now dulled with pain and fatigue. Usually his face had a boyish cast, but now it was drawn and wan and he looked even slimmer than his normal 170 pounds.

But, finally, he straightened and set his shoulders. The horse stood patiently, waiting to see what was to come next. Warner breathed deeply, taking air into his lungs in big gulps even though it hurt his ribs and stomach muscles where they'd pounded on him. Warner was much stronger than he looked. He'd been working horses since he was twelve years old. He was wide shouldered for a man of his weight and slim hipped. Most of his weight was in his shoulders and his arms and his chest and hands. He had big, capable, gentle hands that horses liked. Now he used them to reassure the horse as he slowly looked up in the sky. He said, "Thank you, God. I really appreciate it."

Then he began to allow himself the privilege of rage. Before, after they'd dumped him off in the alkali flat to die, he'd had to use all his concentration and energy and thought on surviving and somehow making it out of the badlands alive. He couldn't think about the *bandidos* then, couldn't afford to spend an ounce of energy on hate and rage, couldn't cloud his thinking with anything but thoughts of survival.

But now he had the horse and he had a way out, a way back to life. The horse, against all reason, had been there to save his life. He was going to save the horse's life and his own in the bargain.

So he stood, enjoying letting the cold, hard rage build. He and the horse would make it to the Rio Grande where he'd get water and food for both of them, and then he'd get reoutfitted and go hunting. Warner Grayson had never shot a man in his life, had never, in fact, ever even shot *at* a man. But all that was going to change. He said, as if he were still soothing the horse, "I know me six sonsabitches is going to die. And they are going to die hard. I just pray that nobody gets to them bastards before I do. Lord, don't even let 'em get a bad head cold. I want 'em just enjoying the hell out of life when I find them, just like me and Red was doing when they come in amongst us."

The words sounded oddly loud in the stillness of the arid plains. The horse stomped a foot as if impatient to get on with whatever was to come next. Warner patted him. He said, "That's all right, ol' pony. I'll tell you all about it while I get you rigged up. Say, what kind of horse are you, anyway? Never saw your like before. But you look like a horse might enjoy a little hunting."

In all his life Warner Grayson didn't reckon he'd ever been so glad to have hold of a horse and that covered a whole countryside full of horses. They'd been his life since he was twelve. By the time he was fourteen he was already a professional, breaking broncs, gentling them, teaching them, retraining using horses, taking the rough spots off workhorses, selling them, trading them, breeding them, buying them. By the time he was twenty he was already known throughout most of' south and southeastern Texas as a man who could fix your horse or fit you out with one that would get you through more than one storm. By the time he was twenty-four he'd managed to buy a little ranch of some five hundred acres on the Nueces River just fifteen miles from the coastal town of Corpus Christi. It had been an ambitious undertaking for a young man with no backing and no way of earning money except with his knowledge of horses. But he'd taken the risk and had immediately set about a program of trying to perfect the ideal cow horse by crossing Morgans and quarter horses and American saddlebreds. It had been nip and tuck and he'd finally had to resort to a side business to keep up the payments on his ranch and the breeding stock he was buying.

He offered a unique service to the ranchers in south Texas and one that had never been attempted before. During the winter, when they got little or no use, the cow horses were let out to roam the range and they tended to forget that they'd ever been domesticated. By the time it came to start getting ready for the heavy spring work, most of the horses had gotten snorty and developed a hump in their backs and an itch to pitch, especially first thing of a frosty morning. It was a chore that the cowhands had been reluctantly doing themselves until Warner had come along and offered to take the "bark" off the whole remuda and start the rancher off with a set of good, gentled working horses that wouldn't be pitching cowboys off and getting them stove up and hurt and just generally delaying the business of the ranch.

It had been a success from the start. Most of the cowboys had anywhere from eight to twelve horses in their string and there might be ten or fifteen cowhands on some of the bigger ranches. Then there was the matter of new broncs that had to be taught that bucking wasn't going to get them anywhere and that they might as well settle down and learn to be useful. Warner had started off charging two dollars a head to get spoiled horses back in shape and six dollars to change broncs into saddle horses. The first year he'd cleared nearly a thousand dollars and nearly killed himself with the work. If he hadn't had such a hand with horses the job would have taken twice as long and put a good many more bruises on Warner's body.

In his second year he found that some ranches had too many working horses and some not enough. With that as a beginning he started acting as a broker and a trader. Then, not long after that, he started taking along a few of his own horses, horses that were part of his breeding program, and selling them at a premium to the rancher or cowhand that wanted one absolutely top-notch horse in his string that could always be depended on, a night horse, a storm horse, a stampede horse.

About then Warner saw that the work was becoming too much for him and he'd taken Red Boyer on as a partner, not in his ranch, but in his custom shaping-up business. He'd been friendly with Red, as he was friendly with most people, but he hadn't taken on Red as a partner because he was such a particularly good friend; he'd asked Red in for the simple reason that Red was good with horses. That was Warner's approach to most everything—you did the simplest matter in the simplest way and didn't try and complicate it with any unnecessary confusion. That's the way he worked horses, simple and straightforward. Horses seemed to appreciate it and he reckoned most people did also.

Some folks called Warner a bronc tamer, a wrangler, a horse handler, a lot of things. But to himself he was a horseman, just a horseman.

# 2

The *bandidos* had ridden into their camp just about the time they were finishing supper, just at that hour of twilight when it isn't exactly dark and yet not light enough to see much more than indistinct shapes. They'd had a good fire going, built out of cow chips and some downed mesquite limbs they'd picked up along the way. They'd bought a half a beef hindquarter off a rancher earlier in the day and had cut steaks and roasted them over the coals along with a pot of beans and some coffee. The weather had been cool enough that they'd figured to get three or four days' worth of meals off the beef before it began to go bad. They'd been on the road for three days, making good time, coming from their head-quarters on the Nueces River near Corpus Christi heading for a ranch near Del Rio to begin their end of winter's work.

They'd been able to hear the sound of the *bandidos* coming for some little time, but they hadn't known who they were or how many they were until they'd suddenly broken the circle of light of their campfire. And, of course, they still hadn't known that the men were bandits, not then. They'd looked like seven rough, mean looking Mexicans, no oddity in that part of Texas. Still, they'd given each other looks of warning, him and Red, as the men had ridden in and sat their horses, looking down at the fire. The one in front had been a fat Mexican with a bandolier across his chest and a knife scar from his right ear, down his cheek, and halfway down his neck. It had been an ugly, raised, red-looking scar. He'd said, his little pig eyes in his fat face looking all around, "Say, what chou got heer, sum fine caballeros? See theese fine horses. Theese mens are caballeros."

He'd been referring to their trading stock which they'd picketed on a single rope up near the camp. But his words meant that the *bandidos* had circled them, scouted them, before riding into camp because only their saddle horses and the packhorse had been inside the firelight. Warner and Red had stood up slowly. Red was still wearing his sidearm, but Warner had taken off his gun belt as being too cumbersome for the business of cooking and eating and had stowed it in his bedroll that was laid out a little way back from the fire.

The fat horseman said, "Say, what chou do weeth so meeny fine horses? For chust two mens?"

Warner and Red had tried to act casual, tried not to show any fear. Red had said, "The others are out gatherin' up firewood. They'll be along directly."

The *bandidos* had begun to fan out, half circling the fire. They were on one side of the circle of firelight and Red and Warner were on the other. The man with the scar laughed. He said, "Ah doan see but two saddles. Theese odder men, dey ride weethout the saddle?"

Warner said, "They're on their way. They're bringing other horses. They ought to be here any minute. We're taking a big horse herd down south. We're out in front, picking the path. That's why our fire is so big, so they can find us."

But he could see the bandit leader hadn't believed him. The man was wearing a sombrero, as were some of the others. But others were dressed pretty much as they were, in jeans and flannel shirts and boots and high-crowned Western hats. But Warner could see more guns than a friendly party of travelers usually carried.

The scar-faced man laughed again. He said, "So, chou bring six or seben horses ahead to find the trail. Then the others come with the beeg herd, eh?" He laughed. "That preeety funny." He looked at them, taking note that Warner was unarmed. "Say, chou know they es a lot of *bandidos* around theese country. You must be beery brave men to come by chouselves. Theese es beery dangerous because of theese *bandidos*. Chou have all these fine horses. *Bandidos* steel horses, chou know."

Then, without being asked, he and the rest of

his men began to dismount. Warner took a step closer to Red. They glanced at each other. They could feel the trouble growing and closing in. Warner glanced back at his bedroll and estimated the distance as too great to just sort of saunter over and pick up a gun. His idea was to treat the Mexicans friendly and show them the customary hospitality of the road until they did something that made it clear they meant mischief. Warner's general policy was to put a good face on matters and hope for the best. But he knew, with a sinking heart, that they were more than likely in trouble. He figured the best they could hope for was that the Mexicans would simply steal their horses and leave them in peace.

Now the Mexicans had drawn closer to the fire and were squatting around it in a semicircle, passing a couple of tequila bottles back and forth. The scar-faced one offered the bottle to Warner, but he just shook his head. He said, "Don't reckon so. That Rio Grande pepper juice is a mite strong for me."

The fat Mexican had a gold tooth. Now that he was near the fire Warner could see it gleaming in the light. His face went angry when Warner turned down the tequila. He said, "Chou doan wan' to dreenk weeth us? Chou sum gringo theenk he too good to drink weeth a poor Mesican?"

Warner had said, "Ain't that. Just ain't thirsty."

One of the other men said something in rapid

Spanish. Warner spoke enough of the language to know the man was asking what they had to eat. Their tin plates were clearly obvious, just back from the fire and the coffeepot was still sitting on some embers that had been pulled back from the fire. The scar-faced one said, "Say, what chou got to eat por sum poor Mesicans? Chou got *carne*?" He gestured toward their tin plates where some well-gnawed beef bones could be seen. "Chou eat *carne*. Maybe chou got no *carne por* poor Mesicans."

The man was goading them. Warner looked beyond the circle of sneering faces and looked at the men's horses. All of them looked ridden down and underfed. He doubted a one of them had seen grain since coming under the grip of its present owner. The country they were in was poor, but there was some fair grazing a few miles south where the country began to improve as it headed toward the Rio Grande. But that was to the southwest. To get to Del Rio he and Red were going to have to cross the edge of the alkali flat they knew so well. In fact, they were camped just on the edge of it, the idea being to get the horses well watered and well fed and then hurry through the trackless land for the twenty miles of it they'd have to cross.

But, Warner thought, as he watched the Mexicans eyeing their saddle horses and the packhorse, their plans might be about to change.

The quarter of beef was wrapped in oilcloth and had been put away in the tarp of the packsaddle. Now one of the Mexicans got up and walked past Red and went over to where the packsaddle was lying on the ground and began pulling loose the canvas cover. Red turned around. He said, "Here! What the hell you think you be a-doin'? Ain't nobody invited you to supper. Wait till yore ast."

Warner said softly, "Red . . . take it easy."

But Red was a different man than Warner. His hair wasn't all that red, more rust colored, but his temper was bright red.

Red took two steps over to where the man was working at the packsaddle canvas and grabbed him by the arm and jerked him back. He said, "Goddamit, hold on. Ain't you got no manners?"

The man whirled and, all of a sudden, there was a knife in his hand. Red had stepped back quickly. His hand had started toward his holster. Warner had yelled, "Red!"

His partner had looked across at him. Then his eyes had strayed toward the other Mexicans. He let his hand drop by his side, away from the handle of his revolver. But he said to Warner, "Hell, do we intend to jest let 'em rob us?"

The fat leader said, "Say, what chou fren theenk? He say we *bandidos*? He ain't so beery nice."

Warner turned back to him. "Well, the man was

going into our pack. He ought to at least ask first."

The Mexicans were facing him. The fat one smiled slowly, his gold tooth gleaming. He said, "Hey, gringo, I doan theenk they es eeny odder mens. I theenk you try an' fool me. Eh?"

Warner swallowed slowly. It was beginning to look plain·that they were in for it. He had turned back to Red in time to see the Mexican with the knife begin to saw at one of the ropes of the diamond hitch that held the pack to the packsaddle. He had seen Red glance his way again, had been able to clearly see the anger rising in Red's face. And he'd known what it meant. He and Red had been partners for three years and he knew that there came a time when Red Boyer just didn't give a damn anymore. Warner had seen that look on his face once when Red had taken on four men in a fistfight. He'd gotten the hell beat out of him—and out of Warner too—but for Red there had been no other way.

Warner had known that it wouldn't be a fistfight they'd be having with these Mexicans. He took a couple of steps backward, sort of casually trying to get near his bedroll and his revolver without appearing to be after anything. But he knew he wasn't going to make it in time. He had said, a little desperately, to the fat one, "You be wrong about our other partners. I'd bet they ain't no more than half a mile from here. Bringing in the big horse herd."

The Mexicans had slowly stood up. All of them except the fat one had been watching Red. The fat one smiled again. He'd said, "Oh, jess? Chou have theese frens who es coming? Chure, but I don't theenk you tell Chumacho de trooth. I theenk maybe you make the lie."

Warner had been half watching the Mexicans around the campfire with the other half of his attention on his partner and the *bandido* who was busy sawing away at one of the pack ropes. Red had glanced his way and he'd seen the anger just about to explode. He'd shook his head, but it was too late. Red had reached out and grabbed the Mexican again and jerked him away from the pack and whirled him around. Warner had seen the Mexican drop the knife and go for a pistol he had in his belt. Red had drawn and shot the Mexican dead center in the chest. Just before Warner had dived for his bedroll and his revolver he'd seen the Mexican go over backward from the force of the slug that had taken him in the chest. Then, an instant later, had come the fusillade of shots that had cut Red down from the back. He'd staggered forward a step and then gone down to his knees and then fallen face forward.

It was the dive toward his bedroll that Warner later figured had saved his life. He'd no more than landed on the ground, still a yard short of his bedroll, when the air where he'd been standing had been filled with whistling bullets. The Mexicans had shot Red and then turned, instinctively, to finish him off too. But the sight of him on the ground had made the fat one laugh and salvaged his life. Chumacho had said, "Look at dis one. He es no getting chot an' he fall down. He es so afraid of theese bullets he falls down from the *boom, boom*."

So, for that instant, the killing mood had been broken and his life had been spared. Besides, if they had killed him outright they couldn't have had as much fun with him as they'd had, off and on, through the night. Only once had he come near to being killed outright again and that had been when two of the *bandidos* had gotten into an argument about which one of them was the best knife thrower. To settle the argument they'd made Warner stand up as a target. Fortunately, they'd both been so drunk that only one had come near him, tearing his shirt and giving him the slight cut in his side. His biggest problem had been the humiliation of having to hunt for their knives in the dark and then to return them to the Mexicans so they could throw them at him again. He had begged to be allowed to bury Red, but they'd just slapped him around and finally let him roll Red's body out of the firelight. In the process he'd managed to get Red's wallet out of his pocket and hide it in his boot in case there were any names or addresses he could write to for Red—assuming he got out of the mess himself.

Of course that hadn't worked because they'd found the wallet when they made him take off his boots so they could scorch his feet. It had been Chumacho who had decided that the most fun would be not to kill him but to handicap him as bad as possible and then leave him in the alkali flat to die. The fat Mexican had told the others that they could have many laughs about that while they were selling "theese fine horses en Mesico." He had thanked Warner for, as he said, "Bringing to theese poor Mesican theese fine horses. Chou are a beery good *hombre* to bring Chumacho such a gift."

Of course they'd hacked up the beef and had themselves a feast. They'd taken out the rest of his and Red's supplies; their sugar and coffee and flour and salt and whatnot, and what they couldn't use or devour they scattered around in the dirt so it would be ruined. Every so often Chumacho would ask him when his "frens" were coming with the "beeg" horse herd, but, other than the occasional kick or slap they pretty much left him alone while they spent their time getting drunk and gorging on the beef and supplies he and Red had brought. He didn't know if it was out of meanness or design, but they wouldn't let him have so much as a drink of water or a bite of food all through the night. The only food he was able to get his hands on was a couple of fistfuls of oats that he and Red had brought for the horses, to sustain them and keep them on keen edge for the hard crossing of the alkali flats. The oats had been a puzzle to the *bandidos*. They couldn't conceive of anyone actually carrying grain for their horses. Their idea was that a horse ate what he found on the ground and, if he didn't find anything, he went without. Warner had watched in sadness and loss as their trading stock had been led into the firelight so that Chumacho could look the animals over. He knew he was seeing the animals fit and well cared for for the last time. A week under the Mexican's hands and they'd be as drawn down and used up as the *bandidos'* sorry-looking mounts.

In the first few hours, as the Mexicans had gotten drunker and sleepier, he'd entertained some thoughts of escape. He knew he could jump on any of the horses, bareback and with no bridle, and let the horse run in any direction and be able to hang on long enough to outrun any sort of chase the Mexicans might mount. But it soon became clear that while the fat leader acted and talked the fool there was nothing foolish about his leadership. If one man drank himself to sleep the fat one would kick a couple of others awake to take over the guard duties. There were always at least two or three of the *bandidos* with an eye on Warner. Sometimes they had amused themselves by kicking or slapping him just to see if they could get a reaction.

But Warner had taken it all quietly and stoically. He was a sensible young man, as intelligent as he was good-natured, and he could count. The day belonged to the *bandidos* and, if he were to ever have a day he was going to have to be patient and hang on somehow and survive. Getting angry was no answer, not against such odds. Red was proof of that. But, of course, if he'd been able to reach his weapon in time to help Red then he'd more than likely be lying alongside his partner.

But it hadn't fallen out that way, so the best he could do was resist the urge to fight back and bear with patience and stoicism whatever they cared to fling at him. It was the only way to survive and survival was the only chance he had to get even.

Of course he hadn't forseen what Chumacho had in store for him before they were to finally let him go. Dawn was just beginning to break when the game had turned serious. Warner had been lying on his bedroll, watchful, but trying to get what rest he could. Of course they had long ago shaken out his blanket and taken his revolver and his saddle carbine and the bottle of good whiskey he'd been having a quiet nip on every night before bedtime.

Then Chumacho had come up and squatted by Warner and looked at him and smiled big so that his gold tooth had glittered even without the firelight to spark it. He'd said, "I thin' chou are much too hoppy *por un gringo*. I thin' chou es wonderin' when we es goin' to keel chou. Do chou wonder that?"

Warner had said, as casually as he could, "I reckon you're gonna do what you want to do no matter what my selection might be in the matter." He'd deliberately yawned. "Six of ya'll and one of me. Ya'll are armed an' I ain't. What difference does it make what I wonder?"

But inside he was very afraid. He figured that they sure as hell would kill him. In fact he'd spent most of the night not wondering if, but when. That was when he hadn't been thinking about his partner. He'd run the action over in his mind a hundred times and he still couldn't see where he could have done ought else than what he had. He reckoned he was just feeling guilty about Red because his partner was dead and he wasn't. But, well, he figured ol' Chumacho was going to tie up that loose end. More than likely they'd kept him just to prank around with and help pass the night. Like worrying a bug with the point of your knife.

Chumacho had laughed out loud. All around him the camp was beginning to stir as the sun got up over the horizon. Chumacho had gotten to his feet and begun yelling rapid orders in Spanish concerning the disposition of Warner's horses and the other plunder. Some of it they would take, the rest they would simply destroy. When it appeared they were about ready to leave, Chumacho sent two of the Mexicans over to fetch Warner to the fire. He was plenty afraid, but he was equally resolved not to let them know it. They could kill him, but they'd play hell making him think he was scared of them. His main thought was how he could get his hands on a revolver and take a few of them with him when he went. At least Red had had that much satisfaction. Just before the two *bandidos* had come to fetch him he'd glanced over at Red's body. He reckoned Red was good and stiff, having had all night to start turning back to dirt. The curious fact of the business had been that the Mexicans hadn't paid the slightest bit of attention to one of their own, the one that Red had killed. They had made no attempt to bury him the night before and it appeared they didn't intend any such ceremony in the light of day. The only attention he'd received had been a brief squabble among three or four of them over the dead man's belongings. Chumacho had settled that with a few kicks and blows and then had emptied the man's pockets himself.

They had drug Warner over to the fire and then a grinning Chumacho had taken him by the ankles and held his feet to the glowing embers while the two that had fetched him held him by the shoulders. Chumacho had grinned at him all through the searing, waiting for him to scream or jerk around. But even though the pain had been terrible the only sign of agony he'd let them see had been the sweat that had run down his face and the look he couldn't keep off his face.

Finally Chumacho had laughed and let him go. The two holding him had thrown him aside. He'd been afraid to look at his feet. He'd still had his socks on when the searing had begun, but now he could see that the material had been burned right off him.

But he had very little time to think of his feet. At Chumacho's directions two of the *bandidos* had thrown him on the back of a horse and the whole troupe had started off, riding east into the alkali flat. Warner had had no idea of where they were going or what was planned for him.

Finally, after an hour's ride, they had stopped and Chumacho had ridden up alongside of him. The fat one had grinned. He'd said, "Chou don' theenk we let chou die as easy as chou fren. No, Chumacho doan like chou so beery mouch. Chou die slow, beery slow."

Then he'd knocked Warner off the horse he'd been astride. After that all the Mexicans had dismounted and circled around him. Chumacho had a big canteen of water in one hand and a bottle of tequila in the other. He'd held out the tequila and said, "Chou dreenk. Chou dreen plenty." He'd laughed. "Make chou feets feel goot."

Warner had been trying to stand, shifting from one foot to the other. The pain was so bad he wasn't sure he could endure it. Even an hour after the searing of his soles he still had to bite the inside of his lip to keep from screaming. He had never been a man to bite too deep into the bottle, but now he grabbed at the jug of rotgut tequila the fat Mexican was offering him. He held it to his mouth with both hands and sucked at it as hard as he could pull down the fiery, foul tasting spirits. It burned his mouth where he'd bit his lip, it burned his throat, it burned his stomach. But, in a few seconds it spread through his body so that he could feel some of the unbearable pain leaving the bottoms of his feet. He had drunk until he'd started to gag and then jerked the bottle away from his mouth and bent over, gasping. He'd been all night without water, and the tequila, while it at first had slaked his thirst, had now left his mouth drier than before. As he stayed bent over, listening to the Mexican *bandidos'* laughter, wondering if he were going to be able to hold down the tequila, he could feel the dryness returning to his mouth. It seemed even worse than it had before the tequila.

But when he'd finally straightened back up Chumacho was handing him a big two-and-a-half gallon canteen of water with one hand and taking the tequila with the other. He'd taken the canteen gratefully, feeling so weak he'd had trouble with its weight. He'd drunk, sparingly at first, but then more and more at Chumacho's urging. The fat *bandido* had said, "Chou plenny thirsty, my fren. You dreenk plenty. Chure, chou dreenk plenty."

So he'd kept on pouring the water down. It had been during that time that one of the Mexicans had grabbed the hat off his head and sailed it up in the air. Three or four of them had fired at it, but without any apparent effect.

Finally he'd had all the water he could hold. He'd handed the canteen back to Chumacho and then stood there, weak and half-sick from the tequila, wondering what was coming next. All around them was the barren desolation of the alkali flat. They were in the worst part, where the ground was so loaded with gypsum that nothing, not even greasewood or cactus could grow.

Chumacho had given him a big smile. He'd said, "Now, gringo, I chow chou how we keel chou."

And he'd hit Warner a hard, driving blow in the stomach. It had bent Warner over and taken his breath. Two of the *bandidos* had taken him by the shoulders and held him upright while the rest of the gang had taken turns slugging him in the stomach. After five or six blows his stomach had emptied and that had been the only satisfaction he'd gotten out of the torture, throwing up on his tormentors. But his triumph had been short-lived. It had only caused them to hit him harder.

They had beat him until there wasn't a drop of fluid left in his body to come out his mouth. Then they'd dropped him in the sand. Chumacho had looked down at him, smiling big. He'd said, "Maybe de beeg burds weel come an' geeve chou the help." He'd gestured overhead where a couple of buzzards were circling.

Then the Mexicans had mounted up and, taking their stolen horses on lead, had ridden away. Just before they'd gotten out of sight he'd caught sight of the fat leader turning in his saddle to wave his sombrero back at him.

He'd lain on the ground for a long time, retching dryly as his stomach roiled. But it was the dry heaves, he had nothing left to bring up. Finally, after what seemed like an eternity, he had managed to roll on his side. He'd lain like that for a time, panting a little, while he slowly explored his stomach and chest, hoping the *bandidos* hadn't broken any of his ribs. But they'd all seemed whole. The Mexicans had mostly been hitting him in the stomach and the abdomen and, while he knew it was going to hurt him a bit and be sore for a time, they hadn't really done him much damage. A lifetime of working with rough stock had turned his slim frame into rawhide and no amount of pounding by such as a bunch of drunk *bandidos* was going to hurt him very badly.

But what could hurt him, could, in fact, kill

him, was all around. He raised up on an elbow and looked. As far as he'd been able to see it was the desolation of the alkali prairie, a place where nothing grew and nothing could exist. As he had become conscious of the sun's ascent into the sky, he'd known that he had to do something, try something. He'd known he couldn't stay where he was for very long. He had to find water. He didn't know where he was or how far he would have to travel to find water, but he knew he had to have it. The only sure place he could think of where he would find water was the Rio Grande. He'd risen slowly to his tortured feet. He reckoned the river to be at least twenty-five miles to the south, maybe more. It hadn't mattered. He had decided that if he was going to die he was going to die trying to get himself some help.

The first few steps on his bare, burned feet had almost taken his breath away. The ground would have been painful to walk over even with healthy bare feet. For his it was a test of his will to put one foot in front of the other and keep going.

It had taken him half an hour to make the first twenty yards. He'd stopped then because he'd come upon his hat. He had bent down slowly against the pain in his belly and picked up his hat and dusted off the sand and set it on his head. Then he'd started walking, south. He'd said, out loud, "Lord, I'm standing in need of some help right now. But I'll understand if you can't get to me just right quick. I'll wait my turn."

And then, hours later, he'd seen that dot in the distance that had slowly turned into a horse.

# 3

He had succeeded in getting his shirt off without losing the horse and now he stood, one arm looped through the cheek strap of the halter so he could have the use of both hands, carefully tearing his shirt into long, wide strips. He was trying to make a bridle of sorts, but it was a difficult task because, of course, the Mexicans had taken away his knife and the flannel wouldn't tear straight. He'd finally located a sharp-edged splinter of a rock that had helped him cut across the seams. When he was finished he'd managed to make a strong enough length of material that was about six feet long and no less than an inch thick at any point. He'd tied one end to each of the metal rings at the corners of the horse's mouth where the halter came together on each side. Of course he had nothing to use for a bit. He was just going to have to hope that the horse had been trained to neck rein, turn away from the pressure of the reins on the side of his neck, rather than plow rein which usually needed a bit.

When he was finished he just stood there, patting the horse on the nose and resting. He looked up at the sky. He figured it was somewhere in midafternoon. He didn't have a great deal more time before it came on night. Not that

that made much difference. Time was his greatest enemy now and he had to keep going be it day or be it night. He had to get water and he had a pretty good idea the horse was badly drawn down himself.

As if to emphasize the point that they should get started, wherever it was they were going, the horse suddenly stamped a foot. He'd been standing just as calmly and patiently as could be expected while Warner had fashioned his makeshift bridle, but now that that was done the horse seemed to be saying, "Well, what are we waiting for? You promised me water and grain. Let's have it."

Warner said, as if the horse had spoken, "I got to admit you be right. But we've got one little problem. I'm way too weak to jump up on you, barebacked as you are. So we will have to walk until I can find something to get a leg up off of."

Limping, he turned himself and the horse toward the south. With the bends and curves of the Rio Grande there was no way to know which direction was the shortest way. But due south was certainly the surest. And sureness was of a necessary vitalness.

The horse came along readily, ambling along with his head down. He was shod and, now and again, one of his iron shoes would ring against a granite or quartz rock. Moving, Warner could see just how done in the horse was. He said, "Ol' buddy, I might be doing you just as big a favor as you be a-doing me. I don't reckon you'd have lasted much more than twenty-four hours out here in this buzzard's nest. And, say, just how in hell did you manage to wander yourself off into this godforsaken place, anyway? You don't look no dumber than most horses so what possessed you to end up here? You are obviously too valuable a horse for somebody to just have let you wander off, especially out on an alkali plain, so how in hell are you going to get here?"

Warner was just as dry and thirsty as earlier and his feet bottoms hurt just as bad but, somehow, having the horse had lifted his spirits. Right then Warner didn't know who was going to end up carrying whom to the river, but he was determined that he and this good horse were going to make it out alive. The horse had appeared like magic and he was now convinced that there was enough magic left in both of them that they would make the river.

First he had to find something to give himself a lift up on the horse. Normally he could have sprung flatfooted onto the horse's back. Or, like when he was a tad of a youngster, gotten a toehold by spreading his big toe and the next one and getting a grip behind the horse's knee and using that to climb up on the animal's back. But he was too weak for that now.

He trudged along, his feet beyond pain by now,

looking for a rock or a little mound or anything. From where the Mexicans had left him, and to the five or six miles he'd somehow managed to make to where he'd discovered the horse, the country had gradually been improving. In the distance he could see an occasional stunted mesquite and now and then little patches of brambles and greasewood. The land was losing that caked, cracked, dried look that so well defined the alkali prairie. But he was beginning to lose that burst of energy and good feeling that he'd felt when he'd known he'd finally and for sure had the horse. As he stumbled along he could feel the weakness and lack of will lying on his shoulders like a heavy weight, forcing him toward his knees, urging him to just sink down and rest. But he knew better than that. He knew that once he sat down he'd lie down and once he did that he'd never get up.

And then, like another answer to another prayer, he saw the two-foot hump of an anthill. He knew the ants. They were big as bumblebees and angry as a bad-tempered drunk. He didn't mind getting stung; he doubted if he'd even feel it. But if the horse got stung he'd bolt and Warner knew he had no way of holding the animal. The only way was to walk straight to the hill, step up on it, and mount without ever stopping the horse. The anthill looked to be about fifty yards away and he began getting ready. First he stopped the horse and lifted the bridle over his head to the riding position. Then he took a position on the horse's left side and guided him toward the mound so they'd pass on the right side. He'd step on the mound with his left foot, spring upward as much as he could, and swing his right leg over. He could only hope the horse had been ridden bareback before. Some animals who'd known only a saddle were startled and scared by a rider suddenly landing on them bareback.

But he'd just have to find that out when it happened. Once aboard a horse, even bareback, he was plenty hard to dislodge. But then, that was when he had his strength. Now, he didn't think it would take much to shake him loose.

The anthill was approaching. He shifted both his hands to the horse's mane to get a grip, watching the anthill coming up, calculating his steps so he could hit it with his left foot. It was even higher than he'd expected, looking like a miniature volcano some two-and-a-half-feet tall.

Then it was there and he stepped on the top in stride, rose and jumped, swinging his right leg over the horse's back and hanging onto the horse's mane with all his strength. The horse snorted and jumped forward and, for just a second, Warner felt himself sliding off to the side. But he leaned forward, burying his face in the horse's neck, hanging on and pulling on his mane, and slowly settled himself astride the big animal. The horse had started into some kind of gait that

Warner hadn't recognized. It was faster than a trot, but nowhere near as rough. But, for the time being, Warner just wanted the horse to walk. When he felt he had his balance he sat up straight and took hold of his makeshift reins and slowly pulled the horse down to a walk. Listening to the horse's breathing he realized the horse had even less left than he'd thought. Just that little burst had left the horse blowing and snorting.

But now they were down to a slow walk. After a moment Warner became aware that an ant was biting him on his left foot. He didn't so much care, but he didn't want it to get on the horse. As carefully as he could he lifted his foot and brushed the ant away. After that he just rested atop the horse and let the animal carry them toward the south, toward the river. Now, with nothing to do but stay atop a smooth walking horse, he could at last relax and let the pain work its way all the way through him, let it go as far as it would. He didn't try to fight it with either his mind or his body, he just let it flood and rage. After about fifteen minutes it seemed to level off and stay constant. He just stayed atop the horse, rocking slightly with the motion of the animal. Finally, when he was sure the pain and the hurt had done their best he allowed himself a small smile. "Hell," he said aloud, "if that's the worst of it I can stand that all day long."

After that the agony started to recede, even the

angry sadness about his partner. He wasn't going to feel guilty about Red, he was going to get even for Red. And he was going to get even for himself. He reached down and patted the horse on the side of the neck. He said, "Horse, I don't know what kind of mule you are, but you are a mighty well mannered one. Except you don't ever say a damn word. Where you from? Who put this here halter on you? I now see you got a notch in your ear so that makes you either Spanish or Mexican and means you belong to somebody. But right now you belong to me and I am going to get you water and grain and even a mare or two if you're so inclined once you've rested up."

It had been funny that he'd only noticed that the horse was a stallion once he'd had him caught. Which was just as well. Knowing the horse was a stud might have made him overly cautious and he might not have caught the horse as easily as he had. Stallions were noticeably more fiery and nervous than a gelding and his nerve might have left him if he'd seen he was stalking a stallion. It was funny because it wasn't the sort of thing Warner would have missed even at a glance. But his focus had been so directed to just getting his hand on that halter he hadn't really noticed anything else.

Now, after almost an hour of plodding straight south, Warner began to gently see how the horse reacted to his crude bridle. With just a little rein pressure the horse turned obediently to the left and then to the right. Warner halted the horse with just the slightest pressure on the bridle. Warner said, "Hell, this horse don't need no bit in his mouth. I don't know who trained this animal, but he done a hell of a job."

To start him up again Warner just touched the horse's flanks with his bare heels and lifted the bridle. The horse immediately started into that canter that was just above a trot but not quite as fast as the slow lope of a cow horse.

But he immediately pulled the horse back down to a slow walk. They had a long way to go yet and he had to save all the horse he could.

He slowly rode south as the sun began to descend. He really had no idea how far it was to the river. It could be ten more miles or it could be twenty. Even with his mind working at its best he would have been uncertain because he hadn't known the place from where he'd started. Now, hurt and tired beyond his endurance, and half crazy with thirst he was only able to think in short stretches and even that was hazy. But the horse kept plodding along and he was content to sit and wait and hope. It did seem to him that the country was gradually beginning to improve with every mile they made. Not that that was saying much, but the wintered out mesquite and huisache trees and bramble bushes were beginning to increase. It gave him hope because it was at least some kind of sign that they were headed in the right direction.

Then, just a little before twilight, the horse stumbled and almost went to his knees. Warner could feel him beginning to tremble even as he tried to scramble to the ground as fast as he could. The sudden emergency had sent a flash of energy through him. The horse was the wild card in the deck. He knew how much he had left inside himself; he didn't know in just how bad a shape the horse might be in. And if the horse quit then he was finished.

The horse was trembling harder and beginning to sweat even though it was coming cool as the evening came on. Warner had seen the signs plenty of times before. It was the last indication a worn-out horse gave before he fell over and died from exhaustion or hunger or the lack of something he had to have. In the case of this horse Warner knew it was water. He knew a man could go longer than a horse without water and he had no idea how long this particular horse had been wandering around the arid alkali plain. He didn't know what to do so he patted the horse and soothed him as best he could. He cursed himself. He shouldn't have ridden the horse so long. He should have gotten down and relieved the horse of at least the burden of his weight. It might have meant the difference of miles.

He looked around frantically as the horse began

to stagger slightly. Ahead, about two hundred yards, he could see a little mesquite thicket. Maybe if he could get the horse in among that he could keep him upright. At that moment keeping the horse on his feet was the most important factor. Once a horse went down he almost never got up again. So, as gently as he could, Warner lifted the bridle over the horse's head to take him on lead and walk beside him. Patting him and talking quietly and urging him on, Warner started the long walk to the little grove of mesquite. Gone was the pain in his feet and his chest and belly; gone was the mental fatigue and haziness. Energy was pumping through him and his brain was working as fast as it could.

Little by little, in short, stumbling steps, the horse began to let Warner lead him across the prairie. He was still wavering and trembling, but it seemed as if the gentle movement were taking his mind off himself. Warner spoke to him softly, encouragingly. He said, "Come on, ol' buddy, you can make it. Ain't no hill for a stepper. You're blooded stock. High bred. An ol' ordinary horse would've laid down, but you ain't gonna do that. Just kept puttin' them feet one in front of the other."

They went along, Warner staying just even with the horse's head, holding the bridle loosely in his hand. The horse shambled along, his head down, a little of his tongue showing. Warner would have given a new saddle to see some slobber around the horse's muzzle, but he knew the horse's mouth was as dry as his own.

Then, about fifty yards from the mote of stunted trees the horse lifted his head and made a little whinnying sound. He hadn't lifted his head very high and it had been a poor excuse for a whinny, but it made Warner suddenly alert. Was the horse smelling another horse? Had he somehow walked right back into the midst of the Mexican *bandidos*? But he couldn't believe that. Nobody in their right mind, not even Chumacho and his bunch would be dumb enough to ride back into the alkali flat. But something had taken the horse's attention.

Twenty yards away the horse raised his head even higher and flared his nostrils. He made the whinnying sound again and actually began to pick up his pace. Warner pulled back gently on the makeshift bridle. He said, "Whoa, ol' buddy. Where the hell you think you be a-going? Ten minutes ago you was about to fall over and die. Now you want to race. What the hell's got into you?"

The thought crossed his mind that the horse was acting like an animal would when he smelled water. But that was impossible. They were at least ten miles, if not more, from any hope of water. The only thing he could figure was the horse was so far gone he'd taken the blind staggers. He'd seen an old cow horse do that just before he'd died. Had suddenly bucked his rider off and then galloped straight into a barn and knocked himself down. Men who were supposed to know said that horses, when they got to acting that way, were seeing things from other times. The cowboy whose horse had died had said he'd mistaken the side of the barn for the door.

Walking by the horse's shoulder Warner was having to pull back on the bridle to slow the horse by the time they arrived at the mesquite thicket. It was just a little grove of stunted mesquite, the tallest not much over Warner's head, and the whole patch not more than ten yards across with the trees fairly close bunched. Mesquite did that in hot dry country, shading each other and mingling their roots to share what water there was underground. It was why they were able to survive when all other growing things died. Warner had always thought that men could take a lesson from the mesquite in how to get along. Of course he'd never been brainless enough to tell anyone he thought people could learn from a tree.

He led the horse deep into the grove, trying to get him some support from the gnarled trunks of the twisted little trees. The horse kept trying to surge forward, his head down and his neck stretched. Warner said, "What the hell's the matter with—" Then he turned and saw it. It was a sump, a little pool of water no more than five or six feet across and nearly covered over by the tangle of weeds and brambles surrounding it. Warner said, "My, God!" and flung himself full-length on the ground and began pulling back the leaves and weeds and brier vines that were covering the sump. Even though it was dim in the grove there was still plenty of light to see the prize the horse had led him to.

A sump was a seldom found phenomenon in that dry country. It occurred only occasionally where a break in the heavy clay underburden beneath the sand and subsoil allowed a little of the subterranean water that flowed so abundantly beneath the rocks and clay to leak to the surface. Usually, unless the break occurred in such a place as the grove of mesquite, it could never produce any standing water because it would evaporate in the heat faster than it could collect. Warner knew that the sump he'd found would be dry in the summer, even with the mesquite cover. But as he frantically clawed back the weeds and under-growth he, too, could smell the water. It was foul and stagnant smelling, but it smelled wet. Beside him the horse had pushed forward and was straining to reach his muzzle down toward the water.

Then Warner got a space clear and he could see down into the dank darkness of the sump. It was slimy and green and thick, but it was water. Even in the relative coolness of the mesquite grove it had evaporated back down until he could just barely touch its surface by stretching out his arm. He swished his hand around in the scum and could see that, under the surface slime, there was good water. It might be full of alkali and taste like hell, but it would save the horse.

The horse was frantic to get at the water. Warner had gotten up on his knees and, with a sinking heart, he realized the horse could not stretch his muzzle down far enough to even get a taste of the water. Warner was afraid he might try and kneel down in his haste and his franticness and, if he did, Warner knew the bank of the sump might crumble and the horse could break a leg or sink into the quagmire of the sump. He was afraid also that the horse was so weak he'd never be able to perform the awkward and unnatural motion of kneeling down without falling over or hurting himself some other way.

Using what strength he could he managed to get the horse back from the edge of the water hole. He tied him to the limb of a mesquite tree and then began urgently trying to think of some way he could get some water into the horse. He tried first with his hat, getting on his belly and leaning down into the hole as far as he could. But all he managed to do with that activity was get his hat messy and clean off some of the scum. No, he had to find some way of bringing the water up. He thought and then he stepped out of the thicket and looked around. There were rocks aplenty scattered around amid the sand and cactus. Some were the size of grapefruit, some were as big as hay bales. The only good thing about them, as far as rocks went, was that they were volcanic and, therefore, not as heavy as, say, granite or ordinary country rock. As quickly as he could he started grabbing up rocks of a size he could carry. They might have been light for rocks, but they were a terrible load for him. But he took strength through desperation and was able to lift and carry several valise-size chunks of rocks, staggering through the scrawny trees, and dropping them into the small pool of water. He carried six of that size, then seven and eight and finally nine before he had to fall on his knees by the sump and pant. The horse was straining toward the pool, excited now by the freshened smell of the stirred-up water. Resting and gasping for breath Warner looked into the sump. He was damned if he could see much improvement. Of course he didn't know how deep the sump was and therefore he couldn't gauge how much new material it would take to raise the water level.

But he was out of selections. He had to get the water level up, had to get some in the horse even if it was so scummy the horse had to chew it. He started back to hauling rocks, hurrying now because the falling sun was signaling night and he had to get the chore done before the light failed him.

After ten more trips, carrying smaller rocks now, he lay on his belly and extended his arm into the sump. He could plunge his hand into the water up to his wrist. His efforts were working. But it still wasn't high enough and, out of fear that the water might drain off through some crevice before he could make use of it, he redoubled his efforts. His strength was long since spent and he had no earthly idea what he was using to carry the rocks to the sump with. He thought that maybe he'd already died and that all the effort he was expending was just another form of the way a dead man's leg or arm sometimes twitched and jerked around after the rest of him had quit working.

Finally the water was only a foot from the top of the sump. The horse, like him, had found the energy to do what he shouldn't have been able to do. He was pitching and lunging around, almost wild to get at the water, in danger, any second, of either tearing his bridle loose or breaking off the branch he was tied to. Warner got to his head, somehow, and petted him and soothed him and gentled him down enough so that, with trembling fingers, he could untie the bridle he'd made out of his red, checkered flannel shirt.

And then he couldn't hold the horse. In two steps the animal was at the edge of the sump and plunging his head into the green water. Warner just stood by, panting, watching him. He let the horse drink for perhaps a moment and then, with great difficulty, pulled him back. He said, with what little breath he could muster, "Can't, can't, drink much now."

Then he stood holding the horse, forcing the animal, who was now trembling with eagerness, to wait. It was a hard wait for Warner. There was just so much water in that sump and the horse might well drink it out of his reach. If he did there'd be no water for Warner because he was way past the rock carrying stage.

Finally he let the horse drink again for another minute. Then Warner pulled the horse back and lay down on his belly with his hat in his hand and, reaching as far as he could, was able to sweep a layer of the scum away and dip up a little water in the crown of his hat. He opened his mouth and tilted his head back and let it run down his throat. It was foul and full of alkali and slimy and nothing had ever tasted quite as good to Warner ever before in his life. The horse was in beside him, crowding him, half kneeling, reaching as far as he could with his muzzle. He was just able to get his lips to the water and make a sucking sound as he pulled a little more of the liquid down his long throat. "Damn you!" Warner said as he watched the water level recede. He tried frantically, almost leaning too far, to get a little more of the water in the crown of his hat. But the best he could do was scoop up a little in the curved brim. He brought it carefully up to his mouth and drained off what he could. Then he looked back down in the hole. The water was too far down, both for him and for the horse. But he reckoned the horse had had enough to get them to the Rio Grande. As for himself, well, he could go back to sucking on pebbles.

He rested them both for what he thought to be an hour. That was another thing the Mexicans had taken, his watch. And the watch had been a present from his grandfather on his eighteenth birthday. It wasn't a very expensive watch, but he'd valued it, especially the inscription.

When he thought his body was up to it he led the horse out of the thicket and then walked him along until he found the hump of a basalt rock sticking out of the sandy ground that was high enough to give him a step up. He flipped the cloth bridle over the horse's head, stepped up on the rock, and mounted. He was a horseman again.

By now it was night, though, with the moon as full as it was, it was nearly as easy going as twilight. He studied the rising stars and then set the horse on a due south course and let the bridle go slack in his hand as he relaxed and just moved along with the animal The water had done the horse a world of good; he could tell by the way the horse stepped along with a little more strength in his stride. A couple of days' rest and a few buckets of real grain and some good hay and the old boy would be as good as ever. While slouching along he wondered how old the horse was. Naturally he hadn't taken the time to mouth him, but he guessed a long four or a short five wouldn't be too far off and he favored him more as a four-year-old. Four was a nice age for a horse, especially a stallion. They'd made their neck conformation and had developed their frame about as well as it was ever going to develop. And they were old enough to have gotten over the fool coltish ways. Yes, he liked four-year-olds. You could really work with them and yet you still had plenty of years to get some good work out of them.

He yawned. On top of being hurt and so exhausted it was an effort to just sit the horse, he was beginning to get sleepy. But then that would figure since he hadn't gotten any sleep the night before, what with the Mexicans taking turns hitting him and kicking him while they stole all his belongings. He looked up at the sky, judging it to be somewhere around eight o'clock by the low position of the moon. He wondered how far it was to the river, but then switched off that line of thought. A man as thirsty as he was could go crazy thinking about a river of water. It might be brown water and it might be so thick with silt you didn't know whether to drink it or plow it, it was still water. He decided to put the thought out of his mind and let the horse worry about the river.

Any animal that could have smelled that little sump from that distance ought to be able to smell a whole river full of water from a hundred miles away. The horse would find the nearest bend of the river. Of that he was sure. He let his chin nod down to his chest and thought he'd just close his eyes for a moment.

There was, he thought, no doubt that they'd been uncommonly unlucky about the *bandidos*. Thirty years ago or even fifteen or ten such an attack would not have been unexpected. Even five years ago neither Warner nor Red would have dreamed of leaving themselves so open to bandit attack in that country so near the border. They'd have traveled by night, they would never have built any sort of fire and they would have been alert and on the ready for any sign of trouble. In fact it would have been doubtful that only the two of them would have been traveling such country with so valuable a commodity as good horseflesh. They'd have hired an extra gun or two to be on the safe side. But that had been then. Over the years the army and the local law and the people who worked the land had gradually thinned out the bandit gangs that once had roamed so freely. Lynch ropes and Winchester repeating rifles had supposedly cleared the land of the *bandidos* to such an extent that it was said a man could stake his horse in the middle of a pasture within sight of the Rio Grande and expect to find him there a week later. That was part of the reason, the biggest part, that had caused Warner and Red to treat the desperadoes with such uncertainty and why Warner had not had his gun at his side. Five years past, even three, or two, they would have both started shooting at the sight of the gang and inquired of their business later. But they had not been expecting *bandidos* because it was thought that the *bandidos* had taken their affairs to safer climes than south Texas. But this gang of Chumacho's were either new to the business and didn't know the territory or they were making a desperate hit and run and then fleeing to Mexico with whatever they could gather up.

Warner thought on those matters as his head grew heavier and his neck weaker. Well, whatever had brought the killers to his camp, whatever bad luck, was going to be the same bad luck for them that brought him to their camp.

He yawned again and let his shoulders slump forward, his hands braced against the horse's shoulders. His eyes dragged shut again and he rode along, lulled by the rocking motion of the horse.

The moon grew high and then passed out of sight and, a little later, the stars began disappearing down the eastern horizon. A few high clouds sailed across the light blue sky, reflecting the light off the falling moon. And then, at about three A.M., the horse walked into the shallow waters of the Rio Grande. He did it without hurry, without panic, just a good horse coming to water. He stopped in two-foot-deep water and bent his head to drink. Still asleep, Warner slid down the horse's neck and awoke in astonishment to find that he was no longer dreaming of water, but immersed in it.

He drank and then he rested in the water, letting it soothe his pains, and then he drank some more and then rested some more. The horse, his thirst finally quenched, stood quietly in the water and watched Warner. Finally, when Warner began to fear he was drinking too much, he got painfully to his feet and splashed over to the horse. The horse was no longer helpless, no longer as dependent on him. He could take it into his head to run off at any time and Warner still had serious need of him. He came up to the horse's head and, with painfully cut and bruised fingers, untied the knot at one of the steel rings on the halter. That gave him a lead rope, still attached to the ring on the other side of the halter, of some six feet. He slowly led the horse up on the bank and then upstream for a hundred yards or so to where some willows drooped beside the banks and there were a few patches of grass. It wasn't much, but the horse immediately set in to graze and even to mouth down some of the willow leaves. The rope he'd made out of his shirt gave Warner enough room so that he could sit down and lean back against a willow tree while the horse ate what he could. Warner looked at the river and then he looked north toward where the trackless waste lay that he and the horse had somehow traversed. He shook his head slowly and then he looked up at the sky. He said, "Thank you, Lord, I am much obliged. I know your opinion on vengeance, but I am still intending to give you a hand on that matter."

To him it was a wonder that the horse had come straight to the water. Once they'd left the alkali plain, and that could have been as much as five or six miles back, the country gentled up greatly and there would have been enough grazing to have tempted the horse to stop. But, without guidance of any kind, he'd marched straight to the river and dropped Warner into it. Warner looked over to where the horse was reaching up, grappling with his lips to pull down some willow leaves. He said, again, "What in the hell kind of horse are you? I never saw your like before."

But sleep still wanted to come to him. After a little more time of rejoicing at his deliverance he tied his end of the cloth rope around his wrist and then curled up on the ground and went to sleep.

He awoke to a full sun, a sun that had been up almost a whole hour. He was startled when he opened his eyes and then it took him another few seconds to place where he was. The bridle rope was still tied around his wrist. The horse had left off grazing and was now just standing patiently over him and switching flies with his tail and stamping a foot impatiently every now and then. Warner sat up and groaned involuntarily. He'd stiffened up over night and it seemed as if he hurt in every part of his body. He was going to have to get up and get to moving around before his muscles would loosen up and release him from some of the soreness. One thing at least—the soles of his feet still hurt, but the pain was bearable. He was sitting cross-legged and he could have looked at them if he'd wanted to but he preferred not. He didn't know how badly they'd been hurt and he didn't want to know until he could get to a doctor and see what help was available. For all he knew he might have been crippled for life. He'd walked on them; of course he'd walked on them. He hadn't had any choice. But he'd also seen loose flaps of skin flopping around with every step. Oh, the Mexicans had done a job on him all right. There was no doubting that. He'd have to wait to find out how bad.

He got to his feet and almost immediately became aware of the sound of wagon harness and the rumble of a buckboard. He walked away from the river, leading the horse. A little road, more like a wagon track, ran right alongside the river. Not more than fifty yards away, coming from the west he saw a buckboard being pulled by a span of nice looking mules. As the wagon got closer he could see that it was driven by one old man. The wagon appeared to be loaded with supplies. Warner dared hope that the man might have something he could give him to eat. The idea of food almost made him weak. His stomach had been completely empty going on for better than thirty-six hours. Of course it was still full of water and Rio Grande mud, but that didn't take the place of food.

He limped out into the middle of the road as the wagon came on at a good pace. The driver pulled up just short of Warner and stared at him with a mixture of wariness and curiosity. Warner circled the mule team, still leading the horse. He came even with the driver, a weather-beaten, dried-up, old man who could have been any age. From the sacks of flour and tubs of lard and other cooking supplies in the back of the wagon Warner figured the man worked for a ranch in the vicinity. He gave the man a howdy but only got a curt nod in return. Warner said, "I reckon I look a wreck which is pretty close to the truth. Me and my partner got jumped by a gang of *bandidos* evening before last. Kilt my partner and took damn near everything I had."

The old man was still looking at him suspiciously. He said, "Yeah, I heered they was a bunch of them murderin' desperadoes runnin' loose in the country. 'At the reason I ain't overanxious to stand here jawin' with you. Where'd they jump you?"

Warner pointed north with his chin. He was holding on to the side of the wagon with both his hands, feeling so weary he felt he could drop in his tracks. His feet were starting to throb again. He said, "Right up close to the top of the alkali flat. Then they carried me out in the middle of it and give me a good drubbing and turned me loose without food or water." He looked around. He said, "I wouldn't have made it if I hadn't come across the horse."

The old man gave him a doubting look. He said, "You made it 'crost thet alkali patch 'thout enny food 'er water an' no relay of horses?" His voice said he obviously didn't believe Warner.

Warner said tiredly, "Yes. That's what I just told you." He motioned back at the horse that was waiting patiently. "If I hadn't run across this horse and been able to catch him I'd have never made it to water. I'd have died out there."

For the first time the old man seemed to become aware of the horse that was at the end of the cloth rope Warner was holding. He said skeptically, "You found a horse in the middle of the alkali desert?"

"Yes."

"That horse?"

"Yes."

"Then he ain't yore horse."

"No. I told you I run across him."

" 'N you walked him down?"

"No, I didn't walk him down."

"How'd you ketch him then?"

"I tricked him," Warner answered. He was growing very weary of the conversation.

"How'd you trick him?"

"I just did. Look, I told you I was about to starve to death. Ain't et in nearly two days. Would you have a bite of anything you could spare me?"

There was a grease-stained paper sack on the seat and both their eyes went to it as Warner asked the question. The old man sort of stiffened. He said, "Alls I got is a few biscuits I been savin' fer my lunch. I still got a good fifteen mile to make 'fore the ranch an' it'll be past noon way these here mules travel."

"Fine," Warner said. He pushed away from the wagon. "But if it wouldn't put you out too much could you tell me the direction of the nearest town and how far it is?"

The old man jerked his thumb over his shoulder. "Del Rio. 'Bout ten miles back. Can't miss it."

Warner couldn't believe his ears. They must have been pointing southwest instead of due south to be this close to Del Rio. Or else the Mexicans had set him down at a spot farther west than he'd figured. But it didn't matter. Del Rio was only ten miles away and he and his old horse could make that distance without feed or water.

The old man was looking curiously at Warner's makeshift bridle. He said, "What kind o' rig is that thar?"

"Only kind I had material to make. That's my shirt. I had to tear it into strips to make a bridle for this horse."

"What kin' o' horse be that one?"

Warner shrugged. He said, "I don't know." He was starting to feel mighty weak. He thought the quicker he was on the road to Del Rio the better. Even at a slow pace they could make it in two, two and a half hours and he knew he could get help in Del Rio, knew a man there that could make just about anything come out right.

The man scratched his chin. "Fine lookin' animal. An' you say you jest found him?"

Warner didn't particularly like the man's tone or the way he was asking the question. He said, "I reckon you heard me say that. Yes, I found the horse wandering loose in the middle of an alkali plain. And, yes, I intend to consult for his owners. By the way, what ranch are you off of?"

The driver pointed with his right hand, never letting go of the onside rein. He said, "I work for the Sombrero. Work for Mr. J. L. Slocum. You'd taken a look at the hind end of them mules you'd've seed the Sombrero brand."

Warner put down the impulse to tell the man he

had better things to do with his strength than inspect mules. Instead he said, "Well, tell Jake Slocum that Warner Grayson will be a little late getting to his horse herd on account of some unexpected trouble."

The man stared at him, then said, "Be you *that* Warner Grayson? The horse wizard?"

Warner said, "I don't know about the wizard part, but I'm Warner Grayson and I'm going to be late getting to the Sombrero on account of the trouble with the Mexican bandits. I wish you'd tell Jake for me."

The man was getting animated. "Hell, I seen you jest last year when you come through. Never seed a man with such a hand for horses in all my born days. Hell, whyn't you tell me who you wuz? Man can't be too kereful with strangers on the road these days." He began to open the paper sack. "Here, I got bacon and biscuits in here. Plenty for the both of us. Mr. Slocum would skin me 'live he heered I left you on the road hungry." He opened the bag and showed it to Warner.

But Warner had turned away from the wagon and was busy untieing the cloth rope from his wrist. The sight of the food had made him almost faint. But if he was worth feeding only because he was Warner Grayson the horse "wizard" then he didn't care for any. A man's ability ought not to have anything to do with whether you helped him out or not when he was in trouble. He said,

"No, thanks. Reckon I can hold up until Del Rio. Wouldn't want to short you on your lunch."

Now the old man sounded alarmed. He said, "Why, Mr. Grayson, you must be plumb tuckered out. Why don't you jest ride on out to the ranch with me in this here wagon. We can eat on the way and you kin git a rest. I reckon an all-night trip across that gawdawful alkali flat would kill nearly anybody. Tie yore horse on behind."

But Warner was busy turning the lead rope back into a bridle by tieing the loose end back to the other steel ring. He pitched the bridle back over the horse's neck. He said, "No, thanks, mister. But I will take the borrow of your wheel for just a second." He led the stallion around until he was in position and then put his left foot on top of one of the wagon's wheels and vaulted up and onto the horse's back. He reined the horse around and pointed him west, toward Del Rio. He said, "Well, tell Jake I'll get there quick as I can. Might take me a day or two to heal up and then I got one ranch right there at Del Rio, but I'll be on out to his place next."

The wagon driver was leaning over the side of his wagon and peering at the ground. He said, "Mr. Grayson, do you know you be leavin' bloody tracks?"

Warner said, "Yes. I been doing a right smart bit of that lately."

"Something the matter of yore feet?"

"Yes. Those Mexican *bandidos* tried to roast the bottoms. I reckon some more blisters have busted. Course walking across those rocks on the badlands didn't help them much neither."

The old man said, "Mr. Grayson, I shore wisht you'd git in this wagon and let me carry you to some help. It gits back to Mr. Slocum I left you out here in this shape he's gonna run me off. He sets considerable store by you. As do the cowhands. They hear about this they liable to string me up."

Warner said, evenly, though he still didn't care for the man, "Don't worry about it. I got business first in Del Rio." He touched the sides of the horse and the stallion immediately hit a brisk walk. He called back, "So long."

Behind him the wagon driver yelled: "But at least take some of these here biscuits an' bacon!"

Warner called, without looking back, "Thanks, naw. I'm saving my appetite for a steak in Del Rio."

Then he moved the stallion up a notch into that ground-eating canter of his. He wasn't going to press the horse, but the animal seemed to have so much more vitality that he thought he'd let him frisk around for a mile or two.

But, Lord, he thought, how smooth the animal was. He knew there was a bunch of action going on below but the stallion's back stayed just as level as if he were sitting in a morris chair.

While riding he thought about Del Rio and about his friend there, Wilson Young. It was a bright, sunshiny morning, almost warm enough that he didn't notice the absence of his shirt. With each mile he and the horse passed he was feeling greater and greater relief and amazement at his narrow escape. So far as he was concerned he was one up on death and he had every intention of putting his stolen time to good use. He had survived against impossible odds and, if he could only make it a little farther, he'd maybe get somehow back to normal. But damn, he thought, why did his sense of the rightness of things have to get between him and the biscuits and bacon? All right, so the man hadn't had no more manners nor feeling than the mules he was driving. What the hell did that have to do with a starving man and biscuits and bacon?

He thought about Wilson Young and smiled. Wilson would have eaten the man's biscuits and bacon. In fact he'd have eaten all of them and then had the man turn around and drive him into Del Rio. But that was Wilson Young and you didn't measure regular people up against him. Wilson had once been the most notorious bank robber in Texas. No, that wasn't right. Wilson had said to him, "Warner, a lot of folks think of me as a bank robber. I rob banks, but I ain't just a bank robber. I will rob anyplace where there is money collected up. Except churches. I won't

80

rob churches. I'm a robber so I leave the churches alone out of professional courtesy to the preachers. Does a barber charge another barber for a haircut or a shave? It's the same thing."

But Wilson was now no longer a robber of any kind. Through influential friends the governor had been persuaded, some three or four years back, to issue him a conditional pardon based on his staying out of the robbery business and in general letting other folk's money alone. Some said it wasn't so much the influential friends who'd persuaded the governor as the frustrated lawmen who, when they could lay hands on Wilson Young, couldn't keep him. He was known as perhaps the fastest and most deadly man with a handgun that anybody could ever remember seeing. Wilson Young didn't draw a gun, it just appeared in his hand. One second his hand was empty and the next it contained a revolver that was aimed exactly where he wanted it aimed. But even though he had robbed and he had killed, no one could say that Wilson Young was a bad man. Even his enemies conceded that he lived by a code of fairness that was almost unfair to his own interests. In more than one instance he'd been shot by men he'd been walking away from because he knew they didn't have a chance against him. He'd always explained it, dryly, by saying, "I don't kick cripples."

Now, for the last few years, he'd occupied

himself by owning and operating the Palace, an emporium he called the "finest cathouse and casino southwest of Saint Louis."

In spite of his thirst and how bad he was feeling Warner smiled to himself at the thought of Wilson Young. He hadn't seen him in nearly a year, but they were close friends. Back in Wilson's robbing days he'd gotten his mounts from Warner because it was well-known that a Grayson trained and selected horse would get you there and bring you back unless you found some way to fall off. Grayson had been no more than eighteen when he'd first met Wilson Young and he'd been so nervous he nearly hadn't been able to talk. He'd heard so much about the man that he'd expected some bloodthirsty monster to come swaggering in. Instead had come this gentle-acting, kind-talking man of a little over average height who could have been anybody. But even then Grayson had recognized there was something different about him. It might have been the way his eyes seemed to see everything at once or the quick way he could move without seeming to be in a hurry. It could, have been a lot of things; Warner had never been able to put his finger on it. But he'd liked the man from the first. On top of everything else he could be droll as hell, even with the wicked and evil-looking gang of men he'd surrounded himself with.

On that occasion Warner had sold him a horse.

He'd sold him anywhere from two to three mounts a year ever since while he was in the bank robbing business. There'd never been a squabble about the price or a question about the horse's ability. Wilson Young had made it plain he wouldn't be buying horses, horses he trusted his life to, from Warner if he didn't trust his ability and judgment.

Wilson Young was, Warner reckoned, about six or seven years older than he, being maybe thirty-four or thirty-five. But he was still as coltish as a kid and greatly given to playing jokes on friends and anybody else foolish enough to walk into his loop. His domestic condition was a little difficult to understand. He lived with two beautiful young Mexican girls that he claimed he'd won in a poker game in Monterrey some five years back. They'd been dancers in a cabaret show and Wilson was supposed to have got to playing poker with the manager of the show and, when the manager ran out of money, he'd started betting girls. Wilson liked to say that he could have had the whole show, all eight of the dancers, except he feared for his life with that many hot-blooded women around.

But it wasn't as loose an arrangement as it seemed. Evita was really the only woman in his life. She took care of Wilson's needs and ran the whorehouse with an iron fist and an eye on the cash register. Her cousin, Lupita, who was a couple of years younger at twenty, lived with them, but that was all. Or at least that was what Wilson told people.

The sun was up good enough that he judged it to be some time after nine o'clock. He figured he had to be getting close to the town; he knew he'd better be getting close because he didn't know how much longer he could last. Little waves of nausea and dizziness would come sweeping over him in intervals and sometimes the surrounding countryside went to reeling around like a drunk crossing a slick patch. He was starting to meet horsemen coming toward him. They gave him a polite enough good morning, but they also cast curious looks his way. He reckoned he was something to survey. Here he was, riding along on this exotic horse that was shedding hair like a goat, no saddle, no boots, no shirt, and a piece of cloth for a halter bridle. He knew his skin, even under a winter sun, was reddened up and he felt like he'd lost enough weight to look like a scarecrow.

After a little he began to catch sight of the roofs of the town. Then he and the horse topped a little rise and he could see Del Rio plain as day. It appeared to be no more than half a mile away. He wanted to put the horse into a canter and hurry, but it seemed as if all the energy had suddenly run out of him at the sight of the town. He could feel the last of his reserves, that "whatever" that had carried him through his long ordeal, draining out of him like water flowing from a canteen. He tried not to think of how weak he was, how hungry, in what pain, how unsteady. He tried to just focus his eyes on the town and keep the horse going that way.

Then it seemed as if he couldn't see anything out of the corners of his eyes, just what was directly in front of him. He got to the town and turned down the main street and rode toward the river. He knew where Wilson's place was, he'd been there half a dozen times, but he couldn't seem to get it fixed in his mind. He kept riding down the street, going slow, but he felt that he and the horse were somehow weaving from one side of the dusty road to the other. He could see people and it seemed that they were staring at him, but he couldn't find Wilson's place. Finally he stopped the horse. A man came up and stood by his horse and looked up at him. Warner said, his voice croaking a little, "You d'rect me to tha Pal'ce? Lookin' my friend Wilson Young."

The man said, "You're right in front of it, mister."

He stared. He wanted to say thanks, but he could feel himself slipping off the side of the horse. He felt hands take hold of him. He saw the blackness coming and then it had him. After that he didn't remember anything. He wanted to say, "Look out for my horse. Good horse," but the blackness wouldn't let him. He felt himself being carried. It flashed through his mind that it might be the *bandidos* again and he wanted to struggle, but he couldn't make anything work. He finally decided to hell with it. As dark as it was it was probably time to go to sleep anyway. With a sigh he fainted dead away. He had run completely out of anything to keep going on. Even his nerve had passed out on him.

# 4

Sometime later he was sitting in the bedroom of Wilson Young's living quarters that were over the saloon. They'd put him in a straight-back wooden chair and he'd come to with two mighty beautiful young women rubbing some kind of lotion all over his naked body. Even with nothing left he'd managed to make enough of a squawk that Wilson Young had finally brought him a towel to cover his private parts though he'd made fun of him in the bargain. He'd said, "You ain't got nothing worth putting on display or charging admission to see. Especially for these ladies who've had me to look at for several years."

They'd given him some beef broth and then fed him some mashed up avocado with lemon juice and Wilson had given him a drink of brandy. There hadn't been much talking, not that he could remember. The most immediate need seemed to be to get him smeared with the clear jelly the women were using. They were using it especially on the soles of his feet, keeping one foot immersed in a small pan of the stuff while they slowly rubbed the jelly on the sole of the other foot.

Wilson had said, "Ain't no use arguing with them. They both are experts in the treatment of frazzled out human beings. I think Evita is a witch doctor or something. That stuff they are rubbing you with is called aloe vera, or something. Supposed to be the cat's whiskers for burns and cuts and gunshot wounds. Though I don't know about that last. I've been shot since I've had Evita and I didn't see myself getting better no faster than ordinary. Stuff ain't nothing but cactus juice."

Evita had looked up from her work. She'd said, "That is because you are an old man now. Chou don't got no stren'th in chou body no more."

Wilson had said amiably, "You keep on talking like that, woman, and I'm liable to show you some 'stren'th' on 'chou body.' Say, when you gonna learn to speak English, anyway?"

While all that had been going on he'd wanted to yell out, "Will somebody bring me a goddam steak! Ain't you never seen a hungry man before?"

But even in his slightly dazed condition he knew he couldn't gulp down a lot of food. They'd brought him some more beef broth and then a little bowl of stewed chicken with dumplings in it. With even that little he could feel the strength slowly coming back to him. When the girls had finished Wilson had loaned him a pair of fine whipcord britches. He'd protested that he was still covered with that aloe stuff and didn't want to stain the saddle pants, but Wilson had just waved him off. He said, "The stuff ain't supposed to stain. Besides, I got plenty more and there'll be a bunch of suckers in here tonight just aching to give me some money to buy some more. I hate to think I wasted all those years robbing banks when the real money was right here and they don't try and put you in jail for the taking of it."

Wilson had also given him a white linen shirt and long, heavy, soft socks. It was amazing how nearly of a size they were. He was maybe half an inch taller than Wilson but they were both built on exactly the same mold. Wilson said, as he was putting on the socks, "I reckon you'll be wearing them for a while to come."

He replied, "Hell, I can't get boots on over these."

Wilson smiled slightly. "I reckon you ain't taken a real good look at the working part of your feet. And if I was you I would give it some time before I took a glance. Now you climb up in that big bed right now and get some rest and we can talk later. You still look like somebody coming off a two-week drunk."

Warner suddenly remembered. "My horse! I come in here on a horse."

Wilson said, "Yeah, I seen your horse. Especially the bridle. The horse is fine. We got a stable around there in the back and he's getting the best of care. He don't look in a whole lot better shape than you do. When you get to where you know 'sic 'em' from 'come here' we'll have a talk. I'm almighty curious as to how you managed to come by that horse."

Warner stood up, but the effort was almost too much. He started to weave and had to grab the back of the chair to keep from falling. Wilson grabbed him by both arms and helped him to the side of the bed. He sank down on it. It had a big, soft ticking and a quilt bedspread. He said, "Say, how did I come to get here?"

Wilson laughed. "That's what I'm waiting for you to tell me."

Warner thumped the mattress. "Naw, up here. In your bedroom. I just remember seeing Del Rio in the distance. That's all. It's a blank after that. Don't tell me that horse brought me here and then climbed the stairs and deposited me at your door?"

Wilson said, "It wasn't quite that way, but that's pretty close. There was a commotion out on the street in front of the saloon and I walked out to see what the hell was going on. Figured one of my gamblers had cut his throat in the street right in front of the place just to spite me for him being sucker enough to gamble against the house. Then somebody told me there was a half-dead man laying in the street and that he'd said my name. I went over and had a look and nearly said to just box you up and send you on out to the cemetery. Boy, you was a mess. Took about fifteen minutes before I even recognized you. After that we carried you up here and then them two Meskin women I'm stuck with taken off what little clothes you had on and set to work even before you come around. We kept holding camphor oil under your nose to try and clear your head. But you was still fuzzy up until you noticed you wasn't wearing a stitch. Now lay on up there in that bed and get some rest. I'll give you about a couple of hours and then I'll have you a steak cooked and you can tell me all about it. I'm more anxious to hear what happened than you are to tell me. But I'm afraid you'd pass out again on me if you tried now. So get some rest."

Warner said, "I ain't real sleepy, I'm just so goddam give out. I need one more drink of water."

While Wilson poured him out a glass from the pitcher by the bedside, Warner said, "I swear they ain't nothing more precious than water when you ain't got it. Yesterday about this time I'd've sold my right leg for that glass you're filling."

He took the water and gulped it down. Then he handed the empty glass back to Wilson and lay back on the pillows. "God," he said, "that's good. Better'n poontang."

Wilson gave a short laugh. "Let me hear you say that tomorrow. Now you go to sleep."

"I'll rest, but I don't figure to sleep."

He closed his eyes. Wilson watched him for about ten seconds and then quietly left the room,

91

closing the door behind him. Warner never heard a sound from the instant he closed his eyes.

Five hours later Warner was sitting at a table somebody had brought into the room eating a steak with mashed potatoes and gravy and drinking lemonade with a good deal of sugar in it. He ate half the steak and some of the potatoes, but then he had to stop and rest. He was too full. He'd have never believed, the day before, that there was enough steak in Texas to fill him up, but he couldn't even eat all, straight through, of what wasn't a particularly big T-bone. Wilson Young was sitting across from him in a turned around chair, resting his arms on the chair top and taking sips from a glass of brandy and pulling on a little Mexican cigarillo. It was just after four o'clock.

Wilson said, nodding at the steak, "I reckon your stomach shrunk. Well, now that you need to take a rest you might as well tell me how you come to look like you'd tried to stop a runaway locomotive bare-handed. Boy, I ain't never seen so many bruises on one man's body since the first night I slept with Evita."

The woman was just going out of the room with the empty lemonade pitcher. She turned at the door and shook her fist at Wilson. Even as weak as he was Warner couldn't help admiring the almost perfect symmetry of her small frame. Her breasts were large for a woman of her size, full at the sides and erect, and even though her hips were small, they flared seductively inside the satiny dress she was wearing. She said to Wilson, "I din't put no brusis on chou that night, but chou give me somethin' 'n et wasn't money. You gonna get chou brusis."

Wilson just smiled and shook his head. He looked back to Warner and said, "All right, what the hell happened?"

Warner shook his head for a moment, wondering where to begin. It all seemed like some strange nightmare that had happened to somebody else. Except he knew it wasn't a nightmare because his feet still hurt. The aloe vera ointment had helped greatly, but he'd finally gotten up the nerve to pull down one of the socks Wilson had loaned him and had taken a look at the soles of his feet. They looked like he'd been walking on glass, and hot glass at that. He didn't reckon there was much left of the original first half inch. The fire and the rocks and the sand had pretty well worn that away. He said, "I don't know, Wilson. Best I can say is I reckon I went to a gunfight carrying a willow switch. Whatever happened seemed like there was never a time when I had a chance to do anything about it."

He went on, then, to tell Wilson the whole story, beginning with the Mexicans riding into the camp, the initial confusion as to just what he and

Red ought to do, and ending with what he could remember of the ride into town.

Wilson had listened silently, sometimes sipping brandy and sometimes taking a draw on his cigarillo. It took Warner what was, to him, a surprisingly long time to tell the events. But each little bit had seemed so important he hadn't wanted to leave anything out. When he was through Wilson whistled lowly and said, "Boy, howdy. Warner Grayson, you ain't supposed to be here. You ain't supposed to be sitting in that chair with a steak in front of you and a new pitcher of lemonade on the way. You are supposed to be laying dead out there on that alkali flat somewhere." He stopped and looked at Warner for a long time. Then he said, "I ain't in the flattering business. So I'll just say straight out that I ain't sure I know of another soul that could have pulled off what you done. And that includes myself and Chulo and every other sonofabitch I know that thinks they are about halfway tough. What you done can't be done. It ain't possible. Them *bandidos* sentenced you to death as sure as whiskey will make you drunk. They thought they was having a mean game with you. Warner, you can't be here. It ain't possible."

"It was the horse, Wilson. It was the good Lord put that horse there. If it hadn't been for the horse I wouldn't have made it."

Wilson said, "The good Lord may have put that

horse there, but they ain't another man in ten states could have caught him barehanded and on feet that couldn't be walked on. Caught him with a hatful of sand and rocks and twigs. Shit! No, Warner, ain't nobody else could have caught that horse and then made him work for you like he did."

Warner said, "I don't even know what kind of horse it is. I thought I'd seen ever' horse there ever was, but I never seen one like him. The only thing I know is that he's got to be blooded stock."

"Oh, he's blooded stock all right. High-bred blooded stock."

Warner had started to eat again. He said, "But what he was doing out on that alkali prairie I'll never know."

"I don't want you gambling in my casino, Warner. You hear me? Man as lucky as you are could close me up in a day. Go on and eat the rest of that steak and potatoes and then you ought to eat some pie or something."

"Strange how hard it is for me to eat right now."

"Likely you got out of the habit."

When he was through with his meal and had a piece of pie sitting in front of him along with a cup of coffee and a tumbler of brandy, Warner said, kind of lowly, "Wilson, what the hell should I have done? I mean, I don't feel like I let Red down, but I don't feel all that right about it either."

Wilson Young said, "Kid, you're just feeling bad because he's dead and you ain't. You done the right thing. You bought yourself some time. If you'd've had a gun or could have got your hands on a gun, them Meskins would have cut you down just like they done your partner. Fact of the matter is there doesn't sound like there was a hell of a lot either one of you could have done. You weren't looking for *bandidos*, you weren't expecting any, wasn't supposed to be any around. It's just here lately that we'd heard about this bunch crossing the border ourselves. So you sure as hell, way up north like you was, had no way of knowing was a bunch of desperadoes running loose."

Warner grimaced. "I still feel bad about Red."

Wilson responded, "Of course you do. But Red made the mistake. He turned his back on the main bunch and threw down on the one was messing with your pack. What'd he think them others was going to do once he'd shot their man, stand around and cheer? Hell, no. If he was going to shoot—and I don't think he should have, not at least until ya'll could have both been armed and come to some sort of plan—he should have fired into the biggest part of them and killed as many as he could. Hell, he could have knocked that one he was standing by over the head with the barrel of his pistol. Red lost his head. He got angry. He got mad and let it cloud his judgment."

Warner said slowly, "That sounds like something my granddaddy used to tell me. He said the only use getting mad could be put to was in an angry contest and they didn't hold them often enough to stay practiced up."

Wilson said, "Your granddaddy was a smart man. You kept your head. And you're alive. Of course the fact that you're made out of wang leather didn't hurt you none. You can't walk on those feet of yours, Gray, you can't do it. It can't be done."

Warner took a bite of pie. He said, "They got to get well in a hurry. I got business with six *bandidos*. How you reckon I can go about finding them?"

Wilson blinked. He said, "Ain't you had about enough of their society? You plan to go pay them a visit?"

Warner said, "They paid me one. I like to keep up my social obligations."

Wilson said, "I hope you're kidding. I know you're kidding. You just stick to horses, Gray. That's what you're good at."

Warner looked at him. His face had gone expressionless. There was none of the boyish cast about it now. It was hard and flat. He said, "Wilson, who would know about that gang?"

Wilson looked at him a long moment, then said, "If anybody knows it will be Chulo. You remember Chulo?"

Of course he remembered Chulo. Nobody forgot Chulo. You could just as easily forget an earthquake as forget Chulo. Chulo had been with Wilson Young for as long as Warner could remember. Wilson called him the "black Meskin" and a lot of other names that nobody but Wilson could call him. Not if they didn't want to get flayed alive. He was simply the biggest, meanest, ugliest looking hombre, Mexican or white, that Warner had ever seen. He was weathered and tanned on top of his natural complexion to a swarthy color just short of deep mahogany. He was about three or four inches taller than Wilson Young and easily weighed two hundred and twenty-five pounds. He had a hawk-like nose in a hatchet face and a huge mustache that drooped around his mouth. His left eye was covered with a black patch, the eye extinguished in some fight so long ago that even Chulo didn't remember when he'd lost it. Wilson Young made him wear the patch because he said the old dried-up socket was too ugly to look at. The last touch that completed his face was a knife scar that ran down his right cheek from just below the eye to the corner of his mouth. Warner hadn't seen much of Chulo since Wilson had become an honest citizen, even though Chulo supposedly worked around the casino and whorehouse. Mostly Warner remembered him from the other days, from the owl-hoot days, when Chulo was constantly saying, "I want to fuck sum weemins an' rob one Mesican bank."

Warner said, "Is Chulo here?"

Wilson answered, "He'll be back tomorrow. He's gone over into Mexico on a little trip for me." He poured them both some more brandy and motioned for Warner to go on eating his pie. Wilson was silent for a moment and then he said, "You ain't really serious about going looking for that gang, are you?"

Warner just looked back at him, chewing slowly. He didn't say anything.

Wilson said, "You remember when I used to buy horses from you?"

"Of course. Hell, you still do."

"No, I mean back in the days when I was collecting bullet scars."

"Yes."

"You remember, and it hasn't been that long ago, maybe four or five years, about hitting me up to join my outfit?"

Warner looked down at his pie. He didn't say anything. It had seemed like a mighty exciting idea at the time though he doubted that his grandfather, even if he had already passed away, would have approved.

"Well, do you?"

Warner nodded slowly. He said, "Yes, I suppose so."

"And what did I say?"

Warner was feeling more and more uncomfortable. He said, "You said a lot of things. But mainly you said I wasn't cut out for it and you couldn't afford to get either me or you killed on the chance it come up."

Wilson said, "I told you there'd come a time when you'd hesitate, when you'd want to think, when you wouldn't react. And that hesitation would get you killed and maybe whoever was with you. You remember that?"

Warner took a swallow of the brandy. He knew it was the finest liquor money could buy, but he didn't much care for the taste of it. He did like the feeling it gave him when it commenced to spread around in his stomach. He said, "Well, yes, I remember that. It ain't exactly the kind of compliment a body is likely to forget."

Wilson said, "The world is made up of two kinds of people—them that hesitates and them that don't. It's that simple. And that's the reason you ain't going looking for that bunch of *bandidos*. They'll get taken care of, don't you worry. But likely they are right now back over in Mexico spending the money off whatever they stole. But they'll be coming back and reports I'm hearing is that they are likely to run into a mighty warm reception. They done considerable harm to a lot of people and the feeling is that they need to get discouraged right quick before they get others to thinking like they used to, that there's easy pickings over here."

"You think it's just one bunch?"

Wilson said, "As it happens, that's what Chulo has gone to Mexico to see if he can find out. Some concerned citizens around here come to me and asked for his help." He stood up. "It's getting on for evening. I'll be getting a little gambling trade in here pretty quick. Reckon I better go put on my frock tailed coat so I'll look like a proper casino proprietor."

"What about the cathouse? How do you dress for that?"

"Are you crazy? Evita runs that place with Lupita's help. You think she'd let me around them girls? Hell, I ain't even allowed in and I own the damn place. I'm tame now, Warner. Just a house kitty now."

"Yeah," Warner said. "But save the jokes. My ribs hurt too bad to laugh."

Wilson was wearing an open-necked blue shirt with blue gaberdine saddle pants. The bone-handled .44/.40 caliber revolver, Colt manufacture, he'd been carrying ever since Warner had known him, was at his side. Warner didn't know that he'd recognize Wilson Young without a side gun on. But he felt damn certain he wouldn't recognize him in a frock coat.

Wilson said, "Finish your supper. Them girls are going to come up and oil you down again pretty soon. But you might ought to get some rest before they arrive. You reckon you need watching? I got most stuff set over there by the bedside table that you might need. But I could send one of the girls from the cathouse to keep an eye on you and do any fetching and carrying you might need." He half smiled and added, "I can't imagine you needing her for anything else the condition you're in."

Warner said, "Naw, I can get about all right. If you was any kind of friend you'd've sent that girl out to me while I was out there on the alkali flat. I wouldn't have give a damn what she looked like so long as she was carrying about a gallon of water."

Wilson stood up. He said, "I'll look in on you from time to time, but I reckon you'll sleep most of the night away. It's good dark now and I reckon as soon as them ladies get you ready for bed you won't have no trouble nodding off. You hurting much?"

Warner shrugged and almost winced. But he hid the look that started across his face and said, "Naw, not much. I'm still damn well *aware* of my feet, though."

Wilson said, "Believe it or not, that cactus squeezings that Evita has damn near soaked you in is the real stuff. It'll cure a hurt faster than anything I've ever seen and is just the absolute original genuine stuff for burns and bruises and whatnot. I don't know why it works, but it does, though I never heard of it until I caught hold of Evita. But you still ain't gonna be bouncing around tomorrow morning. I never seen nobody with more black-and-blue marks on 'im. I reckon you'll be lucky if you can walk far enough to piss without hitting the bed."

Warner suddenly said, "Say, that reminds me. This here is your bedroom. I can't take your bed."

"Warner, one thing a man who owns a cathouse ain't never short of is beds. You just make yourself at home. And take you some more of that brandy. You may not like it but it'll help you sleep."

"What about my horse? You know something about that horse?"

"No, not really. But that's a Pico horse. I'm certain of that. What he was doing out where you was I can only guess."

"A Pico horse? I never heard of no breed called Pico. What are you talking about?"

But before he could answer, Evita, followed by her cousin, Lupita, came bustling into the room. They had already changed into their evening's finery, but they were also carrying towels and a pan of what he recognized as the cactus grease. Lupita appeared to have what looked like a flannel nightgown over her arm. He wanted to tell her that unless she was bringing it for herself she might as well take it back, but it didn't appear they were going to give him much time to protest or argue the way they came at him.

Wilson paused at the door. "They are going to

have their way. My advice to you is to save what strength you got left and not put up no fight."

Evita snapped her fingers at Wilson. "You! Señor Beegshot! Chou geet downstairs and make your job."

Wilson's look said, See what I mean? But he said, "You rest tonight, Warner. We'll talk about that horse in the morning. I think you'll find it a pretty interesting story. Anyway, he's getting good treatment down in the stable and is coming around mighty fast. Of course didn't nobody try and beat the liver out of him like you had done for fun."

Wilson left and the women took over. They paid no more attention to him than if he was a load of wet wash they were tending to. They got him up from the table and took him over to the bed and undressed him without ceremony, taking off the clothes it seemed he'd only had on a few hours. After that they rubbed him down with the cactus lotion, paying special attention to his feet. Indeed, they took the heavy socks Wilson had loaned him, loaded them up with the aloe vera, and then pulled them back on his feet. After that, in spite of what protests he could muster, they insisted on putting the flannel nightgown on him. He'd mumbled something about it hardly being cold enough to wear anything but Lupita had told him sharply, "Chou need the heat. The heat is good for chou hurts."

They treated him, he thought, like he'd gone and gotten himself hurt on purpose and was now causing them trouble just for meanness. He said, "I didn't ask for this, you know."

Evita was pulling back the covers. She said, "Chou are as beeg a baby as Weelson. Now chou geet under the covers and chou be quiet. Chou body needs the warm."

He said, "Hell, Evita, I just come out of the goddam desert. Don't you reckon I had enough warm already?"

But Lupita was pushing him down on the pillows and pulling the covers over him. Lord, she was beautiful, with her shining black hair and deep eyes that had a devilish sparkle in them. She was slightly bigger than Evita and, as she bent over him, he couldn't help glancing at her breasts. She caught him at it and giggled. She said, "That don't do you no good for a long time. You chust a beeg baby now."

They left him then, but Evita paused at the door and snapped her fingers at him. "Chou don't keek them covers off or chou geet beeg troubles. Now chou sleep."

He had no expectations of going to sleep so early, especially not after the long nap he'd had that evening. But it did feel good to just lie in the soft bed, and the girls had been right about the heat of the nightshirt and the heavy covers soothing his pains. From downstairs he could just faintly hear the sound of music and raucous talk and loud laughter. He lay there quietly, not expecting to sleep, just content to let himself finally relax. But he hadn't counted on the beating he'd taken or how much it had taken out of him and his inner reserves. More than just his feet and his bruises needed to heal. Not even five minutes had passed since the women had gone out of the room, shutting the door behind them, before he was asleep. So deeply did he sleep that he was never aware of the number of visits that Evita and Lupita and even Wilson Young paid to his bedside to check up on him.

He awoke before dawn, coming awake instantly, with his mind alert and knowing exactly where he was. For a moment he lay very still, slowly exploring the limits of a brand-new sensation. He didn't hurt. He didn't hurt anywhere. Not even the soles of his feet ached. For a long moment he lay there enjoying a bliss he'd never understood before, not fully; the absence of pain. It was almost as pleasurable as anything he could think of; a woman, a drink when he really wanted one, a good meal when he was hungry, the feel of a fine horse under him. So he just lay there and marveled at how feeling nothing could feel so good.

And then he sat up and he knew he'd been wrong. The absence of pain had been an illusion.

Smothered in the cocoon of the blanket heat his pain had been lulled into taking a rest. But as soon as he'd thrown the hot blankets off and sat up the hurt had got right back on the job.

He groaned, being as quiet as he could because he could tell the whole house, or whatever you called some sleeping rooms over a saloon, was quiet and still asleep. He reckoned such folks kept pretty late hours.

Finally he swung his legs around, wincing with the sensation, and sat on the side of the bed with his feet not quite touching the floor. He sat like that for a long time. He didn't know about the soles of his feet but he reckoned the rest of him was just sore from the pounding and the misuse his body had taken. If he'd have been a horse and under his care he'd have prescribed light exercise to work the muscles loose and get the kinks out of the joints. He figured he wasn't built that much different from a horse and that he deserved at least as good a treatment.

With his teeth gritted he eased off the edge of the bed and put his feet on the floor. Surprisingly, they didn't hurt anywhere near as bad as he'd expected.

He stood up, testing his balance. Except for feeling a little lightheaded he was pretty sure he could walk without toppling over. Just standing up he could feel that a great weight of the tiredness and loss of strength that he'd ridden into Del

Rio carrying on his back was mostly gone. He didn't reckon that he wanted to go out and wrestle or gentle a bronc, but he was somewhere near back to his old self.

There was a window just to the left of the bedside table. The shade was drawn. He reached out and gave it a tug and let it slowly go up to reveal the window. The window looked out on what he recognized as Del Rio's main street. He knew that just a hundred yards down to his right was the Rio Grande and the International Bridge that crossed into Mexico. It was just coming light and he could see that the streets were deserted though here and there he could see lights coming on in houses and buildings as people got up and lit their lamps and got ready to try and make another day. There was a lamp on the bedside table with some matches alongside. He took a step over and struck one of the matches and lit the lamp and then trimmed the wick until it was burning brightly. He looked around as the light from the lamp drove the shadows out of the corners. It was a big room with several overstuffed morris chairs and a big chiffonier where he figured Evita kept her clothes and a couple of big bureaus and a big, built-in closet that he reckoned belonged to Wilson. The table he'd eaten off the night before was still there except someone had cleared away his dishes and the remainder of his meal. The only thing left was half a pitcher of lemonade. He took three halting, painful steps over to the table and got hold of the pitcher in both hands and hefted it up to his mouth and had a good long drink. He didn't reckon he was ever going to get his thirst satisfied.

There was a bottle of brandy on the bedside table along with a tumbler. He didn't particularly want any. What he wanted was a big cup of coffee and a hell of a helping of ham and eggs with some baking soda biscuits. But he figured that the brandy might take the edge off his soreness and make it easier for him to get around. And he knew he was going to have to use his body if he was ever going to get it well again. So he took the two steps back to the bedside table and helped himself to a tumblerful of the brandy. It went down pretty hard at first, but, once down, it seemed to get right on the job.

He first set himself the task of walking around the room. He made one circuit, shuffling more than walking, and while it wasn't pleasant it wasn't as bad as he'd thought it was going to be. He paused to take half a tumbler of brandy and then started off again. By the time he'd circled the room ten times he could move with fair comfort so long as he didn't make any sudden moves.

When he felt he was as loosened up as he was going to get he sat down on the bed and took the flannel nightshirt off over his head. It caused him to use muscles he hadn't tested and the effort almost took his breath away. He sat for a moment, getting his breath back and then looked at his feet. They had undergone an amazing improvement overnight. Of course they still didn't look like anything you'd want to walk on, but he could see signs of healing. They were pink with new skin, but the deep cuts seemed to have closed and the bloody spots where the blisters had formed and then popped and then formed again were just shiny new skin. He thought to himself that that cactus juice must be the real article. He put the socks, which were still damp with lotion, back on. All his feet needed, he figured, was not to get roasted again for a while and stay off sharp rocks and cactus spines and they'd be back to normal by and by.

There was a mirror on one of the low bureaus and he got up and walked over to it. He looked his chest over and his back and what of his legs he could see. As near as he could tell, judging by the black-and-blue marks, the Mexican *bandidos* hadn't missed too many places with their kicks and blows. He was just one great big bruise. But that wasn't anything to concern him. Coming up as a bronc twister he'd figured that bruises were a natural part of the way a man lived. They just went with the hat and the spurs. Of course that had been when he was first learning. It had been a good long time since a horse had done the deciding of when it was time for him to get off.

The girls had folded the clothes that Wilson had loaned him and put them on a chair. He got dressed, having to move a little slowly and having to sit down to draw on his pants. After he was dressed he looked in the closet he judged was Wilson's. There were plenty of boots, but not anything he figured he could get on over the thick socks. Finally he found an old pair of *hurraches*, a kind of Mexican moccasin. With the thick socks they fit just about right, though, if anything, they were a little loose. He hadn't reckoned Wilson had such a big foot, but then the *hurraches* were old and probably had stretched considerably.

When he was finished he reckoned he'd have a look around and see if he couldn't scout up some coffee. He could have eaten a live pig for breakfast, but he could hear how quiet the place was and he didn't want to wake anybody up. He didn't reckon Wilson got up at dawn much anymore. More than likely that was when he went to bed.

Warner let himself out of the bedroom and found himself in a hall with a stair leading off each end. Being as quiet as he could he passed three or four rooms and came to the top of the stairs. He went halfway down and ran into another door. It was locked. Thinking about it he reckoned it was the entrance to the saloon and casino and was locked to keep unwelcome visitors from coming up to the living quarters. He went the other way, went down the stairs, found a door, and stepped out onto the main street of Del Rio. If you hadn't have known, a body would never have connected the door to the saloon since it was set so far away from the main entrance to the casino.

The town was beginning to stir. There were people on foot along the boardwalks and here and there shopkeepers were opening their places of business. A few riders and wagons went down the street heading for the International Bridge. He set his hat a little straighter on his head and started up the street looking for a cafe.

He hadn't walked in flat-heeled shoes in a long time, especially Mexican sandals, but he didn't draw any more than the normal looks curious townsfolk throw at an obvious stranger. He found a likely enough looking cafe in the second block down from Wilson's place and turned in the door and found a table and took a seat. He took off his hat and set it on the side of the table, taking note that it didn't look much better than he did. And with small wonder. His hat had been thrown about, rode over, used as a feed bucket, a water bucket for a horse, a scum skimmer, and a pillow. It was dirty and stained and misshapen and still bore the dried marks of the slime from the sump. But it was a good hat and, if he could find a place to get it cleaned and blocked, it would be as good as new a hell of a lot quicker than he would.

A fat woman came over to take his order and, though he felt like ordering a dozen fried eggs and a side of bacon he knew his stomach still wasn't back in shape. He contented himself with four eggs and some ham and biscuits with cream gravy. She brought his coffee first and he smelled it a long time before he took the first sip. There'd been a time, he thought, when he'd despaired of ever smelling coffee again. But that had been a lack of faith on his part and he was just a little ashamed of himself. His granddaddy had taught him that a man has got to believe he'll always come through no matter what the odds. The old man had said, "Warner, once a man gets it set in his mind that he can't do something or that he will fail he might as well look up at the sky and accuse his Maker of turning out a poor piece of work. Because that's what he'll be—a poor piece of work. But it won't be his Maker's fault. Man sets his mind the wrong way is like a spavined horse. He ain't good for nothing."

Warner knew he was going to have trouble with Wilson, but he was just going to have to convince his friend to help him. He had no one else to turn to to help him get reoutfitted. He wasn't going to ask for a loan. He knew there wasn't anything much that Wilson liked better than to get in a match race with somebody that just thought they had a fast horse. Del Rio was the headquarters for brush track racing in that part of the country and Wilson had a standing order in with him for racing stock that could go anywhere from a quarter of a mile to a half mile. And, just coincidently, he had, back at his ranch, a two-year-old colt that he had earmarked for Wilson. The colt was still a little young, but given six or eight months he was going to be hell to beat at any distance short of three-quarters of a mile and especially at the shorter distances they generally ran. He figured the colt was worth seven or eight hundred dollars if he was worth a nickel. He was an outstanding example of breeding quarter horse to Morgan and then back to quarter horse. If Wilson would advance him the money to put him on the trail of the *bandidos* and keep him there, no matter how long it took, he'd let Wilson have the horse for whatever the amount was. He figured the Mexicans had stolen better than two thousand dollars' worth of horseflesh from him and Red, not to count two saddles and a pack outfit and their traveling gear and their firearms. All told he figured it come to right at three thousand dollars. He intended to have the money back, plus interest, plus their hides. And nothing Wilson could do or say was going to stop him from going and finding them and killing every last one of the bastards.

His food came, brought by the surly-looking fat woman. He ate slowly, not wanting to come at his stomach in a rush. The eggs and ham went down easy, but he was forced to slow down on his sixth biscuit. He had two cups of coffee and then put on his hat and stood up and called for his account. It was at that instant, with the fat waitress coming over, that he realized he was standing there without a cent in his pockets.

It had never entered his mind when he'd come in the cafe, but then he'd never gone around in anybody else's pants before. He stood there, not quite sure what to do, while the waitress was toting up his ticket. It came to a dollar and a quarter. He started in to tell her that he'd gotten stripped of his clothes out on the prairie and that he'd borrowed some off Wilson Young and had got up before the house was awake and walked out without realizing he didn't have any money and if she'd just wait he'd go down to the Palace and be right back with the money.

She barely heard him out before she turned her head and yelled out, "Virgil! We got a deadbeat in here!"

It was a small cafe and there weren't many customers, but they all looked up at her loud voice and stared at him. A few seconds later a beefy man came walking out of the kitchen wiping his hands on his grease-stained apron. He was starting to go bald, but there was no mistaking the power in his hands and arms and shoulders. He said, "What's this we got here?"

Warner started in again to tell his story, but the man cut him off before he could even get started good. He said, "Say, we don't serve no free breakfasts to no bums 'round here. You come in here ain't had a shave 'er a haircut in a week, wearin' ol' Mexican sandals an' clothes look like you stole an' set in to tell me some cock an' bull story." He put out his hand and shoved Warner backward. He said, "You jest set down thar' in that cheer an' we'll wait'll the sheriff comes by an' let him see what he thinks. An' fer yore information, Wilson Young lives on a ranch 'cross the border. He don't sleep over his place of bid'ness. Now set down!"

Warner felt a strange peace settle over him. He squared his shoulders. He had been dealt just about all the bad hands he was going to play for a while. He said, levelly, "Now, mister, I am going to walk out that door over there and I'm going to go down to Wilson Young's place and get you your money because I owe it to you. You may try to stop me. You may give me a whipping which wouldn't take much doing because I am as weak as a kitten right now. But if you lay one finger on me you had better go right on and finish the job. You better kill me. Because if I get out of here alive I will come back and let some air in you. And you can depend on that."

116

The beefy man stared at him, suddenly uncertain.

Then, over the man's shoulder, Warner saw Wilson Young enter the cafe and glance around like he was looking for someone. He didn't know if he was glad or sorry that Wilson had arrived when he did.

# 5

They were sitting upstairs in what Wilson called the "whore's kitchen," the big room where the girls cooked and ate and sat around when they weren't on duty. But it was still only about ten o'clock in the morning and Wilson said none of them got up until noon so they had the room and the big table they were at to themselves. Evita had got up and brewed them some coffee and gone back to bed. Wilson had just finished explaining how he'd heard someone moving around and had gone to check on Warner and found him gone. He said, "I figured you was testing out your legs and most likely looking for some coffee. I also figured you didn't have a red cent on you. Started to wait and see how you got out of that one, looking like you do, but figured you couldn't stand much more roughing up. And damned if you didn't pick Boucher's place. He just loves folks that can't pay because he'd rather fight than make money. Mean sonofabitch."

Warner said calmly, "Maybe so."

Wilson laughed. "So you was gonna go back and plug him, huh?"

"If he'd've hit me, yes. I sure as hell wouldn't have been his match physically, not for no wrestling match, not the shape I'm in. Give me a few more days and we might see if he could get his hands on me before I wore him out. Then we'd see how well he could fight down on his knees trying to get his breath."

Wilson looked at him curiously. He said, "Whatever happened to that good ol' boy I used to know was about as gentle as the horses he trained?"

Warner said, "I reckon some of him got left out there on that alkali flat. Or got left to bleach in the sun with his partner."

Wilson shook his head. He said, "I can see that you have made up your mind about this matter. When you first brought it up last night I thought you was still slightly out of your head. But you appear to have made one hell of a recovery. Maybe there is something in that cactus juice Evita whips out at the drop of a body."

Warner said, "I'm feeling better. I don't know about my feet yet."

Wilson leaned around the edge of the table and looked down and laughed. He said, "Them are Chulo's *hurraches* you got on there."

Warner said, "I thought they was a mite big for your size, but they was in your closet. Even with these thick socks I'm kind of rambling around in them."

"How does the rest of your body feel?"

"Sore."

Wilson nodded. He looked thoughtful. Then he

got up and got the pot off the stove and poured them more coffee. When he'd sat back down he said, "Warner, you're a smart man. Too smart, I think, to go outside your limits. And I think trying to hunt down a bunch of *bandidos* when that ain't your line of work is going outside your limits."

"They didn't kill me the first chance they had."

Wilson blew on his coffee. He said, "No, but it wasn't for lack of trying. They just didn't reckon on how tough or how smart you was. Take that trick you pulled about the water in that sump hole. I'd wager there ain't ten men in the county—no, in this state would have had the brains to have put them big rocks in there to raise the water level where that horse could drink. Especially considering the shape you was in and the horse with the blind staggers. Gray, I'd bet you didn't have more than a half an hour to get water in that horse or he'd have died. Where in hell did you get the strength to do it? I know them volcanic rocks are fairly light for their size, but you was plumb out of vigor. How could you even think under them circumstances?"

Warner said mildly, "There wasn't much thinking to it. I just used what was at hand."

Wilson said, "Warner, my point is—anybody that's that smart ought to be smart enough not to play the other man's game. I know considerable about gambling and the first rule is don't ever sit in at a table you don't think you can win at.

And, Gray, you ain't a gun hand. This is shooting business and that's not your game. It's out of your line."

Warner said, "Wilson, I'm going to need outfitting. I'm going to need some money. I've got that horse, but I reckon it belongs to somebody else. Will you stake me? I ain't asking for a loan. I've got a coming racehorse at my ranch on the Nueces that will win you plenty of races. He's a big colt and you'll be able to ride him yourself instead of getting some little jockey, like they've got to doing here of late. I figure the horse to be worth eight hundred dollars, but he's yours at whatever price will put me on my feet and get me on the trail of them sonsofbitches I intend to kill."

Wilson looked at him and shook his head slowly. He said, "Will you listen to yourself, Gray? You just said you planned on killing some folks. Granted they need killing, but have you ever said that before? Ever in your life have you ever said you were going to kill anybody? Have you?"

Warner's face looked bleak. He said, "You wern't there, Wilson. You don't know what it was like. No, I ain't ever considered killing anybody before, don't think I ever used the term even in jest. But then nobody ever done me the way those *pachucho* bastards did. Wilson, I've had plenty of time to study on this. I know, it don't seem like much time to you, but some of those minutes out there on that gypsum flat seemed like days and weeks. Man can do an awful lot of serious thinking when he's in the sort of trouble I was. Now you can argue with me, and you can say you won't outfit me or help me. All that will do is slow me down. I'll get the stake somewheres if I have to walk home to my ranch and sell every horse I got to raise the money. I'd sell the ranch but it's mortgaged to the top of the water trough."

Wilson got out one of the little black Mexican cigarillos he favored. He took a moment to light it and get it drawing. Then he blew out a lungful of smoke and said, "Before we talk about outfitting and getting on the trail for the chase, let's talk about something else."

"What?"

Wilson said casually, "You're a good shot, Gray. And you're fast. In fact I'd say you was better than a good shot with a handgun, I'd say you was excellent. Never saw you shoot a rifle, but I'd reckon you'd be the same. You got them real good reflexes, couldn't be a bronc rider without them. And you've got plenty of nerve and you've got the steady hand and the good eye."

Warner was nodding. He said, "Yes, and at a pretty early age I had some teaching from a man named Wilson Young and a few other men that rode with him. And I don't reckon you can get better schooling than that. We busted many a cap while the bunch of you was waiting around for me to get you remounted on fresh horses and see to your wore-out ones. Yes, if you are aiming to get me to say I owe a lot in that regard, why, it's the easiest thing in the world. For a while there there wasn't a tin can or a empty whiskey bottle safe in my range."

Wilson smiled slightly, working his mouth around the cigarillo. He said softly, "Gray, that's just what I'm talking about. You are a hell of a tin can shot and a hell of a tonic bottle shot, but that ain't the same as shooting at other men. You ever fired a gun at another man?"

Warner stared back at him. He had been expecting this ever since Wilson had talked about hesitating. He said, "Wilson, how old you figure I am? I never told you so you'll just be guessing."

Wilson shrugged. "Twenty-four. Maybe a year older. What the hell's that got to do with it?"

Warner said, "Because you make the same mistake about me that a lot of people do, especially people who think they're trading horses with a kid. I'm twenty-eight, Wilson. And I'm a hard twenty-eight. You might recollect that both my parents died from the fever when I was a young'un and I was raised by my granddaddy. That was one hard old man and he passed his hardness along to me. No, I ain't never shot nobody because I never had no reason to. But if I had to've, I would've. And I got to shoot one now. I know I got this baby face and I've seen to it that I've made good use of it, with women and with horse traders who reckoned they were getting the best of a kid until they took a closer look and figured out they'd been skinned. I don't act tough and I don't talk tough because that ain't my nature. But there have been a few who've found out to their sorrow that I ain't just the good-natured, friendly ol' boy they thought I was. Them Mexicans didn't kill me right off because they didn't think I was dangerous to them. Well, now they will learn to their sorrow that they made a miscalculation."

Wilson cocked his head. He put the stub of his cigarillo out in a saucer. He said, "Well, maybe I don't know you as well as I thought I did. But I'm only talking as your friend when I say that I've heard this before. In fact, I've benefited by it before. There are lots of folks running around carrying guns think they can shoot them. And some of them can. And some of them think they can plug another man as easy as they can pick off a deer or a rabbit. They think that right up until it comes down to the actual doing. Once, about six or seven years ago, I got trapped in a lady's bedroom by a gentleman carrying a double-barreled shotgun. He had me dead to right. I was ten foot from my revolver with a hysterical woman in the way. And the man knew who I was and knew I had a price on my head. I think all the rewards put together come out to around seven thousand dollars. A power of money to that man. And all he had to do was pull the trigger and he'd have splattered me all over the wall." Wilson leaned forward. "Except he couldn't do it. He thought he could do it, he said he could do it, he told me he was going to do it, but, in the end, he started shaking. I walked over and took the gun away from him, got dressed, and left."

Warner said, "What was he, a shopkeeper or a bank clerk?"

Wilson grinned slightly. He said, "My, my, little boy must be cutting teeth. Getting a little sassy. No, he was a top hand on a big ranch. Man used to guns and used to trouble. But he hesitated."

"There you go again. You think I'll hesitate."

Wilson said, "I had a friend. Some time back." He stopped talking for a moment and looked away. A tinge of sadness touched his face. "We kind of started out on the owl-hoot trail together, both of us around seventeen. Name was Les Richter. He was a little like you in some ways in that he kind of give the impression of being a little soft, a little easy. Not that he was. We rode together some six or seven years. Done a fair amount of robbing together, but I don't reckon Les ever really had his heart in it. He was like me in that he'd kind of been forced into outlaw ways because there wasn't nothing else. It was right after the Civil War and the Yankees had taken over the place. Anyway, Les was a good steady gun hand. You could depend on him in a fight so long as he knew it was a fight. Point I'm trying to make is that Les wasn't no stranger to shooting and getting shot at. He would fire his guns and he generally hit what he shot at." Wilson stopped again. After a moment he said, "But then there come a time Les had to go up against a man over a matter didn't have nothing to do with the outlaw business. It was a private matter and Les went into the confrontation not quite sure he was in the right. Happened right down the river in Laredo. Not much over a hundred miles from here. The other fellow was a hard case, he didn't care if he was in the right or in the wrong. So he didn't hesitate. Les did. I killed the man later, but he killed Les. Or rather Les's hesitation killed him because he was the better gunman of the two." Wilson had been looking off in the distance. Now he turned and looked at Warner. He said, "I would have never thought Les Richter would hesitate."

Warner looked at his empty coffee cup and then yawned. He said, "Wilson, you and I can debate this here question until the cows come home, but it ain't going to settle it. I'm going after those bastards. That's not a question that's open to discussion. As to whether or not I'll hesitate, as you call it, well, we won't know about that until the time comes. This is your game and they ain't no doubt you know considerable more about it than I do, this business of shooting other men.

But you don't know considerable more about me than I do. So all this talk is just scattering the dust and causing more work for the girls. You going to stake me or not?"

Wilson laughed. He said, "I wish you wouldn't beat around the bush, Gray. If you've got something to ask me, why, just out with it. Of course I'll stake you, you jug head. Even loan you one of my guns. You can't buy one in the store. Colt makes 'em special for me."

Warner said, "I'll write you out a bill of sale for that running horse I got on the ranch. Bay colt, branded W-nine. So in case I 'hesitate' you'll be able to get some of your money back."

"You don't got to do that, Gray. I'm going with you."

Warner suddenly sat up in his chair and squared his shoulders. "Like hell you are. I ain't had no wet nurse in a good many years. I reckon I'll handle this myself."

"Gray, it ain't just for you. The community is all upset about this matter. I've halfway promised I'd lead a party after this bunch."

"Well, it's a free country. You lead all the parties you want to. But I'm going after this bunch solo. I want every last greaser sonofabitch to know who it is killing them."

"You have your mind set on this?"

"Yep. But I do need a damn good horse. You still got any stock you've bought off me?"

"I've got that chestnut mare I got from you about two years ago and that four-year-old sorrel. You are liable to be on the trail longer than you think. I'd reckon the sorrel has got more stamina."

Warner raised his eyebrows slightly. "On top of the rest of it you are now going to tell me about *horses?*"

Before Wilson could answer Evita and Lupita came into the room. Evita said, "What are you two doing seeting here doing nozing? Why don' chou eat some breakfast or sum'zing?"

Wilson said, "Why don't you just *fix* some breakfast or 'sum'zing'?"

Warner watched Lupita as she moved around the room. Just looking at her, and with his body still damaged, he could feel an old familiar sensation make his neck want to swell. He was going to have to ask Wilson just what the situation was on her. He could see her casting little glances as she went about the business of fixing a meal. She asked how he was feeling and he said he was doing pretty good. She said, "We need to put more of the aloe on chou preeety soon."

He looked over at Wilson. Wilson was looking up at the ceiling, a half smile on his face.

He stayed until the girls had finished cooking and then he asked Wilson where he could take a bath and could he borrow his shaving equipment.

Wilson took him down the hall. They had a bathtub right there in the place. The water came in by pipe from a big cistern outside. Wilson said, "'Course it's cold. But it's a right big bathtub."

And it was nearly the biggest he'd ever seen. Wilson said, "We got it for the girls that work here. Some of them old boys they have to entertain ain't real careful about their personal care and the girls like to rinse off as often as they can. I'll fetch my shaving stuff."

Before he could walk out Warner said, "Wilson, I want to ask you something. I—" He blushed slightly. "It ain't really none of my business, but I was just wondering."

Wilson said, "No, Lupita ain't one of the working girls here. And she ain't my girl. Evita is all I can handle. Lupita, she's loose and she's handy. She does her own choosing. So far as I know she ain't chose nobody lately. Though she does appear to me to be taking an extra special amount of concern in your case."

Warner said, "That's 'cause I'm hurt."

Wilson grinned like a Chesire cat. He said, "Well, I see them *bandidos* didn't beat your sense of humor out of you. Reckon you had better get slicked up if you're a-gonna do some courtin'. Though you musta not been hurt as bad as I thought if you've already got that on your mind. I'll get my razor."

It felt good to soak in the clean water, even if it

wasn't warm. But then, not ten minutes after he'd finished shaving and undressed and gotten into the big wooden tub, the door had opened and Lupita had come in carrying a steaming bucket of water in either hand. He'd made a wild grab for a towel, but she paid him no more mind than if he was sitting in a tent. She poured in the hot water and said, "Chou need the warm to take out the sore. I geet some more."

He'd sat there, stunned, not quite knowing what to do. He'd figured it would take her some time to heat up two more buckets so he hadn't made any preparations for her swift return. Next thing he knew she was back and pouring more boiling water into the tub. It would have been a treat except he didn't know how to cover himself or even if he should. And then she sat down on the side of the tub and started soaping him. He made a mild protest about the seemliness of the matter, but she just shushed him. She said, "Who chou theen wash you when they bring you upstairs? Chou theenk theese is the first time I see chou? Hah!" She kept on washing his back. "*Es muy importante* chou be clean for the magic of the aloe."

She finished up by inspecting the soles of his feet and then left him. He lay in the pleasantly warm water, thinking that this was maybe the first time he'd ever bathed in a bathtub in a whorehouse, especially one that was more round than anything else. Finally he hoisted himself out

130

and dried off and put on the pants Wilson had loaned him. He was feeling more than a little tired and he figured to get in a nap. Wilson was just now eating breakfast so he reckoned they didn't take lunch until midafternoon. Well, he thought, some folks worked some hours and others worked different ones.

He got back to the bedroom he was using, took off his trousers, and got under the covers. Sinking into the bed he realized he still had a ways to go in his recuperation. He didn't have much staying power and he doubted he was strong enough to hold Lupita down. And he still hurt, his feet especially. They no longer throbbed, but if he stayed on them very long they got tender and then painful. He was going to have to learn to be content. His mind wanted to have started after the *bandidos* the day before, but his body wasn't ready.

He was about to doze off when Lupita came in, and, without ceremony or permission, jerked the covers back off him. She had a bottle of what he figured was the aloe lotion in her hand. He started to make some comment about folks ought to knock on doors, but he doubted it would do much good. She went to work, paying special attention to his feet and his chest and the lower part of his back. When she was finished she pulled the covers back up, collected the clothes he'd been wearing, and left the room. He shook his head and turned over on his side, glad to be clean and resting. He had been dying to touch Lupita while she'd been greasing him down, but something had told him it wasn't the right time. Just before he went to sleep he wondered what he was going to do for clothes now that Lupita had carried off all the ones he'd been wearing. But, right then, he didn't much care.

Wilson said, "I call it a Pico horse because that's the name of the man that imported the horse, brought it into this country. Course he didn't bring in only the one that you found, there was six in all."

They were sitting in the Elite Cafe, a better class of eatery than Warner had found on his own that morning. They were both eating a steak with potatoes and boiled onions. It was about four o'clock in the afternoon, a time Warner found mighty strange to be eating a steak lunch. But when you were with a cathouse and casino owner you kept his hours.

Wilson continued. "The breed of horse ain't a Pico. That horse you found in time to save the both of your lives is what they call an Andalusian. It's a Spanish horse from a area in Spain right up near where Morocco or some such place joins in. It's a half brother to the Arabian. They both go way back, way the hell back. I reckon they're about the oldest breeds I ever heard of."

Warner stopped eating. He said, "Andalusian, Andalusian. You know, seems I read that name in a book somewheres. I got all kinds of books on horses. Yeah, he is kin to the Arabian. Hell, that's what puzzled me out there in that desert. He looked like an Arabian, but then he didn't quite. You know what I mean? Close, real close, but not quite there."

Wilson nodded. "Yeah, but the Andalusian is supposed to be a shade quicker than an Arabian without giving up anything in endurance. I figure any other horse would have died out there on that alkali flat. Though how in God's name he got there is anybody's guess."

Warner said, "And you say some man named Pico brought over six of them. Whatever for?"

Wilson shrugged. He said, "I don't know all that much about it. In fact, what I've been telling you about the breed I got from Pico himself. His whole name's Avery Pico. Kind of an old rip. I don't mean he's all that old, forty or so, but he's a drinker and a hell-raiser. I had to throw him out of my place a few times."

Warner said, "You still ain't told me what he was doing with such a breed of horse. I swear I sometimes still think I dreamed that horse up. Until I actually go around to the stable and see him I ain't really going to believe it. A mustang or some old range horse, yeah. But an Arabian cross? Shit!"

Wilson said, "The horse is real. Anyway, this Avery Pico's a kind of strange old boy. He and his wife moved here about six or seven months ago. Bought a small ranch west of town down right at the river. Wasn't a big place, maybe two thousand acres, but it was as prime pastureland as we got around here."

Warner said, "Must have cost him."

Wilson nodded. "Man seemed to have plenty of money. I don't know where he got it, but he spent it like he had it. And I don't even know where he came from, come to think of it. He wasn't a Texan. Had some strange-sounding accent. Might have been from Virginia or California or some place like that. But he had this idea of importing these Spanish horses. Said he was going to breed them to either American saddlebreds or just plain cow horses and turn out the perfect animal to work cattle. Yeah, I believe he was going to use crossbred mares and turn out a outstanding cattle horse for a fair price. Said the endurance and quickness of the Andalusians would carry over into the common cow horse and produce a new breed."

Warner looked skeptical. He said, "Where was the cow sense supposed to come from? Horse can be fast as hell and strong as hell, but he better be able to think better than a cow or he ain't no good to a cowhand."

Wilson shrugged. He said, "From the cow

horse, I reckon. Like I say, he talked a lot of nonsense, but if a man spends his money in my place he's got a right to talk all the nonsense he's a mind to. Said those Spanish horses cost two thousand dollars apiece. At least that's what he said it cost him to get them here."

"Two—" Warner rolled his eyes. "I never even heard of a two-thousand-dollar horse outside of them racehorses they run up in Kentucky and places like that. Hell, that's a power of money to pay for a horse. He still think this is going to work?"

Wilson said, "Pico is dead."

"Yeah?"

Wilson said, "Got raided by a gang of *bandidos*. From what his wife says we ain't got no reason to doubt it was the same bunch you and Red run into. They got all his horses, maybe twenty all told including them Spanish horses, and killed him when he run out to try and fight them off, which was a damned fool thing to do. Run out in the open like that. Killed him and one of his hired hands. The best we can get out of Mrs. Pico is there was ten or eleven of the bandits. Pico got two of them and she thought a third rode off wounded. That was about ten days ago, maybe two weeks. You could figure they carried them horses back across the border, had themselves a fiesta on the proceeds, and then come back across for another helping."

"But, Wilson, that horse I found couldn't have made it for over a week on that alkali flat. That's a fact."

Wilson shrugged. "I ain't saying he did. But he could have got loose from them when they first stole them off Pico's place and then got lost and went to wandering around. Hell, the damned horse just got here from a foreign country. He wouldn't know the area. He might have got to grazing north and just kept going until it dawned on him the land was getting a little poor. Just because he's a foreign horse wouldn't make him any smarter than any other horse. I believe it was you told me not to never be surprised at what a horse will get up to."

Warner said, "It could have happened that way." Then he looked off toward a corner of the cafe and shook his head. He said, "But what kind of odds do you reckon it took to put me and that horse together right there, in that place, at the same time? And under them circumstances. Me at the end of my run and him so drawed down he was forced to be gentle. Didn't have strength enough to be anything else. You're a gambler. Give me odds on that happening."

Wilson got out a cigarillo and lit it. Except for a few men drinking at the bar they were the only customers in the cafe. At least the only customers having a meal. When Warner had woke up he'd found a fresh pair of Wilson's saddle pants and a new, crisply ironed shirt piled on the wooden chair. There'd been a new pair of the heavy, soft socks as well. Warner kept meaning to ask Wilson what he was doing with such socks in south Texas, but it kept slipping his mind. What he mainly wanted was to get out of the damned socks and the damned Mexican sandals and put a pair of boots back on. But he knew his feet needed a couple more days even if they were healing much faster than he could have dared hope.

Wilson said, "I don't think odds go that high. Just be thankful. That's why I can't believe you want to stick your hand back in the fire. Once is enough for even the slowest child."

Warner ignored him. He rubbed the thigh of his pants. They were jeans, but they were of a much softer material than the rough denim he was used to buying that were made by the Levi-Strauss company. And the blue shirt he reckoned Lupita had brought him was of a soft cotton. He said, "I ain't shore if I can go back to my old brand of clothes after wearing yours for a couple of days. You don't mind looking after yourself, do you?"

Wilson said, "Chulo ought to be back late tonight or early in the morning. That is if he didn't get tangled up with a woman or a bottle of liquor that was bigger than he is. He ought to have found out if it was the same bunch. Not that

I think there's much doubt. Mrs. Pico said there was a fat man seemed to be leading the bunch. But he never got close enough for her to see any scar."

"What was she doing at the time?"

"Said she was firing a rifle out the window of the ranch house. Which I don't doubt she was. She's got a lot of sand, that lady. She sent one of their *vaqueros* in with the news and the doc and the sheriff and a couple of deputies went out. Question is, do you want to take that horse back out to her or do you want me to send somebody out with it?"

Warner grimaced. He said, "I ain't much of a hand for getting around grieving widows. Wouldn't know what to say."

A waiter came over to take away their dishes. They were sitting at a table that looked out on Del Rio's main street. Mounted men rode by, the hooves of their horses throwing little puffs of dust in the air. Wilson Young drew on his cigarillo and looked out the window. He said, "I don't reckon you are gonna find a grieving widow. Ain't my business to say, but I don't think it was a love match. Pico was considerably older than his wife and she is a mighty handsome woman. Mighty handsome. I'd put her close to your age. Kind of a strawberry blond-haired woman. I wouldn't be surprised if the idea for those Andalusians didn't come from her."

"You are saying a rich man bought himself a wife."

Wilson gave him a level look. He said, "I ain't saying anything. Don't get me confused with some old woman hangin' out the warsh and gossipin' over the back fence. I'm just saying what I said. I'm also saying that it struck me she knew more about horses than he did. You understand me?"

Warner said, "I reckon I'd like to take that horse out there. Truth be told I'm pretty well taken with that horse. I feel like he's lucky for me. Of course I don't know what kind of horse he really is because I haven't tried him, not under any kind of conditions. But the sonofabitch has got enough heart for three or four horses. You reckon she might loan him or rent him to me? I think it would be fitting if I used the horse that saved me to run down her husband's killers. What do you reckon?"

Wilson sighed. "Warner, I keep expecting you to come to your senses and go back to being the Warner Grayson I know whose business is horses. Have you forgot you've got a dozen ranchers expecting you to get by and smooth out their remudas? You want a bunch of cowboys getting all bruised up riding spoiled stock that's been turned out all winter?"

Warner picked up his coffee cup, saw that it was empty, and set it back down. He said, "They can wait a while. They are a month from any real work. Besides, like you say, I'm going to need some time to heal. I couldn't take the bruising myself working a rough string. Besides, what if I'd died out there? What would the ranchers have done then? Now, about Mrs. Pico. You reckon she might consider loaning me that horse? That is if he's fit?"

Wilson said, "Well, I don't see why she wouldn't. Especially considering she wouldn't have him back if it wasn't for you. You going to at least send word to the ranches that are expecting you?"

Warner said, "I might not need to. This other business might not take that long."

Wilson laughed and said, "Shore. You been man hunting for as long as I've knowed you. Shore, Gray, I know you got this figured down to a gnat's eye. Boy, you are something. I mean, you are really something. You remind me of a friend of mine, Justa Williams, except he's got reason to act like he knows what he's doing. He's rich."

Warner said carelessly, "Say, is Charlie Stanton still around?"

Wilson looked blank for a second and then the puzzlement cleared from his brow. He replied, "Oh, that kid you let help you winter before last when Red was hurt there for a little while. Hell, Gray, you ain't thinking of sending him out to work those ranches? You'd lose every customer you got. Hell, he ain't no more than eighteen or nineteen."

Warner said comfortably, "I wasn't near that old when I started."

"Yeah, but you got something special. Everybody knows that."

"I wasn't the only one got it given to me. I think that Stanton boy has it too."

"Gray, he ain't even cowboying. He works in a goddam dry goods store."

Warner said, "I told him to lay off that work as a cowhand. All that's good for is getting you busted up by them damn longhorn cattle. Why God ever wanted to invent such a beast and call it a benefit to man is more than I can imagine. I'd as soon try and work a herd of bears. Or mountain lions. Damn cattle kill more horses than Mexican tick disease."

As they walked back to the Palace, Warner trying not to limp, Wilson looked over at him curiously. He said, "Tell me the truth—how you feeling other than your feet? Seems like you done a pretty good job on that steak."

Warner said, twisting his shoulders from side to side, "I don't feel all that bad. Still sore. But I'm getting my strength back."

Wilson said casually, "If you feel up to it I'll tell Evita to send you one of our girls. In fact you can just keep her with you while you're here. She'd probably appreciate the rest."

Warner hesitated and then he said, "What do you reckon would happen if I was to just kind of give Lupita a little caress? Little gesture. Maybe a little kiss on the cheek?"

Wilson half smiled. He said, "There, my son, you are on your own. When I won them two girls in that poker game I thought I'd found me a bird nest on the ground. But Evita made it clear as a bullet through the head that it was me and her and Lupita was off-limits even if she was legally mine. Listen, I've slept in the same bed with both them girls, all three of us naked as the day we seen daylight and it has never crossed my mind to even *think* about touching Lupita. All I can do is wish you luck. I don't know nothing about that section of the country. Now. What about that Pico horse?"

Warner said, "I reckon I'll take him out myself. But I think I'll wait until tomorrow. I'm hoping I can wear boots by then. I'd hate to show up at that lady's place wearing these here Mexican moccasins."

Wilson said, "Well, you are looking better. First look I got at you I give you up for dead. But I don't reckon you be through with the nursing yet. Them women get their claws into a man they don't let go no more than a cat does a mouse."

Warner's feet were starting to get tender. He slowed. He said, "I just can't get used to your damn hours. I never et lunch at four in the afternoon in my life."

Wilson said, "Actually, they ain't my real hours. Most times I stay over to my ranch in Mexico. It's just with Chulo gone and this here Mississippi riverboat gambler I hired to run the casino both being out I've had to hang around. Soon as Chulo gets back you and me will probably bunk in over at my ranch."

They went in the private door of the Palace. All Warner had on his mind was getting off his feet and taking a little rest. But he'd no more than got in the room he was using than Lupita came in with a steaming bucket of saltwater. She jerked him upright and swung him around, peeled his socks off, and plunged his feet in the hot water. She said, "Theese salty water weel make chou feet tough. Es very necessary."

"Aw, hell," he said. "I need some sleep, Lupita."

She was going to the door. She held up a finger. "Chou keep chou feet in theese water for one hour an' theen I come back and sleep wit' chou."

He stared after her. Hell, for that kind of prize he'd keep his feet in tequila and horse piss. But after a while his eyes got heavy and he lay back on the bed. By straining his legs he could just keep his feet under the water.

If he didn't go to sleep.

# 6

He damned near hadn't recognized the horse when they'd led him out of the stable. True, he'd been brushed and curried and washed down, but even that and the two days of rest and good grain and hay didn't seem enough to account for the dramatic improvement in the horse. He was lighter in color than Warner had remembered. He looked like a mixture somewhere between a dun and a light brown, but it was hard to tell the way his coat shimmered.

Warner had looked him over with a critical eye, finally mouthing him and deciding that the horse was a young four. He'd walked around him, feeling his legs, checking his hooves. As near as he could tell the horse had come through the ordeal without losing his place in line. Warner couldn't get over how the horse had bloomed and filled out with just the little good care he'd gotten. It was a sure sign of how fit and durable the horse was.

The stable boys had saddled and bridled him with a rig of Wilson's. Warner had checked the girth, something he did on every horse he rode, and then stepped aboard. The horse had stood stock-still while he mounted, but then, with him in the saddle, he'd wanted to go prancing sideways. Warner had put it down to youthful exuberance, but he'd still checked the horse immediately. He'd said aloud, "Listen here, buster, I'll decide when we move. Not you. You're the horse, I'm the boss. Let's me and you get that straight going in so we don't have no trouble about the matter at an inconvenient time."

The stable boys had laughed. Warner had given them a wink and then put the horse in that stylish little canter of his and rode out into the street and turned north and then west on the river road.

His feet felt pretty good. Lupita had come in and caught him sleeping with his feet out of the water. She'd brought in a fresh bucket and then sat beside him on the bed and made sure he kept his feet immersed. He'd tried to kiss her on the neck, but she'd pushed his face away and scolded him. Then he'd tried to kiss her on the cheek and she'd given him a light slap. Figuring it couldn't get much worse he'd bent his head around and kissed her on the lips. All that had got him had been a kiss back.

But that had been as far as it had gone. As he'd tried to lean her back on the bed she'd suddenly reared up and given him a good scolding, again, for taking his feet out of the saltwater. After that she'd made it clear that until the nursing was over there wouldn't be anything else.

Well, the nursing was damn near over as far as he was concerned. He had boots on his feet again, even though they were a little uncomfortable. Wilson had gone over to his ranch across the river and found an old pair of his boots that were stretched out and soft. Lupita had greased his feet and, with regular socks, they'd fit.

He rode along the river road, following the directions to the widow Pico's ranch that Wilson had given him. It was a fine, early spring afternoon, a little warmer than could be expected and it felt fittingly good for him to be a-horseback again, especially on such an animal. His only complaint was the horse's flowing mane and overabundant tail. He didn't begrudge the animal the tail, especially when the flies would get thick that summer, but he thought the mane ought to be roached, or at least cut back. But then he remembered how he'd held himself aboard the horse with that very same mane and he found he couldn't say much.

About a mile out of town he pulled the horse up. He figured the animal was fit enough to be put through his paces. He was on a broad stretch of prairie and, except for a lone house here and there, he and the horse pretty much had the place to themselves. He touched the horse lightly with his spurs, putting him into a lope and a gallop, all the while reining him around in circles and figure eights, seeing how responsive he was to the bit and how quick and surefooted. The horse performed without a fault, even to Warner's exacting expectations. Warner said aloud, patting the horse on the neck, "Either somebody did a hell of a job of training you or you got breeding goes back more than a year or two."

He was wearing a side arm that Wilson had loaned him. It was a Colt caliber .44/.40, which was a gun that fired a .40 caliber cartridge set on a .44 caliber frame. Wilson always said that a .40 caliber bullet would stop anything you could hit where you were supposed to hit it and the .44 caliber frame, being bigger, made the gun steadier in the hand with less barrel deviation. The revolver had the standard six-inch barrel that Wilson generally favored for everyday work. But, on some occasions, Warner had seen him carry a four-and-a-half-inch barrel as well as one with nine inches. It all depended on what Wilson was expecting to run into. He'd given Warner a full holster rather than one of the cutaway jobs he wore when he was around town. The full holster kept the gun from bouncing out if a rider got into some rough going. It wasn't as fast to draw out of, but Warner had already made up his mind that he wasn't going to get into any quick draw contests with anyone. If he saw anyone coming he planned to shoot, he'd already have the gun in hand.

Now he wanted to see how the Andalusian handled the sound of gunfire. His stock was routinely exposed to it because a cowhand never knew when he might have to fire a pistol and he damn sure didn't want a horse exploding under him at the same time.

Warner put the horse in a slow walk and pulled the pistol and fired straight into the air. He felt the horse tremble slightly, but other than that he didn't react. Still keeping the horse walking he lowered the gun a little closer to the animal's ear and fired again. The reaction wasn't much different. Warner put the horse in a lope and fired straight ahead, the muzzle blast occurring not more than a foot from the horse's right ear. This time the horse didn't even flinch.

Warner nodded, satisfied, and put the revolver away. This old plug wasn't a half-bad horse.

He rode the rest of the way to the Pico ranch deep in thought, oblivious to the horse and to his surroundings. Ever since he and the horse had rescued each other some part of his mind had been scheming with a plan as to how he might find the bandits, lure them, and reduce the odds so that he could do the job by himself. Warner had always been quick and smart even though circumstances hadn't allowed him to go beyond the sixth grade of the local school. But his grandfather had been a reader and he'd picked up the habit from the old man of always having a book handy, something he could spend his rare few minutes of leisure with. His grandfather said that books weren't just words, but spurs for the mind.

His grandfather said they made you think. And so Warner had early on learned to set his mind to a problem and work it through until he could see a way to make an end result that was to his satisfaction. He'd never been one to parade this ability and most of his reading was done in solitude since the old man had passed on.

But here was this problem about the *bandidos*—he intended to bring about a result that was going to be entirely to his liking and he was going to do it in his own way. And that in spite of what his friend Wilson Young, or anyone else for that matter, might think or want.

He and Mrs. Pico were sitting out on the shaded porch of her ranch house drinking coffee. Warner hadn't wanted any coffee, but she'd seemed to feel they ought to have something so he hadn't said no even though, truth be told, he'd much rather have had a big glass of cool, well water.

The ranch house was of the type built in the area except that it was bigger than most. It was built out of whitewashed adobe bricks and topped with red clay tiles. There were three outbuildings, the biggest of which was also built out of adobe bricks. He figured that's where the Andalusian stallions had been stabled, it being cooler than the other two barns which were built of sawn lumber. Mrs. Pico had been shocked and then thrilled and then grateful when he'd ridden up on her horse.

But even through all those emotions she'd never seemed to get excited. It went with Wilson having called her a "cool customer." He'd also said she was tough, though she certainly didn't look tough. She was tall, for a woman, and willowy with that reddish blond hair that could look so many different colors depending on the way the light struck it. The most amazing thing about her had been that she was wearing pants. True, they were obviously riding pants and made for her out of the kind of material that women wore, but Warner didn't reckon he'd ever seen a woman in pants before. She had on flat-heeled boots with tops that came up almost to her calves. They looked like cavalry boots, but she'd informed him that they were English riding jodhpurs and were quite popular in Kentucky and Tennessee and Virginia, where she was from.

Warner would have called her not quite beautiful. He reckoned Wilson's description of her as handsome was close to the mark. She was not full breasted as was, say, Lupita, or at least she wasn't unless the silk blouse she was wearing did not reveal her bosom. But there was a seductive flare to her hips, especially in the tight, thin material of her riding pants. All in all, Warner had decided, he wouldn't kick her out of bed. He'd also decided that there might be a problem getting her in the bed in the first place as she seemed to be more interested in horses and ranching than anything else. He had arrived and she'd come out, coolly, and then there'd been some confusion and surprise and then joy about the return of her horse. They'd stood out front for a while with her mostly saying, "I can't believe it, I can't believe it." And then a *vaquero* had come and led the horse away to the big, adobe brick barn and she'd invited him into the house and sat him down and given him a drink of brandy. Without much interference from her he'd told her the whole story. The only time she'd interrupted was when he'd been describing the bandit leader. She'd said, emphatically, "Yes, yes, that's the man. The man who stole our horses and killed Avery."

He had taken note that she hadn't said "killed my husband" but "killed Avery." It might not have meant much, but it went along with Wilson saying that he doubted Warner was going to find a grieving widow.

Her biggest reaction had been when he'd described finding the Andalusian in the middle of the alkali flat and how he'd worked to get his hands on him. "Oh, my," she'd said, "Oh, my. That poor colt. That poor, poor animal."

He'd given her a look, wanting to say, "Say, what about poor me? I was on that flat myself."

But he'd gone on with the story. When he'd gotten to the part about the horse almost dying if they hadn't found the sump hole she'd said, "What a miracle. No, what a nose. Horses raised

151

where the water is in short supply have such a nose."

He'd said, as politely but as pointedly as he could, "Well, he had the blind staggers. If his nose had been a little better he might have pointed us toward that water a little sooner."

When the story was finally finished she'd thanked him and then, almost as an afterthought, inquired after his well-being. He'd just told her that his feet were still a little sore and let it go at that.

Now, sitting in the shade of the porch, drinking coffee, she said, "So I suppose you could say Paseta saved your life, Mr. Grayson."

He looked up. "Who's Paseta?"

She said, "The stallion of course. The Andalusian. Paseta is his name. Don't you name your horses, Mr. Grayson?"

He said slowly, "Well, no, ma'am. Never quite seen the need. I know which ones is which just by the look of them. And if I was to get confused I reckon I could check the brand." He smiled. "I ain't met many horses I figured could remember their name even if you gave them one."

She said, "But it's a sign of affection, a feeling between you and the horse."

Wilson had told him her name was Laura, but Warner had neither offered to use it nor been invited to. He put his coffee cup down carefully on the little round table that stood between their two chairs. He said, "Well, Mrs. Pico, I reckon me and you have got a different viewpoint on the matter of horses. I'm in the horse business. They ain't pets to me and I seldom use one horse two days in a row. I work them too hard for that. I don't give a horse a name and I don't tell him mine and we still seem to get along fine. I've had horses I was fonder of than others, but that was because they was better horses and done their work like they should. Long as a horse keeps it straight in his mind that I'm the one supposed to be on top and he's the one on the bottom then we get along fine. Any time I get one that's confused about that issue I get rid of him or bring him around to my way of thinking if he's young enough."

She said, "Surely you must feel something different for Paseta? Surely you realize you wouldn't have lived if he hadn't been there?"

Warner said dryly, "Yes, and I don't reckon he'd have found his way out of that alkali flat if I hadn't come along. So I figure me and him is just about even. I will say, though, if it had been any other breed of horse I don't believe he would have lasted on that gypsum flat. While I could still see a sign I found horsehair all over that area and I got to figure it was his. I figure that horse was in the worst of that flat for a good two or three days. Any other breed of horse would have died. I know I thought I was seeing things

153

when I got my first look at him. Then, when I got closer, and saw I didn't recognize him as any breed I'd ever seen I was pretty sure I'd gone out of my head."

She looked toward the barn. She said, "It was very lucky for you that I had hand trained Paseta to come to me or else your hat trick wouldn't have worked."

He wanted to tell her that about half the horse owners he knew trained their animals to come to the sound of a feed bucket, but this woman appeared to believe she'd invented horses so he decided to let it go. He just said, "Yeah, lucky."

Her voice went sad. She said, "And now he's the only one of my babies I have left. The others are gone, all gone." Then her eyes went fierce. "But I think I killed one of the bandits. Avery ran out in the yard like a damn fool waving his pistol and shooting in the air. What did he think—that the noise was going to scare them away?"

"But three was supposed to have been hit. Two killed here."

She said, "Oh, my two *vaqueros* were firing. And I think that finally Avery got it in his head that they were not playing a joke, that they were here to steal our horses. But he was drunk." She squinted her eyes in disgust. "As usual. I think he finally shot one. But I *know* I hit one out the window with the rifle. I kept trying to shoot the fat one, but he was very elusive. Damnit!"

After a silence he said, "I'm going after those bandits."

She said, "Yes, I've heard they are getting together some sort of a vigilante group to go after them the next time they come across."

He shook his head. "Naw, I said *I* was going after them bastards. Excuse me. Them *bandidos*. By myself. I have taken this whole business personal and I ain't going to wait until they decide to come back across. And I ain't going with any group. I got my own plan."

She looked at him uncertainly. "One man against six? Or maybe more by now? There were ten when they first came here, seven when they attacked you and six when they left. But they'll have gone back to Mexico by now. They could be a dozen."

He leaned forward and spit far enough so that his spittle didn't land on the tiles of the porch. He rolled the brim of his hat in his hands. He said, "I don't give a damn if there's fifty. They gonna wish they'd never seen me. I got me some heavy tallying to do. And I need to borrow that horse of yours. And any others you got."

She gave a little start. She said, "Loan you Paseta? After I've just gotten him back?"

He said, "Ma'am, I ain't gonna lose your horse. I'll fetch him back to you none the worse for wear and maybe a little the better for the experience. I know it's a hard thing for me to ask of you, you being so fond of the horse. But I'm afoot. Them bandits took everything I had that a saddle would fit."

She said, her voice faltering a little, "Of course, Mr. Grayson, I'm greatly in your debt for saving my horse. But isn't—I mean . . ."

He said, "Couldn't I borrow or rent or buy another horse? Yeah, I sure could. There ain't a rancher in this part of the country wouldn't trust me with his best animal. You may not have heard of me but, like I say, horses are my business. So I could get another horse. Wilson Young has got some fine, fast horses, most of which I sold him. But I got a special reason for wanting to use that horse of yours."

She was looking uncomfortable. She said, "What would that be?"

He said, "Well, first I think it would be fitting. Second, I believe by now them bandits has discovered what they had when they stole your other horses. I'd bet my shirt that that second raid they made over here came right through your ranch to see if they might have missed any of those high-priced horses. Because I don't reckon they knew what they had any more than I did when I first come upon your horse. I want them to get a look at another one." He stopped. Then he said, "But that's two reasons. The third is the most important."

"And what's that?"

"That I don't know just where or for how long this hunt might take. And I want the best horse under me for speed and endurance I can find. And that would be that horse of yours. He's proved he can handle rough country."

She didn't want to do it, he could see that. She said, "But I hear they are already making plans to catch or kill the bandits when they come back. Why don't you join forces with them?"

He said, "Because our interests ain't mutual. Their main intent is to wipe out the bandits. I plan to do some of that myself, but I'm interested in recovering my property as well. And yours too, for that matter."

She suddenly sat up straight in her chair. She said, "You think there's a chance you could get my horses back?"

He nodded slowly. He didn't feel like he was lying more than was necessary. He said, "If I can get my hands on one of them bandits, especially the fat one, he's going to tell me where he sold my horses and your horses. See, he took some horses off me that was worth, all things considered, just about as much to me as them two-thousand-dollar horses of yours."

She had her fists clenched. She was no longer the "cool customer" she'd been. She said, "But he will have sold them."

Warner nodded. He said, "Of course. But I guarantee you he will tell me who he sold them animals to and where they are. Then I will go and get them."

She said, "But it will be in Mexico!"

He spit again, wishing he had a glass of water. He had to work saliva up in his mouth to keep it from going dry and then it got too thick. He said, "So? I been to Mexico before."

"But how will you get them back? Some Mexican *ranchero* isn't going to care if they're stolen."

Warner half smiled and said, "I hadn't planned on discussing it with him."

"You mean you'd steal them?"

"How can you steal something that belongs to you?"

She sat back in her chair and looked at him. She said, "I just hate to think of my poor baby having to go through more hardships after what he's just been through."

He almost winced at the use of the word, but he said, "Lady, I know more about keeping a horse fit than anybody you've ever set eyes on in your life. I ain't planning on starting this afternoon. Your horse will be ready and he won't get put through nothing he can't handle."

"And you think you might recover my other Andalusians?"

"That's what I'm talking about." He spit again. "There would be a fee for that, of course."

She cocked her head slightly. "How much? You musn't base your thinking of what the horses are worth on some drunk horse talk by my husband. I mean my deceased husband."

"I ain't," he said. "It'll depend on the time and trouble it takes me. Same way I charge for anything to do with horseflesh."

She hesitated. Then she said, "Do you have a plan?"

He stood up, then said, "Yes. Whyn't we go inside where it's cooler. Tell you the truth, I got me enough sun in that little spell I was in that bad country to last me a long time. And now it's shining under the porch roof. Besides, I need a paper and a pencil so I can kind of draw you out what I got in mind. And I could use some water. Just plain old water."

They got inside the pleasantly cool, somewhat dim house. Warner didn't generally notice furniture and such, but he could tell the place had been done up top-notch and pretty well leaning to a woman's touch. Laura Pico brought him a big square of wrapping paper and a pencil and then went back to fetch him a jug of water and a glass. He took time to down two tumblers of water before he set himself to the task. They were at her big kitchen table.

He made a mark off to the right of the brown wrapping paper. He said, "Now here's Del Rio. And right along here comes the river. Now west of here is your place." He made a circle about two inches in diameter. "And up here, about thirty or forty miles north is where my camp was when them bandits jumped me. And here—" He made a big circle in the upper center of the paper, to the east of her ranch and just a little more to the northeast of Del Rio. "And here," he said, "is the alkali flat." He drew a little dotted line down from the center of the alkali flat to the river and then west to Del Rio. "And that's the route me and your horse took to get to the river Jordan. Which it damn sure looked like to the both of us." He studied the map a minute and then said, "Now here"—he pointed with his pencil—"on upriver about forty miles is Comstock and Amistad and some mighty rough country. The good grazing stops not ten miles north of here." He made a mark on the paper at the river about an inch or two west of where he'd indicated the Pico ranch was. "I figure that bunch crossed about right here. Maybe they come over from Villa Acuña or farther inland. But I'd bet my hat that they made a stop at Villa Acuña either going or coming and they is folks knows their where-abouts. Now that first raid, the one when they stole your livestock . . ." He deliberately didn't mention that they had also killed her husband. He continued, "I figure they come through here first, figure they'd been watching the place. I figure they grabbed up what stock of yours they could lay their hands on and then drove them to the northwest. I don't know if they hit any other places on that raid or not. Did any of the other horses they stole come home?"

"Yes," she said, "but they were just range stock. Mares we were going to breed to the Andalusians. I think five or six have come back. We had about thirty on grass at the time. No, about then ten or twelve would have been up here in the corrals getting ready to be bred."

Warner said, "Anyway, they probably hit a few more small ranchers and gathered up what they could. They either peeled back to the west or come around you to the west between here and Del Rio. I don't figure they went east of Del Rio because that country has got some big ranches on it and is pretty thick with cowhands and ranch workers." He tapped the map again. "And I figure they crossed about the same place west of here the next time they come, the time they took hold of me and my partner." He drew a line up from the river to the west side of the alkali flat. "That's about where me and Red was camped. Right there. And all they had with them was the horses they'd started with. No fresh stock, no pickings off the countryside. That means they'd damn near followed their steps the first raid. I reckon they'd figured on pushing on north and swinging back to the west, taking what they could. But then they found me and Red, robbed us, dropped me off in the badlands, and hightailed it on home with their ill-gotten goods."

She said, "So? What are you getting at?"

He chewed on the pencil a moment. "What's west of you here?"

She shrugged. "Not much. The western end of our ranch runs out of good grazing. The ground gets rocky and the grass has to fight with the cactus and the brambles and the mesquite groves. I'm not sure if it's privately owned or is state land."

"Won't matter," he said. "It's all the room I need to operate. Grass stay pretty good to the north?"

"Oh, yes. For at least ten or fifteen miles."

He kept studying the map, tapping his teeth with the end of the pencil. He made a mark north and a little east of Del Rio between the town and the circle he'd drawn for the badlands. He said, "Howard Trevor's ranch is right in here. In fact that was the ranch me and Red was aiming for the night we camped on the edge of the alkali flat. Figured to cross it in one day and start in to working Howard's horses. Then, when them Mexicans dropped me off to die they rode out of that flat heading southwest, heading home with my stock and goods. But I wonder if they hit Howard's place on their first sweep. I'd bet marbles to money that they did and that that's when your horse got loose and run off. Naturally, him not having been in the country long enough he was turned around and didn't know which way the barn was. Probably saved him from the bandits. He kept going up north in that badlands and they didn't want to look for him there. I need to check with the sheriff or Wilson to see if Howard's ranch got depredated."

"Poor baby," she said. "Lost and no water or feed."

He said, "You will say that, won't you?" He was sorry for the words the minute they were out, but he hadn't been able to hold back. She'd been irritating him talking about horses the way she had from almost the first moment.

She said, "Will what?"

He said, "You will use a term of endearment for a working animal." He figured that now he was in it he'd just plow straight ahead. She could loan him the horse or not, just as she chose.

Her face flamed slightly and she shook her head so that for the first time he could see that she had a tiny little blue bow in the back of her hair. It wasn't holding her hair together, it was just there as an ornament. She said, her voice hard, "Better a term of endearment on an animal that causes you no harm than a brute of a man that gets drunk and abuses you with his mouth and his hand."

He said quickly, "Listen, I'm sorry. I opened my yap when I had no business to. What you call that horse is your affair. It's your horse. You can call him for supper for all that it matters to me. I ain't interested in but one thing right now and it's

163

them goddam bandits. Now, you going to loan me that horse and some others or not?"

She looked at him, her color slowly returning to normal. He could see the anger going out of her. Finally she said, "Tell me some more about this plan of yours."

He pointed at a spot on his crude map about four miles upriver from her ranch. He said, "It's a rough guess, but I figure they'll come across right here the next time they come. Or within a mile of the spot. I figure they've crossed right here at least twice before, either because it's a beeline from where they are coming from or because it's a good spot to cross the river, shallow or narrow."

She said, "That doesn't make all that much sense. I would expect them to vary their plan. Change it."

He said, "My grandfather used to say that a man might get fatter or thinner but his boot size stayed the same. Naw, them bandits will cross there. They've crossed there safely, going and coming, at least twice. They got no reason to change. You need to remember that just because you're mean as a snake don't make you as smart as one. I don't reckon this bunch is carrying too many schoolbooks in their saddlebags."

"And then what?" she asked.

He made another *X* on the paper to the north of where he'd indicated the bandits might cross. He said, "I'm going to bait me a trap about right here."

"With what?"

He gave her a look. He didn't much like the woman, but that had nothing to do with catching *bandidos*. If she wanted to act cool and tough and hard that was her business. He said, "Why, with horses. What'd you think? They're horse thieves. You don't catch horse thieves with a herd of longhorn cattle."

She said, "You're going to locate some horses there and hope they come?"

"That's right. Course, I might let out a few feelers to sort of point them in the right direction."

"I want to be there." She said it hard and fierce.

He laughed. He couldn't help himself. "Like fun. I need help, not hindrance."

She said, "I can shoot and I can ride better than most men."

"Well, I can't," he said. "And that would just make me look foolish. No, I've done turned down Wilson Young's help, so that ought to give you a pretty good idea that I intend on doing this one solo."

She said, "Why don't you want me along?"

They were standing side by side at the big kitchen table. He turned on her with a flat look. He said, "Because you wasn't in the middle of that goddam alkali flat dying of thirst with your feet roasted like you would a frying chicken.

165

That's why. Now, I want to get up a herd of about ten or twelve. Want to get them all slicked up and shiny and be feeding them grain and hay so them dumb bandits will think they are valuable horses. The way they go through stock they don't know a good horse from a range cull."

"They knew my Andalusians."

He said, "I don't think so. And that's why I don't think they carried them very far inland in Mexico before they sold them. I've known some professional horse thieves in my time and they don't steal poor quality horses. They steal high-bred animals because, as one told me one time, the penalty is the same for stealing a good horse as it is for a nag. All them Mexican bandits look for is to see if a horse is fattened up and well cared for. They figure that makes the horse valuable on account of the way they treat their own stock. Why, a professional horse thief would have no more come through here and mixed in twenty or twenty-five common range mares with them prime Andalusian stallions than he'd have kicked a stump with his bare foot. Soon as he seen what he had in them Spanish stallions he'd've gathered them up and lit out for safety. What would he want twenty mares along for? More animals to herd and you're mixing mares in with stallions. My gawd, what a bunch of horses to try and drive. And you say some of them mares was starting to come in season? Wow! I reckon

I'd rather have seen that than gone to a circus. I wouldn't be surprised if they didn't lose more than just that one Andalusian."

She had been studying his face while he talked. It was really the first time she'd looked at him as a man, as a person. She said, "Are you married?"

The question surprised him a little, but he didn't let his face show it. He shook his head. "Naw."

"Got a girl?"

He shook his head again. "Oh, I done my share of courtin', but I never found one could put up with my way of life."

"And what's your way of life?"

"Mostly gone. You can't establish yourself in the horse business by staying in your own backyard." He turned his head and looked toward the kitchen pump. He said, "Can I have another glass of water?"

She took his empty tumbler and filled it and watched him drink it down. When he was through she said, "You must have gotten awfully thirsty out there."

He said, "I don't reckon I'm ever going to get filled up again. Now. What about them horses and that Andalusian in particular?"

She said, "It's getting late in the afternoon. Why don't you stay to supper and we'll talk about it."

He said, "Well, considering I'm afoot I don't reckon I got much choice. What was you thinking of having?"

She said, "Well, I've got a smoked ham hanging in the root cellar. We could have that and some fixings. I've got a big pot of pinto beans made and I could make biscuits with some redeye gravy. Have you ever had cold tea with sugar and lime in it?"

He said, "No, but it sounds good."

She said, "It'll quench your thirst faster than water."

"Then I'm for it. And I don't see where you got much choice but to loan me them horses, especially that Andalusian."

"What makes you so sure of that?"

He said, "Because, lady, I can tell you want them other five stallions back more than anything else in this world and you've about decided I'm the one can get them for you."

"What makes you so sure of that?"

He turned his young, shrewd eyes on her. He said, "Because you are all of a sudden being nice to me. And you ain't the kind does that unless you figure there's something in it for you."

She laughed and said, "Why, Mr. Grayson, what a pretty way you have of paying a girl a compliment."

He said, "Ma'am, I'm a man who will do or say anything so long as it pleases the ladies and don't scare the horses."

She gave him a look. "Is that a fact?"

He returned her look. "Yes," he said, "it is."

# 7

Chulo said, "*Es El Gordo por seguro*."

Wilson Young said, "For sure? That fat bastard with the scar?"

Chulo nodded. He said, "*Si. Es por* chure. *Por seguro.* I doan know why nobodys es keel that mean sondebitch. I theenk he es juan mean *pachucho*."

Wilson said, "Scar and everything?"

"Chure," Chulo said.

Warner said, "But you didn't see him?"

The big Mexican shook his head. "He nowhere I go. He es en Monterrey, maybe. That es what some peoples say."

Wilson said to Warner, "After what you told us we was kind of figuring it might be El Gordo. At least that's what we call him. His name is Chumacho. I don't know what else. Nobody has ever laid their hands on him. But he's been seen over here a bunch of times, especially back when them *bandido* raids was common as cactus. He's done more mischief over the years than any sonofabitch we haven't hanged. It would take some loco bastard like him to start raiding again as grown up as this country is."

They were sitting in the kitchen of Wilson Young's *ranchero* that was just across the river from Del Rio in Mexico. Wilson had bought the land and built the house while he was waiting for the governor to make up his mind about pardoning him. Now he made it sort of his bachelor quarters when he wanted to get away from the casino and cathouse. It was not really a ranch. He had about a thousand acres, but he made no attempt to raise cattle. He let his neighbors use his pasture to keep the grass cropped down and the only animals he kept on the place were his riding horses and his racing stock. The house was very similar to Laura Pico's except it was smaller. It had only two bedrooms and a big kitchen and a parlor that was strewn with saddles and chaps and other horse and ranch gear. Sometimes Wilson let Chulo sleep in the spare bedroom, but he always made him bathe in the big cistern he had outside first. As a consequence Chulo usually slept in the barn when he stayed on the place.

Now they sat at the table talking and discussing the bandits and what Chulo had found out. Wilson Young was drinking brandy, Chulo was drinking rum and Warner was drinking well water. There was a big bowl of cut limes in the middle of the table and, every now and again, he'd squeeze a little of the juice in his glass of water. Laura Pico had been right about the tea with lime in it cutting his thirst better than just plain water. But Wilson hadn't had any tea so he'd just settled for the lime and water which, he'd decided, was what really done the quenching.

Warner'd spent the night at Laura's and then had rode out early on the Andalusian horse and found out in town that Wilson was at his place in Mexico. He'd stopped to eat breakfast in town, glad to be getting back to some sort of normal schedule. He was still sore, but he was feeling stronger and stronger with every hour of sleep and every meal. He'd crossed the river at the International Bridge and then, following the directions Evita had given him, had found Wilson's place. He had not seen Lupita at the Palace and he had not looked for her. He'd arrived at about ten o'clock to find Wilson up and stirring around with his first cup of coffee. Wilson had expressed surprise that Laura Pico had loaned him the Andalusian. Warner said, "Why not? Hell, she wouldn't have him if it wasn't for me."

Wilson had shrugged and said, "Well, the way she felt about them horses I'm just surprised. If she'd've had them as colts I think she'd've breast-fed them."

He'd said, "Watch your mouth, Wilson. This ain't one of them working girls you got staying over your saloon."

Wilson had raised his eyebrows saying, "Well, my, my, ain't we the gentleman. Where'd *you* sleep last night?"

Warner had said evasively, "Wherever it was I didn't see you there."

Wilson had yawned. "I come over here early yesterday evenin'. I can take that place just so long and then I got to get out of there and get over here for some peace and quiet. You take you a run at Lupita yet?"

"Not yet."

Chulo had arrived about an hour later, dirty and smelling of every flavor in Mexico and looking for a drink. He had some scratches down the right side of his face and a welt across his forehead and one finger was tied up with a dirty, bloody rag. He'd said, "A leetle troubles. Es notzing."

Chulo and Wilson had talked in rapid-fire Spanish that had been too fast for Warner to follow.

Warner asked, "Well, where does this El Gordo locate at? He got one place?"

Wilson said, "No, not really. They's a couple of *chiquita pueblas* about ten, fifteen miles in from the river, little villages. He's in and around there, but nobody knows if he stays one place steady."

Warner said, "But Chulo never actually saw him?"

"Said he saw some of the men who'd been with him on this last raid. Said he talked to one of them. I think he broke his neck." He looked over at Chulo. "You break the man's neck? The man who didn't want to talk to you?"

Chulo shrugged and took a swig out of the rum bottle. He said, "Theese man es beery *el stupido*. He doan want to tell Chulo what he wan' to know. Maybe I am a leetle mean with heem."

Wilson said, "You broke his neck, you dumb Meskin. How many times I got to tell you if you kill somebody they can't tell you a goddam thing?"

Warner said, "They call this guy Chumacho. Is that his name or a calling name?"

Wilson shrugged. He said, "It's a nickname. Nobody seems to know what this fucker's real name is. They call him Chumacho because that's about as bad as you can call somebody."

"What's it mean?"

Wilson said, "Well, it don't exactly translate, but it kind of means you can't get no meaner. You're the meanest sonofabitch around and you ain't never done nothing that you're sorry for or ashamed. It means he'd gut his own mother if he thought she'd swallowed a peso."

"And Chulo says he's gone to Monterrey?"

Wilson gave Chulo a disgusted look. He said, "This damn dumb bastard don't know where he went. He *thinks* he went to Monterrey because some little kid on the street said it. He don't know shit. I sent him down there to find out what was going on and all he wants to do is fuck weemins, as he calls 'em, and drink whiskey."

Chulo said, yawning, "I beery tired. I fuck

173

meeny weemins an' drink a lot of wheesky. I doan sleep for two days and two nights."

Warner said to Chulo, "Do you know where Chumacho sold the horses he stole? Especially the Spanish horses from Mrs. Pico."

Wilson answered for him. He said, "Ain't nobody knows except El Gordo. He's got a couple or three men you might say work steady with him, but the rest he just picks up for each raid."

Warner shook his head and sucked on a lime. He said, "What do you reckon punched this ol' boy up to start raiding into Texas again? He must know it's dangerous as hell."

Wilson said, "I doubt if he gives a shit. You got to be around these folks awhile to understand that they ain't got many choices. My guess is he stole from the peons until they didn't have nothing left for him to steal. Maybe the *Rurales* got after him. You know who they are?"

"Yeah. The Mexican rural police. I hear they ain't nothing but bandits themselves."

"But they got the badge. No, I didn't figure Chulo was going to find out much about El Gordo, not around his home country, them two little villages El Milagro and Boquillas. The peons are scared to death of him. But what it seems like he's doing is convincing some small-time, half-assed *bandidos* that it's safe to go back to stealing across the river. So he gets six or seven new men

174

to go with him. Naturally, if there is any danger they're the ones get put up front. He's come over twice with about a dozen men. This time he only got back with five. He's telling folks that everybody made it back all right, that the missing ones have gone off to the big towns to spend all the money they made. And, of course, nobody is going to dispute him."

Warner said, "And he was coming over here before? Before the country got so settled?"

"Yeah." Wilson shrugged. "Bastard leads a charmed life. He ought to be dead by now but he ain't. That's why I been telling you it's time you got back to gentling horses."

Warner looked away. He said, "Not just yet."

Wilson said, "Goddamit, Gray, has your head turned to rock? I can't make it much clearer that this pig fucker is dangerous as hell. You'll get your ass killed! Goddamit, this ain't your line of work."

Warner didn't say anything, just kept looking away.

Chulo got up and raised his arms over his big shoulders in a stretch and a yawn. He said, "I theenk Chulo go to sleep now. Chulo beery tired."

He turned to walk through the jumbled parlor, heading toward the back bedroom. Wilson yelled after him. He said, "No, you don't! You go out there and stand under that cistern spout. And use some soap. And take off them filthy clothes."

Chulo said, whining, "Ah, Weelson, Chulo beery asleepy."

Wilson said, "Chulo gonna be beery fucking sorry if he goes in Weelson's bedroom dirty as a pig. You get within seven foot of that bed and I'll shoot your damn ears off."

"Weelson, chou are too hard on poor Chulo." He hung his head. "Doan I go an' do like chou tole me?"

"Go wash off, damnit. You got to get clean sooner or later. The smell off you would stunt livestock. Now go warsh!"

But, instead, Chulo went out the front door, yawning and carrying a half-full bottle of rum in one hand. Wilson Young watched him in disgust. He said, "Now he's going out and smell up the barn. Probably won't be able to get a horse to go in there for a week."

Warner said casually, "I don't reckon there's any way to figure when El Gordo might be coming back to visit?"

Wilson looked at him. He said, "You asking me to predict the mind of some goddam half-crazy, double-dumb, Mexican bandit? The answer to that, my young friend, is whenever the mood strikes him. One day he'll get up and go to telling anybody that will listen that there's some easy pickings over there across the river in Texas, that we're all asleep or cowards or ain't got no guns, or are down with the fever. Whatever sounds right in his mouth. He'll tell some of them dumb peons that ain't got a damn thing to lose including their lives, which ain't worth living anyway, that all they got to do is follow him over the river and they'll be richer than they ever dreamed. He'll have his two or three regular men, of course, and they'll gather up whatever fools they can convince and they'll all get drunk and across they'll come. Without no more plan or forethought than a fool a-fuckin'. They could come tomorrow or they could come in a month or they might not ever come again. For all we know Chumacho is laying somewhere with a knife in his guts and has crossed this river for the last time. You got to remember, it ain't real smart to try and steal horses in this day and age."

Warner said, "Then why do they do it?"

Wilson shrugged. He said, "Gray, you talk like a man ain't spent much time on this side of the border. They steal and get hung or shot because it's more fun than starving to death. Don't you know how poor these folks are?"

Warner said, "It ain't that I never give no thought to it, Wilson. It's just that I don't see where being poor ought to make you cruel in the bargain."

Wilson said, "It ought not to. And it don't most of them. This here Chumacho is just a mean sonofabitch. He'd be mean and cruel if he had a million dollars. Where'd you say you spent the night?"

Warner stood up and stretched. He said, "I'm starting to get hungry. I know you ain't got nothing to eat around here that me and you can cook. Let's ride across the river and get us a steak."

Wilson got up. He said, "Com'on outside with me for a minute. I want to see something."

"You going to give me some more advice, Uncle Willy?"

They were going out the front door. Wilson turned right and headed them down toward the river. He said, "Gray, don't you reckon it's about time you went back to work? You appear to be just about all healed up now. I know you're out some livestock and I know they killed your partner, but a man ain't never gained a foot forward by looking back. Let it go. Sure, I'll stake you. To a working outfit. A trail outfit. Even loan you that revolver you're wearing out of friendship. Even a horse tamer needs a firearm at his side."

Warner said, "You never did tell me what dry goods store Charlie Stanton is working at."

Wilson stopped and turned his head and looked Warner in the face. He said, "You are crazy as hell. You can't turn your business over to an inexperienced kid. For God's sake, Warner, he's been sacking potatoes for the last six months."

Warner didn't answer him other than to ask again where Charlie Stanton worked. He said, "What happened to his daddy's ranch?"

178

Wilson gave him a disgusted look. He said, "Went bust. Charlie works at his uncle's store. You ain't got a lick of sense, you know that?"

"I can't help it. I got to do what I got to do."

Wilson said, "You know who you remind me of? You'd never guess in a hunnert years. You remind me of Chulo. Chulo. That's right. How you like to be compared to him?"

Warner said, "Seems to me he's made you a pretty steady hand through the years."

Wilson said, "*That* aside . . . He is and was the hardest headed man I ever met until you come up with this latest stunt. Back in them bad old days when we was robbing banks in Texas and fleeing to Mexico just one jump ahead of the law he always wanted to rob a Mexican bank. He used to hold up a finger and say, 'I like to rob juan Mesican bank.' I never could convince the dumb sonofabitch that we couldn't rob banks in both countries and still have someplace to run. He couldn't understand it. Just like you are too rock headed to understand that this horse thief business ain't none of your affair and the best you can do is forget it."

Warner just said quietly, "Give it up, Wilson. You've had your say."

Wilson Young threw his hands in the air and said, "Shit!" Then he started on down toward the river which was about two hundred yards away. As they walked the ground began to slope off toward the edge of the water. Here and there were a few mesquite and post oak trees. All of the cactus had been dug out or burned off and the grass was cropped short by the few cows and horses that were wandering around grazing.

Wilson walked on a few yards farther and then stopped. Down toward the river, ten or twelve paces away, was a small mesquite tree. Wilson pointed at it. He said, "You reckon you can hit the trunk of that tree?"

The trunk was about twelve inches across. Warner said, "I reckon."

"Lemme see you."

Warner drew the revolver Wilson had loaned him, thumbed back the hammer, took deliberate aim and fired. He was gratified to see small pieces of bark fly out from almost the dead center of the trunk. He put the revolver back in the holster and looked at Wilson.

His friend said, "That's pretty good. Now do it again and this time shoot before the tree dies of old age."

Warner said, "Goddamit, Wilson, I am not a fast draw artist like you are and I ain't going to practice to be one."

Wilson said, "I ain't talking about fast drawing. I just want you to draw the weapon, point it like it was your index finger, and shoot. Don't aim. You can't aim a revolver. You look at what you want to hit and point your finger at it. Just imagine the barrel of the gun is your index finger. Now do it."

Warner drew the gun again and this time did as Wilson had told him. His shot was much quicker and no less accurate.

Wilson said, "Now do the same thing only fire twice. And you better goddam well not fire that gun double action. You thumb that hammer back for both shots."

Warner said, "Damnit, Wilson, I know that. But what I don't know is why we are doing this."

"Draw and fire."

He drew, thumbing the hammer back as his revolver cleared the holster and fired at the spot on the tree that was now becoming visibly chewed up. The first shot was barely away before he had thumbed back the hammer and fired again. His second shot was just to the right.

Wilson said, "That ain't bad." He reached in his pants pocket and took out a handful of cartridges. He handed Warner five cartridges. He said, "Reload."

Warner said, as he put the cartridges in the cylinder of the .44/.40 revolver, "Wilson, what I got in mind don't require no pistol expert. I told you I'm hungry."

Wilson said, "You never know when you might need to be a little better than you are right now. This time I want you to profile."

Warner looked at him. "What?"

Wilson said, "You're firing straight on, you're exposing your whole body, you're making yourself too big a target. As you draw, as you stick your right arm out I want you to let your body turn so you are sort of sideways to the target. If it's somebody going to shoot back at you you give him less to hit. It's the little things, Warner, that can keep you alive."

"Profile?"

"Yes, profile to the target. You just turn your body, bringing your left side back, as you draw and fire. Try it. And fire twice. Always fire twice."

Warner did as he was told. The half-turn movement came naturally to him. If anything, it seemed to make his aim go more instinctively toward the target. He fired twice, taking satisfaction in seeing more bark fly. Enough had been shot away in one spot that he could see the bare wood of the trunk.

Wilson looked at him curiously. He said, "You're a good shot, Gray. Still a good shot. With a little practice you could be a hell of a good shot. But, still . . ."

"Yeah," Warner said. "I know. I might hesitate."

Wilson pointed. He said, "See that limb coming off to the right? Just about four feet high? Aim at that. Fire at least three rounds."

The branch was half the size of the trunk, a hard target with a revolver at ten paces. Warner took a breath, let it out, then drew and thumbed off three

182

rounds. The limb shook and trembled and bark flew.

Wilson said, "You hit it solid twice. The third one barely missed but that was because you ain't thumbing real smooth."

Warner turned and looked at him, holding the smoking revolver down by his side. He said, "Wilson, I appreciate your help, but I ain't planning on getting in no gun duels. I'm going to do what I have to do just as easy and simple as I can without giving the other fellow any more chance than I have to." He said it flatly, plainly, leaving no room for misunderstanding.

Wilson looked at him thoughtfully. He said, "You know, Gray, you've done a good bit of changing here lately. Maybe that alkali flat put some poison in you. You are starting to sound about half mean. Maybe you won't hesitate."

Warner didn't say anything, just turned and looked toward the river. He glanced back just in time to see the revolver suddenly appear in Wilson's hand and hear five shots fired as one. The branch quivered and jerked and then sagged downward as half its diameter was shot away at the spot Warner had marked with his two hits. Almost as fast as the gun had appeared Wilson returned it to its holster. The sound of the gunfire was still reveberating in the air.

Warner said, "Showing off or showing me how it can be done?"

183

Wilson looked at him and slowly shook his head. He said, "I already told you how to do it and I don't have to show off. I was practicing. I practice nearly every day."

As they walked slowly back toward Wilson's house Warner said, "How many other men you reckon can shoot like you?"

Wilson said, "I don't know and I don't care. Just so long as I don't ever run up against one."

Warner said, "Wilson, I'm going to need a small herd of about ten horses. I can get five out at Laura Pico's. They don't got to be quality horses, just something I can feed up and slick up so they look good to a Mexican horse thief. I don't want none of them running horses of yours. They are a little too dear to be using for my purposes. But I wondered if you might have some common range horses about the place."

Wilson cut his eyes at him. He asked, "What are you up to?"

Warner replied, "I didn't ask you if you had any questions, I asked you if you had any horses I could borrow for a few days."

"Or maybe a few weeks?"

"Or maybe a few weeks."

Wilson said dryly, "We might have some bait around here. I'll have my head *vaquero* see what he can gather up."

Warner said, "I'm starving to death. Let's go across and eat a steak. Hell!"

• • •

Warner stood in front of Stanton's Dry Goods wishing Charlie would spot him and come out and talk. He hated to be talking to Charlie inside and maybe have his uncle come up while he was putting his proposition to Charlie. Besides, he didn't much like to go into dry goods stores. A dry goods store wasn't like a general mercantile. It catered more toward the female trade selling canned vegetables and fruit and canned sardines and salt pork and beef and potatoes and apples and flour and other, comestables that the ladies needed to set a table. It also sold all sorts of tonics and waters and powders and the stuff that women took along with yard goods to make curtains and dresses and bed linens and women's clothes and thimbles and needles and thread and such. A man could buy a pair of shoes in such a store but he couldn't buy boots. And he could buy a town shirt and town pants and even a swallow tailed coat and a foulard tie, but he couldn't buy a saddle or a rifle or rope or an axe or anything a man living outdoors might need, not even a pot that could stand hard usage.

And then, just as he was about to give up and go in, Charlie spotted him out the window. A minute later he was out on the boardwalk, his face lit up and his hand out. "Mr. Grayson," he said, "my dawgs! I never expected to see you here."

Charlie was a medium-size kid of nineteen with

a shock of unruly brown hair who looked gangly in town shoes working in a dry goods store, but who Warner knew had a touch with horses nearly as good as his own. There was nothing gangly about the young man when he got a leg on each side of a horse, especially if it was a fierce bronc that could unseat him.

Warner shook hands and said a word or two, but shut Charlie off when he started in to talk and to visit. Warner said, "Charlie, reason I looked you up is I've got work for you, steady work I'd say."

Charlie's face took on a hopeful look. "Horse work?"

Warner said, "Of course horse work. What'd you reckon I dealt in, ladies' high-button shoes?"

Charlie looked down. He said, "Don't talk about ladies' high-button shoes to me. I never been so sick of nothing in all my life." Then he looked up at Warner with no apology in his eyes. "But I reckon you heard our cattle business went belly-up. Two dry seasons and us in there on a shoestring done us in. My uncle give me this work and it brings in a little money so I do it."

Warner said, "I ain't knocking what a man has to do to help his family out. But can you take another job?"

Charlie said fervently, "If it's horse work and it pays any kind of money at all I can. I'm gettin' seven dollars a week here."

Warner said, "This is kind of a two-part job.

First part of it is we are going to hold a small horse herd about ten or fifteen miles northwest of here. I don't know how long that is going to last, but it's going to last until I even a score or until my money runs out. This could be a little dangerous, though I don't intend for it to be so for you and it won't be if you do exactly like I want. But for that work I intend to pay you three dollars a day."

Charlie cupped his hand to his ear. He said, "Come again?"

Warner smiled. He said, "You heard me." Then his face turned serious. "After that I want you to work the ranches with me like you helped me and Red out that couple of times."

Charlie grinned. He said, "Boy, howdy, I can shore handle that."

Warner said, "Red got killed. Never mind asking me how right now."

Charlie said, his voice soft, "I'm right sorry to hear that. Mister Red was a fine man. He always treated me square even when I was first learnin'."

"Well . . ." Warner said. He let a pause pass. "So I'm going to need some help. I won't take you on as a partner, not just yet, but I'll pay you a fourth of what I take in this first season. That will be considerable more than twenty-eight dollars a month. What do you say?"

Charlie said, "We start this afternoon?"

Warner smiled faintly. He said, "It'll take us a couple of days to get ready. Besides, ain't you got to give your uncle some kind of notice so he can find a hand to replace you?"

Charlie looked down at the ground again. He said, "I ain't exactly needed. I reckon I'm more a hindrance than a help. My uncle is just trying to help daddy and us out."

"Well, if you want the job you ought to tell him right away."

"If I want the job! Will a dog suck eggs? Hell yes, I want the job. How big a horse herd we going to hold? Fifty, hunnert head?"

Warner said, "More like twelve or fifteen. Not many more."

Charlie looked puzzled. He said, "Mr. Grayson, you ain't gone in the charity bid'ness like my uncle, have you? You don't need no help holdin' twelve or fifteen horses. You can do that in your sleep."

Warner said, "It's a little more complicated than that. I ain't going to explain it now, but I do want to say again that it could be a touch dangerous. That's part of the reason for the three dollars a day."

"What's the other part?"

Warner said simply, "Because I might get killed and then you wouldn't get that work making the ranch circle like I'm planning."

Charlie said, "Damn!" His eyes searched Warner's face. Then he said hesitantly, "You ain't kidding."

"No. And I don't want to talk about it anymore. If it bothers you say so now. I got plans to make."

Charlie said, with a dry laugh, "Well, if such happens, I reckon it will bother you considerably more than it will me."

Warner smiled slightly. He studied Charlie. For the last two years he and Red had given the boy work. And, even in such a short period, it seemed that Charlie had gotten more mature every year. Not that there was ever much of the gadabout tomfoolery about Charlie. Nobody had to yank him out of his bedroll in the morning. He came awake and up and ready for the day's work. And you didn't have to tell him to do something more than once, or *how* to do something more than once. He was a serious-minded kid who tended to business and earned his money. And now it looked like he was growing into a young man of the same nature.

Which was why Warner wanted him. He strictly wanted him to handle the horse herd they'd be driving and holding, leaving Warner free to concentrate on his real business with El Gordo. He didn't want another gun hand along. He didn't want anyone else to help him with that part of the business; not Wilson Young, not Chulo, not anyone. What he was trying to do was personal and he wanted to handle it personally.

Warner said, "Well, then I reckon we got a deal. You better get back on in there and sell some more ladies' shoes. I got to find my banker. Tell you what, why don't you meet me at the Elite Cafe around six o'clock and we'll eat some supper and make plans."

Charlie said, "Can we make that half-past? We don't close up here till six."

"Yeah. In fact I just ate lunch. Seven would suit me even better. One thing I need to know now. . . . Have you still got a dependable horse?"

"Got more than that," Charlie said. "I taken a page outten your book and been doing a little trading on the side. But I got two good saddle horses I kind of keep for myself."

Warner said, "We can use all the horses you got. I'll rent 'em from you."

Charlie said, "Ain't no need for that. I—"

Warner cut him off. "I'll see you at seven and we can talk all this out then. You'll think of some more questions by then and I might even answer some of them. Now I got to go. I'll see you later."

He walked down to the Palace and went in. The casino hadn't opened and the saloon part was doing scant business. He found Wilson Young sitting alone in a small nook at a back table. He sat down and shook his head at the glass Wilson slid over in front of him. His friend raised his eyebrows. He said, "You joined the Temperance Union?"

Warner said, "Naw. Just that whiskey still

makes me dry. If anybody comes my way I'll take a big glass of water, though."

Wilson raised his hand in the air and waved a finger. Then he said to Warner, "You want to kind of keep this water thing to yourself. Word gets around that the stuff can be drank might ruin my business. How much money you need?"

Warner squinted, running the figures through his mind. He said, "Well, I'm getting my weapons off you though I'd like to buy this six-shooter you are letting me wear."

"Ain't for sale. But I'll loan it to you. Permanently."

Warner grimaced. He said, "You got strange ways, Wilson. You better be careful somebody don't take you for a good fellow."

Wilson ignored him. He said, "What else you going to carry?"

"A double-barreled shotgun. Maybe two."

"I got one of them new scoped rifles. You know, the kind that got a spyglass on top of the barrel you sight through. Got cross hairs."

"I've seen 'em."

"It's a thirty ought six caliber. Single shot. But it reloads right quick. Might come in handy if you need to cut the odds down from long-range." He smiled wickedly.

Warner said, "I ain't planning on doing any of it long-range."

Wilson took a sip of brandy. He said, "My *vaquero* says he ought to be able to get you up a half dozen fair looking hides. They ain't going to pass for blooded stock, but they'll do until your thieves get close. And, of course, that's all you want. You'll handle it yourself from then on. Right?"

Warner gave him a look. He said, "You still think I'm that eighteen-year-old kid you bought a horse off of when you was on the run. Thought I'd skinned you because you was hard-pressed and couldn't bargain."

Wilson laughed. He said, "I could have *taken* the damn horse. Hell, we'd just robbed half a town. You reckon I would have been in any more trouble stealing a horse?"

Warner said, "Yeah, but that wasn't your style then and it ain't now. Then you found out the horse was worth the money I was asking. Surprised the hell out of you."

Wilson said, "You got to understand I wasn't exactly used to dealing with honest men."

"Point I'm making is you didn't think I knew what I was talking about then and you don't now. But you ain't going to change my mind."

Wilson said, "I've given up on that, Gray. You've convinced me you are going to do this your way." He stuck his hand in his pocket. "How much money you need?"

"Make it about eight hundred. I still might have

to buy a good horse or two to dress up my herd. And I'm going to need a pack mule."

Wilson pulled out a wad of bills and started leafing off fifty and hundred dollar bills. He counted out a thousand and pitched it across to Warner and then put the rest back in his pocket. He said, "Take a little extra."

Warner said, "You always carry that kind of cash around with you?"

Wilson said, "You don't think *I* trust banks do you?"

Warner looked at the money. He said, "This is more than what that horse I'm selling you is worth. I'll write you out a deed of sale before I get away."

"Don't worry about it. I'll take it when I get the horse."

Warner frowned. He said, "Wilson, you need the bill of sale before I leave. I might not come back."

The gambler immediately rapped on the table three times. He said to Warner, "Knock on that."

"What?"

"You heard me. Knock on that. And keep your mouth off your luck."

Warner started to knock on the tabletop and then stopped. He said, "Oh, that's silly nonsense. Besides, I meant I might not come back this way."

Wilson said loudly, "Damnit, knock!"

Warner sighed and knocked. He said, "I guess

you want these clothes back. Hell, I don't know if I can go back to that stuff I used to wear after dressing in your style."

"Keep 'em," Wilson said grandly. "I never wear anything twice. Wear a shirt once and throw it away. Where you planning on setting your trap?"

Warner took a drink of his water, then said, "Well, you seem to be taking a load on yourself deciding what my plans are. I don't recollect telling you about any trap or such. By the way, what are *you* going to do about this here matter. Seems I remember you telling me you and the rest of the uptowners around here was making some plans. What is it ya'll have got up? Not a posse or a catch party. Ya'll are too high-toned for that. Was it a committee? Yeah. What are you and the committee planning?"

Wilson shook his head slightly. He said, "Oh, Warner, making sport of your betters. My son, how you have fallen." He shook his head again. "Well, I'll tell you what *we* ain't going to do. *We* ain't going to gather up a horse herd and go set out on the prairie while we wait for that Chumacho and about a dozen more bandits to come along and finish the job of killing us. And *we* ain't going to send some seventeen-year-old kid along to try and do a job only *we* can do and end up losing all *our* customers in the process. What *we* are going to do is wait until we get word from all them spies that Chulo went over and set up about when and where El Gordo is coming across and then we're going to be there to meet him. Course, we could be wrong. Maybe we ought to get us a dozen horses and go set out on the prairie and whistle as loud as we can and see if a fat bandit will come when he's called."

Warner yawned. He said, "I know I oughtn't to make fun of my betters, but I can't help it." He finished his water in a long gulp. "I got to go spend this money while I still got it in my hand. You keep telling me how dumb I am I'm liable to give it back because you'll have me believing I ain't smart enough to be carrying it around. Besides, Charlie's nineteen and he ain't going off to gentle my customer's horses. He's going out with ol' dumb me to help herd that bunch of horses we will be inviting Chumacho to come and steal."

Wilson said, "Well, hell then, you might as well forget about your customers. I thought at least sending Charlie along might mollify them a little. But if you ain't even going to do that then you are still letting the Meskin rob you."

Warner said, "Goddamit, Wilson, I'm just now barely well enough to work gentle stock, let alone them with the bark still on. Even if I started in today I'd be way behind. Red is dead and he was half the outfit, half the work that got done. I will get to my customers as soon as I can. When I do I'll explain it to them. They'll either understand or they won't. But they was getting along on their own before I came along. I reckon they can handle it a little while longer. I need Charlie with me."

Wilson said, "Your business."

Warner said, "One other thing . . ."

"What?"

"I need to borrow one of them good running horses off you."

"One of my racehorses? Why?"

Wilson's table was not only set in a nook that was recessed into the wall so it was like a separate little three-sided room, it was also raised about a foot and a half off the main floor. Warner figured Wilson had it like that so he could sit with his back to the wall and have a good perch to oversee the business in his establishment. They were in the saloon part of the place which was about a third the size of the gambling area to the left of where they were sitting. A waist-high railing separated the casino from the saloon with a little opening about in the middle. As they had been talking Warner had noticed a man come in off the street through the casino entrance and then stand a moment looking around. He seemed to spot Wilson Young for he stared their way for a few seconds and then started walking toward them. He was noticeable because the place was almost empty and because he was wearing a long, dirty, white cotton duster, the kind of garment a man wore when he was on a long ride and wanted to keep his clothes clean. But, as the man stepped through the gate from the casino into the saloon it struck Warner that something wasn't quite right about the man. It appeared he hadn't shaved in a couple of days and his hair hung shaggily out from under his hat. He turned directly and headed for their table. Still watching the man he answered Wilson's question. He said, "Why? Because in case I get into a chase with them bandits I want to have a horse I can change onto off that Andalusian."

Wilson said, "Who's chasing who?"

The man was only a few faces from them. Warner said, "Why, me chasing them."

Wilson laughed. He said, "Yeah. I can see a dozen bandits running from you."

Just then the man came up to them. He stopped about six feet away, below them on the saloon floor. Warner noticed that the man had his right hand in the pocket of the duster. But there was something about it that bothered him. He'd worn plenty of dusters and they had shallow pockets in them. They weren't made for a man to use to carry his get-around materials in. But this man had his hand deep in the duster pocket, almost up to his elbow.

Wilson glanced up at the man. Warner could see that Wilson had both hands on the table, cupped around his glass of whiskey. Wilson said, "Can I help you?"

The man said, "You be Wilson Young? The gent what owns this here place?"

Wilson nodded. He still had his hands on the table. He said, "Yes. What can I do for you?"

The man said, "I lost me better'n a hunnert dollars in here last night. You got a faro dealer that crooked me."

Warner was sitting to Wilson's left, his side almost to the man. He was getting a prickling sensation at the back of his neck. Without moving his shoulders he dropped his hands in his lap and then, very slowly, eased his revolver out of its holster, extending his right leg to make it come easier to his hand. There was something very wrong about this man, something he couldn't quite pinpoint.

Wilson said, straightening up in his chair, "Not here, friend. This is a square house. I got a man who knows every way to cheat there is and his job is to watch every player, and that includes my housemen, and make sure there ain't no cheating. If you lost you lost on the up-and-up."

Warner glanced at the man's boots. Only half of them were showing from underneath the duster. He slid his chair sideways and back, the noise of the legs screeching against the floor covering the soft *clitch-clack* of the oiled mechanism of his revolver as he cocked it. Below the table he aimed his revolver by instinct, aiming for the middle of the man's chest, the raised nook they were sitting on allowing him a much better shot from under the table than if the man had been standing on the same level they were.

The man said, "Goddamit, I don't kere what you say! I know when I been crooked an' this here be a crooked house. Now, by gawd, I'll jest be havin' my hunnert dollars back er know the reason why."

Warner saw two things at once. Out of the corner of his eye he saw Wilson start to slowly slide his hand back toward the edge of the table. At the same instant he saw movement near the middle of the man's duster. Something was poking at it.

Warner fired, the shot making a startlingly loud noise in the cavernous room. It almost seemed to echo. The slug hit the man in his lower left rib, near the center of his chest, ricocheted upward through his heart, and then passed out the back near his backbone. The man, for an instant, had a surprised look on his face. Then he fell over backward, crumpling in a heap. As he fell the revolver he'd been holding under his duster tumbled to the floor, still cocked.

Wilson Young, who had not flinched at the sound of the shot, cast a quick look at Warner and then jumped to his feet, stepped down off the raised level and knelt over the man, ripping open his duster. The man had another revolver stuck down in his belt. Wilson said, "Looks like he came prepared." He reached up and closed the man's eyes. A few people had come hurrying over, talking in a buzz and gawking at the body.

Warner got up slowly and stepped down to the floor. He was surprised that he didn't feel much of anything. Wilson looked around as he came up. Warner said, "You reckon it really was the gambling, that he felt cheated? Or do you reckon it was some old score?"

Wilson shook his head. "I don't know. I never saw him before in my life. But that doesn't mean anything. He looks like he could have been for hire." Then he gave Warner a long, curious look. He said, "What did you see that I didn't?"

Warner said, "The duster bothered me right off. It's as still as a dead cow out there. Ain't no wind blowing to raise dust. Then he had his hand too far in the pocket of his duster. I bet there ain't no pocket in there. I bet it's been slit open or cut off."

One of the men that was kneeling by the body stuck his hand inside the right pocket. He said, looking up, "Nothing there. You could scratch your belly through this pocket."

Wilson rubbed his chin. He said, "I reckon it was my belly he wanted to scratch." Then he looked back to Warner. "Anything else? Must have been something made you sure."

Warner said, "Yeah." He gestured toward the man's boots. They looked clean and fresh shined.

He said, "Wasn't any dust or dirt on his boots. What's he doing wearing a duster inside or on the boardwalk?"

Wilson shook his head and motioned to several men. He said, "Get that body out of here. Bad for business. Take him over to the sheriff's. I'll be damned if I'll pay to bury him." Then he turned, stepped back up on the dais, and sat down at the table. He looked at Warner and said, "Don't you want a drink of whiskey now?"

Warner shook his head. He said, "I'll drink another glass of water and then I got business."

Wilson motioned at the bartender, who was watching the body being carried out, to bring over some more water. Then he said, almost as if he were talking about the weather, "Lot of folks think I have stayed alive because of the speed of my hand. That helps, but it ain't the whole story. No, the main thing that has kept my boots on has been the fact that I can usually tell what a man is going to do before he even knows." He cut his head left to look at Warner. "But today I was wrong about two men. And I don't make that many mistakes, not as a usual thing." He kept looking at Warner, a half-quizzical smile on his face. He said, "Well, Warner, you have just shot your first man. What's going through your head?"

Warner waited until the bartender had set a glass of water in front of him. He took half of it down and then said, "Truth be, I was thinking there wasn't no need for me to have shot the man at all. About the time I saw what I thought was him trying to poke something between the buttons at the front of his duster I saw, out of the corner of my eye, your right hand starting backward. Likely you would have drawn and shot him before he could have exposed the muzzle of that revolver he had hid out."

But Wilson Young shook his head. He said, "No. I saw that little movement under his duster and that was the first idea I had the man had come to shoot me. I'd've been a quarter of a second late." He picked up his drink and took a sip. "And it's that quarter of a second that gets you kilt. I'd already realized I was late and I was going to fling myself to the right, to the floor, drawing as I did, and hope he missed or didn't hit none of my vitals." He sipped at his drink and looked across the saloon where they were dragging the body out. "And then you fired." He smiled slightly. "Like to have scared me out of my skin. I never had no idea you had a gun in your hand."

Warner said, "His boots was too clean. Man don't come in in a traveling duster and shined boots. Wasn't a speck of dust on them. That's when I cocked my revolver under the table."

Wilson said, "And you made that noise with your chair to cover the sound."

"Yeah."

"And you aimed by instinct, making your hand look where your eyes were seeing."

"Yeah."

Wilson shook his head slowly and then finished his drink. He sighed and said, "Shit. Shit, shit, shit! You told me and I didn't listen to you. You're right. I was still thinking of you as that eighteen-year-old I used to know. Well, I have been educated. You do not hesitate." He leaned back in his chair and looked at Warner. He said, "For which I am eternally thankful because I reckon you saved my life."

Warner pulled a face. He said, "Now you're being silly, Wilson. You would have handled it just like you said, fell over and fired while you were falling."

"But it was you saw the danger before I did, Gray. And it was you shot the sonofabitch. I ain't supposed to make mistakes like that. It scares the hell out of me."

"You still don't know about this man?"

Wilson shrugged. "It doesn't make any difference. I can figure on an average of five or six times a year somebody is going to try me for one reason or another. I'm usually a little more ready for it than I was today. You sit in your own saloon and you think you're safe, but you ain't." Then he reached over and put his hand on Warner's shoulder. "You seem to be taking this mighty calmly."

Warner said, "I don't see there's all that much to get excited about. The man come in here with murder on his mind. Am I supposed to feel all upset because I interfered with his plans to shoot a friend of mine? I don't see why. Any more than I'm going to feel sorry for that fat bandit that put me to die out on that alkali flat."

Wilson said, "For the first time I'm starting to get the feeling that Chumacho might just be in a touch more trouble than he knows." He clapped Warner on the back. He said, "You are some piece of work, Gray. I'm in your debt."

Warner waved off the words. "Forget it, Wilson. You don't owe me nothing. I might have died if it hadn't been for them two women of yours."

Wilson smiled. He said, "You better go hunt up Lupita. She's been wondering where the hell you've been."

Warner got up. He said, "I got some business around town right now, spending money."

But before he could walk away Wilson called his name. He stopped and looked back. His friend said gently, "Warner, I'm going to say this for your own good. I know you're tired of hearing it. I just don't want you to begin to take yourself for granted. You were here with me and you shot to save a friend. But you may be alone next time and sometimes it's harder to shoot to save yourself. You don't see it as clear. *Savvy*?"

Warner said, "You're right. I am tired of hearing

about it. But much obliged for the concern. I won't time how I'll react until it happens." He made a gesture with his hand. "Just like this here."

Wilson saluted him with his whiskey glass as Warner turned and walked out of the saloon. In truth Warner was a little surprised himself at how calm he still felt. Maybe it would change later and he would feel something different, but he didn't think so.

# 8

It took two more days to get the supplies organized and the horses gathered up and the other odds and ends tended to, but they had finally gotten on the road. Warner had six horses from Wilson Young, plus one of his racehorses in case it was needed, and seven of the brood mares from Laura Pico. Besides his two riding horses Charlie Stanton had contributed four old range horses to the bunch. In all they were driving seventeen horses with two saddle horses apiece for themselves. After considering all that he had to carry Warner had finally discarded the idea of a pack mule and had bought two mules for a hundred dollars apiece and borrowed a buckboard from Wilson Young. They had the wagon loaded with sacks of grain and oats and four hundred feet of soft rope on a big wooden reel and a couple of salt blocks and even a few bales of alfalfa hay, a commodity that was seldom found along the border and for which Warner had paid dearly. The rest of the wagon was taken up with their foodstuffs; canned vegetables and fruits from Charlie's uncle's store and some salt pork and a couple of slabs of bacon and a sack of dried beans and sugar and coffee and various pots and pans. They'd also brought a ground cloth to put their bedrolls on or to use as a tent in case it rained, which, as Charlie said, "He'd be glad to get wet just to see it."

For weapons Warner had his side arm and two twelve-gauge shotguns. Instead of the 30.06 he'd chosen an old .50 caliber Sharps rifle. Charlie had a handgun and a shotgun. In the intervening days Warner had slowly told Charlie most of the story. He had been frank with him about using the horse herd to attract the bandits, but he had not told Charlie what he was going to do once he had the bandits, especially, El Gordo, in his gun sights. He'd said, "Once they show up your job is done. When I tell you to git or you hear a gunshot you are to head for home. That's why I'm going to give you thirty dollars in advance. If they haven't shown up in ten days then I'll give you another thirty. But you are not to interest yourself in this matter at all. Not in the least. Is that understood?"

Charlie had wanted to argue, had wanted to say he couldn't just run off, but Warner had given him the choice of losing the job or giving his word that he would do exactly as Warner requested and ordered.

In the end he had agreed though Warner could see it had troubled him greatly.

Laura Pico, however, had been a different piece of yard goods. She had seemed to think, or so it sounded to Warner, that the one night they'd spent together had bought her into a game she hadn't been invited to play. When he'd shown up to get the range mares to add to his little herd he'd found her insistent on going along. He'd said, "Laura, I already got a kid with me and, to tell you the truth, I just ain't a good enough shot to protect me and him and you and kill Mexican bandits at the same time."

But that wouldn't do for her. She'd argued and argued and he'd kept saying no steadfastly. Finally, she'd said, "All right, then, you can't use Paseta."

He had just stared at her for a moment and then walked over to the horse and started taking his saddle off. She'd run after him and grabbed his arm. She'd said, "You have to take me along! I want to get my horses back."

"Then get them yourself. To tell you the truth I wasn't much looking to go prowling around in Mexico after your horses as it was." He'd shaken off her hand and gone back to undoing the girth on his saddle.

"And after I was nice to you!"

He'd looked around at her and smiled. "I wondered when that was coming. Well, Laura, I was nice to you too. You know, what I got is just as good as what you got and yours don't work worth a damn without mine. Besides, you can't have it both ways."

"What's that supposed to mean?"

"It means you can't be a man and a woman at the same time. You can't give your word, which you did, like a man and then turn around and take it back like a woman when things don't go to suit you."

She had almost screamed at him. "I want to shoot that fat sonofabitch that stole my horses! That bastard!"

He'd nodded. "I figured it was something like that. Well, he's already taken for the next dance. You'll have to sit this one out. That's what I mean, Laura, you better decide what you mean to say and then stick to it. You don't want me to try and get your horses back that's fine. Just don't try and run no shell game on me. I ain't eighteen years old and your skirt ain't the first one I been under."

He had been just about to pull his saddle off the Andalusian when she had reached around him and pushed it back. She said, "Oh, take the horse. Take the damn horse. You got any other insults you want to pay me before you go?"

He'd shook his head. "No. I reckon that covers it."

She'd said, "Then you can go back to hell, *Mr.* Warner Grayson." Then she'd turned on her heel and gone back into the ranch house, her reddish blond hair bouncing with every step.

Charlie had been holding the horses they'd gathered a few hundred yards back from the house. As Warner had rode up he'd looked puzzled. He'd said, "Was that lady yelling?"

"No," Warner had said. "That's just her natural tone of voice."

He'd had trouble with Lupita, also, but of a completely different kind. When he'd asked her where he was supposed to sleep she'd assigned him to her room and her bed, which was just fine with him. At least it had been fine at first. He had gone to bed at nine or ten o'clock while she was working. But then, somewhere around two in the morning, the place would close up and she'd come in to bed ready to play. It had thrown him off his sleep habits worse than ever.

But that was just as well because he'd planned to mind the herd during the night and look for comfort and then sleep during the day while Charlie was on duty with orders to wake him at the first sign of any visitors.

Now they were a good five or six miles northwest of the Pico ranch and Warner was beginning to look for a spot where he could locate the herd. He planned to go as far west as the sparse winter grass held out and then settle in somewhere about two miles north of the river. His plan was to close herd the horses and then take them down to the river every evening to give them a good drink and then drive them back to the camp for the night. He wanted to appear to be a rancher who had taken his horses to fresh grass while he was letting the first spring grass get a good start without being trampled down and nipped off back at his main pasturage. It was a not uncommon habit though it was done with cattle more than horses. But he didn't think Mexican horse thieves were going to much care about the difference. And, he figured, after about two or three trips to the river with such fine looking animals the word ought to spread pretty quickly over in Mexico that some damn fool gringo was just aching to get his horse herd stolen. His horses would be noticed the first time, commented on the second, and be a cause for plans to be laid by the third. He could only hope that he wasn't making it so tempting that it might attract bandits other than El Gordo. But, if that happened, he would deal with it as best he could.

Charlie was driving the buckboard with his two saddle horses and Wilson's running horse tied on behind. Warner had been riding the Andalusian steadily although he knew he should at least have thrown a leg over the running horse just to make his acquaintance. But the Andalusian was such a pleasure to ride, so steady and quick to the touch, that Warner had been spoiling himself. If anything he'd almost grown fond of the horse, or at least as fond as he was likely to let himself get about a horse. Once or twice he'd almost called him by name like that damn fool woman, but he'd stopped himself in time.

As they moved, slowly to let the little herd graze a bit, Warner had come on the alert for a likely looking piece of ground to make a camp. As they'd gone they'd been picking up what downed wood they could find for a campfire. Warner intended to build a big campfire every night and keep it going. He didn't want any interested parties having trouble finding him.

He was looking for some broken ground or some kind of cover that would provide him a hiding and firing place a little way away from what was going to look like an occupied camp complete with a well-tended fire. But the problem was that the prairie was just too flat and uneventful. He turned the herd slightly north, taking them a little farther from the river than he wanted to go, but in hopes that the ground would roughen up some. He was looking for anything; a small hill, a ditch, a clump of rocks, a dry streambed, anything that would provide cover for one man against a number.

Finally, when they'd come what he figured was nearly ten miles from the Pico ranch and with the grass beginning to thin out worse than it had been, he found what he was looking for. It was a small thick grove of mesquite trees up on a small rise with a little *harranca* running in front of the grove that was almost like a crack in the earth.

He said to Charlie, "Well, I believe we have found the place. Now we got to set up our picket line and build a camp."

They took the reel of three-quarter-inch soft

rope and Warner tied one end about five feet off the ground to the stoutest mesquite he could find. Then, with Charlie driving the wagon, he paid out about two hundred feet of the rope to make a picket line plenty long enough to hitch their small herd to on individual leads. He cut the rope with his pocketknife, tied it to the end of the wagon, and had Charlie ease the mules forward until the rope was stretched tight. He knew it would sag, but, for the time being, it was a tight line some four feet off the ground.

Before he told Charlie to take the strain off, he got out of the wagon and hunted up some big rocks and chocked them under the wheels of the wagon to keep the wagon from rolling backward toward the mesquite tree. His plan was to loose herd the horses during the day, letting them graze on the poor grass and then tying them on lead ropes at night to the long, stretched out picket line. That way he wouldn't have to worry about the horses and could concentrate his nighttime work on watching for the bandits. They'd feed the horses oats and grain and a little hay at night and, in a few days, they should be slicked up enough to make any horse thief get careless.

Charlie had already had all this explained to him so, as soon as he got down from the wagon seat, he began unhitching the mules. Their work was over for the time being and they'd just go into the horse herd. And, of course, big, good-looking mules were especially attractive to Mexican horse thieves since many Mexicans, because of the rough country, preferred to ride mules, who were more surefooted than horses.

Sitting in the bed of the wagon, Warner was cutting off ten-foot-long lead ropes. Any shorter and they'd snub the horse too close. Any longer and it would give the animal too much room to get in trouble. All of the horses were wearing cheap rope halters. Warner had bought some and made some. He'd done the latter while, as a concession to Wilson Young, he'd sent Charlie on a circuit of the four nearest ranches to tell them of his troubles and general state of bad health and that he'd get to them just as soon as he could if they still wanted him. To a man, Charlie had reported, they'd been concerned about him and couldn't wait for him to get better and bring their horses up to snuff.

He got down from the wagon bed and looked up at the sky. As near as he could figure it was as close to four in the afternoon as it was going to get. He said, "Well, Charlie, I guess we better bunch up these horses and take them down to the river for a good drink and then get back up here and get ourselves set up for the night. I hope we have some spectators on the Mexican side that take an interest when we water these horses."

Charlie mounted his saddle horse and they gathered up the strayed horses and mules into one bunch and started them the two miles to the river. As far as Warner was concerned it had begun.

Horses were easier to drive than cattle and this bunch had shaped up quickly so that they'd been no trouble on the trail. Horses, being driven, would usually follow a mare and the older the mare the better. A big black eight- or nine-year-old from the Pico ranch had established herself at the head of the herd early on and pointing the rest of the horses had been mainly a case of keeping her headed the right way.

Which was just as well. As fond of the Andalusian as Warner was getting he could quickly see that the horse didn't know any more about the business of driving stock than a Yankee knew about biscuits and grits. Oh, he responded quickly enough to rein and spur to put a laggard or a stray back into the herd, but he had to be directed to do it. He hadn't the slightest idea that it was his duty to take out after the errant head of stock without any urging from Warner.

But Warner had expected the horse to behave in just such a way, just as he'd thought Mrs. Pico's idea of crossing the Andalusian stallions with range mares to produce a superior cattle horse was about as likely of success as his ever getting along with her on a regular basis.

He was pleased, though, to see the Andalusian's ears prick forward and hear him give a little nicker when they were still at least a mile from the river. It was clear evidence that the horse could, indeed, smell water better than most. At least better than the horses they were driving because none of them had made the slightest sign.

He called across to Charlie, "Better get ready to slow them down. We're less than a mile from the river. Keep a close lookout in case we have trouble."

He had a double-barreled shotgun in his saddle boot and the .50 caliber Sharps tied on behind his saddle. To Wilson's dismay he'd insisted on taking the big gun in place of the 30.06. His argument had been that if he was going to use a long-distance weapon he wanted something as close to a cannon as he could get and the Sharps just about fit that bill. It was a little better than five feet overall with a forty-six-inch barrel on it. It, too, was a single shot, but the shells looked to be near the size of small carrots. Warner had fired a .50 caliber gun before and he knew it had a kick that you had to learn how to handle. But it would fling one of those huge shells nearly a half mile and the gun hadn't been made that was more accurate for that kind of shooting. Against his wishes Wilson had insisted on taking it around to a gunsmith and having the scope taken off the 30.06 and remounted on the Sharps. Warner had protested he didn't know how to use the damn thing, but Wilson had just said to line up the cross hairs on whatever he was shooting at and let science do the rest.

Now, maybe a quarter of a mile from the river, with the rest of the horses smelling the water and getting restless, Warner had Charlie hold them back while he dismounted and untied the big rifle. Using the saddle on the Andalusian for a rest he trained the scope on the river and looked over both shores. It was amazing how powerful the scope was. It was like a spyglass a surveyor had once let Warner look through. It made things seem about ten times closer than they were.

He searched the Mexican shoreline of the river and then looked deeper into the country. He didn't want to be in the midst of watering the horses and suddenly get surprised by a band of renegade *bandidos*. This was one time he intended on doing the surprising himself.

He waved to Charlie to let the horses go ahead on. He mounted up, still holding the heavy rifle, resting it sideways across the saddle and followed as the horses started at a fast lope toward the river.

As they got to the edge he yelled, "Slow 'em down, Charlie! Don't let them get too far out."

They were at a crook in the river where the water was swift running and shallow. A jug-headed horse could get in far enough, in his haste, to either bog in the sandy bottom, or get his legs swept out from under him. But Charlie was in the water, riding back and forth in front of the little herd, forcing the horses to keep at least their hind feet on dry ground.

The Andalusian was too well mannered to make a dash for the water. He waited until Warner gave him permission and then he waded out until he was standing in about a foot of water and lowered his head. While the horse drank Warner put the Sharps rifle to his shoulder and used the scope to scan the land up to three-quarters of a mile back from the river on the Mexico side. Coming from the river the land lay flat for about a quarter of a mile and then it began to rise in a little series of hills. Warner knew they built into a range of north-south running *sierras*, mountains, but that was some thirty or forty miles south. With his telescope he could see the poor huts of the peons who tried to make a living on the poor land raising goats and corn and anything else that would grow. Now and again he caught sight of a peon staring his way, but he saw no sign of mounted men, bandits or otherwise. Never mind, he told himself, the word would begin to get about, especially when they were observed on more than one occasion bringing the horses to water.

When the horses had finished they drove them back to the site Warner had chosen for the camp. He loose herded the horses while he sent Charlie off to the mesquite clump to see how much more downed wood he could find. They had a sizeable load already in the wagon, but mesquite burned fast and they'd need a good bit to keep a fire blazing all night. Fortunately there were several clumps of mesquite a little farther on.

After Charlie had brought in two armloads they set to work staking the horses on the picket line. Charlie kept his saddle horse loose and Warner decided to stay with the Andalusian the rest of the night. When they had the horses tended to Warner had Charlie build a small cooking fire while he set about fixing the meal. Using the tailgate of the wagon as a table he got out a slab of bacon and sliced off a dozen thick slices and arranged them in a big cast-iron skillet. Charlie had rigged a grill over the fire with some fair-size rocks on each side. It was a little high-toned for such a camp but it made food cook evener than just setting the skillet in the embers.

While he waited for the fire to burn down Warner filled the coffeepot with water from the fifty-gallon barrel they'd brought along from Del Rio. Then he threw in a fistful of ground coffee beans and set the big pot near the fire. After he judged the fire to have burned down enough he set the skillet, full of the thick bacon slices, on the grill and turned his attention to taking his big clasp knife and opening three cans of pork and beans and a can of tomatoes. They'd brought six loaves of bread from the cafe in Del Rio, about the amount they figured would hold up three or four days. After that it would be the canned biscuits they'd bought a good supply of in Charlie's uncle's store. But the canned biscuits would not be any treat. They were, as Charlie said, "hard enough to get steady work as rocks." While he sliced up one of the loaves of bread he could hear the bacon crackling and snapping. A light eddy of wind brought the smell of the cooking bacon to his nose. Next to a pretty woman's perfume and the smell of a good horse, Warner reckoned that bacon scent was nearly as good a smell as there was, especially when you were hungry.

Charlie had gone back for another load of mesquite and, as he came struggling into camp with a double armload Warner saw that the bacon was starting to brown. With the point of his knife he turned it over, gave it a few moments, and then dumped in the cans of beans and the can of tomatoes. Then he pushed the coffeepot nearer to the fire so it would be ready when the meal was and got out a couple of tin plates and some eating utensils and a big ladling spoon and laid them to hand on a clean piece of paper the bread had come wrapped in. It was not yet twilight, but the shadow of the moon was showing on the horizon. They were, he thought, running just a trifle late. He wanted to have eaten and have the camp set up before it got good dark.

When the beans and the bacon and tomatoes

were bubbling, Warner took the ladling spoon and dished out half to Charlie and the other half to himself. Then he set the skillet aside, poured a little water in it so the remains in the bottom wouldn't harden and make it hard to wash, and then he and Charlie set in to eat. Warner used two pieces of bread to empty his plate and then one to swab it clean with. They drank water with the meal and, by the time they were finished, the coffee was ready. They each took a cup. Warner said, "Now you got it straight, Charlie?"

Charlie was blowing on the coffee in his tin cup. He said, "Yessir. I'm to sleep in that grove of mesquite back yonder with my saddle horse near to hand. If I hear shootin' I ain't to do nothing. After the shooting stops I'm to wait a few minutes. If I don't hear you holler by then I'm to cinch up my horse and light out just as quiet as can be. I'm to ride straight to Mr. Wilson Young and tell him what I know."

Warner nodded. "That's fine. At first light you are to look the situation over carefully and come on in. That is if things have been peaceful the night before. You'll see me stirring around most likely, getting breakfast ready. But if you see any other folks about you lay low and wait until I whistle you in." He took a sip of his coffee. "Way my luck is running somebody else has already killed that fat sonofabitch and his *amigos*, and me and you is just going to get a little practice tending horses which I don't reckon either one of us needs."

Charlie said, "He'll come, Mr. Grayson. Ain't a bandit within a hunnert miles of here could resist this little herd of horses that ain't all that well guarded and this close to the border."

"That's just it," Warner said, "maybe I'm making it look like a setup. Maybe it looks too easy."

Charlie said, "I don't reckon them Meskin *bandidos* is overloaded with smarts, Mr. Grayson. Besides, they'll take the time and see ain't but one of us standing guard and that'll look like pie to them. There for the grabbing. They'll come. I jest wish you'd let me in on the shooting."

Warner gave him a look and swished his cup to get rid of the grounds that had collected in the bottom. He said, "No more talk like that. It's good dark. I reckon it's time you took your bedroll and went on over and bedded down in that far mesquite thicket. Be sure and tie your horse close to hand and don't take the saddle off him. Just loosen the girth. He'll get plenty of exercise during the day."

Charlie was up and gathering his gear. He said, "I'm supposed to leave you my shotgun?"

"Yes," Warner answered. "You won't need it."

He watched as Charlie loaded his horse with a canteen and his bedroll and slicker, then mounted and started off toward the mesquite thicket. The little clump was only about a hundred yards away, but Charlie had to circle the *barranca* that ran between it and the camp.

When Charlie had disappeared into the night Warner set about his own preparations. First he added a little more coffee and water to the pot. He'd be up all night and, on this first night, not having slept the night before, he was going to need all the help he could get to stay awake.

The first thing he did was pile wood on the fire to make a good enough blaze to cast a strong glow about twenty feet across. Then he took a ground sheet and laid it down and put a bedroll on top of that. He unrolled the bedroll and then stuffed it with sacks of potatoes and apples to give it the appearance of being occupied. But he pulled it back far enough from the fire so that it was in the dim light, making it necessary for the curious to give it close scrutiny in order to discover it was only produce that was asleep. He took the saddle off the Andalusian and set it at the head of the bedroll like a man normally would. Then he tied the Spanish horse a little way down the picket rope so as to have him out of the way of any gunfire, but still close enough at hand to get to him quickly in case he needed the horse. He didn't unbridle the horse, just took the bits out of the animal's mouth and tied him to the picket rope. He already knew he could ride the horse without a saddle and even without a bridle if need be.

When he was done he surveyed the scene around the campfire. The wood was already starting to blaze up good and should burn steady for a couple of hours without need of replenishment. He'd left out all the cooking paraphernalia, thinking back to when the bandits had noticed his and Red's plates. He'd also left out the side of bacon along with some other odds and ends including the two bottles of tequila he'd bought special for the occasion. He could only hope that he got a chance to use them.

Finally he went to the wagon. It was parked sideways to the campfire, sort of running east to west, and north of the camp. If the Mexicans came they'd come from the south, unless they circled, and, in that case, they'd be turned back by the *barranca*, especially in the dark. So, if he'd figured it right, they should enter his camp from the south, just as they had before.

There were two extra bedrolls of blankets in the bed of the wagon and he took one and spread it casually on the ground cloth like the man who'd been occupying it had either gotten up for some reason or was on night herd duty. Then he took the other bedroll and put it beneath the wagon, facing the campfire. He took the three shotguns out of the wagon, checked their loads, and then laid them side by side under the wagon. Lastly he slid the big Sharps rifle underneath and then crawled in under himself. He had forgotten to bring himself a cup of coffee, but he figured he could hold out until it was time to build up the campfire.

The shotguns were not loaded with double-aught buckshot as most would have expected, as Charlie had. Instead, Warner had loaded them with number four shells. Number four shot was half the size of buckshot, but he wasn't shooting to kill. He would be shooting to maim and cripple.

All there was to do now was wait. And hope. He didn't reckon he ought to pray about it since he knew the Bible and knew God's attitude toward vengeance. He did pray for God to forgive him if the Mexicans got unlucky enough to pass his way with greed on their minds and lust for his horses in their hearts.

He yawned and thanked Lupita very much for having ruined his last night's chance of getting any sleep. But, taken all around, it had been worth it. At least this way he'd have little problem sleeping the next day, a chore he usually found difficult to do. His grandfather had been of the fixed opinion that Moses had left one commandment back up on the mount and that had been, *Thou shalt not sleep whilst there is sun enough to work by.* As a consequence Warner had always found it nearly impossible to sleep during the day and, even when it was forced on him, he'd always felt a little guilty.

The night made little noises all around him, but they were just the noises a night usually made, the cry of a night bird, the rustle of brush as some small animal made its way through, the faint sound of wind blowing the grass. Occasionally the water cooked out of the mesquite and made a popping and crackling sound. But none of these were the sounds Warner was straining his ears to hear. He wanted to hear the far-off creak of saddle leather, the clank of bits and bridles, the jingle of big roweled Mexican spurs.

The night drug. It was a dark night with just a sliver of a moon. From his position under the wagon Warner couldn't quite see the whole sky, but he patiently watched the slow march of the moon and stars across the almost cloudless blackness. He thought it was the longest night he'd ever spent. Each time he took out the watch he'd borrowed from Wilson and peered at the white face the black hands would have moved considerably less than he'd hoped they had. Warner had gone to bed at seven or eight o'clock many times. But that had been to sleep. And there had been plenty of times when, for one reason or another, he'd worked all night, either traveling or trying to save a sick horse, but that had been different. Then, he'd had something to do. As near as he could figure this was the first time in his life he'd ever laid under a wagon an entire night waiting for bandits to ride into his circle of firelight so he could cut down on them with a succession of shotguns.

He had to get up four times to add wood to the fire, but he did it with a shotgun crooked in his arm and Wilson's bone-handled revolver at his side.

His only comfort was the coffee which just kept getting stronger and stronger in spite of all the water he kept adding to it. That and the noise the horses made.

Finally the first faint traces of dawn began to show in the east. As the light began to come and he was able to distinguish the horses on the picket line, he came stiffly out from under the wagon. He looked toward the grove of mesquites and could just make out Charlie, sitting his horse. He waved an arm and whistled. He saw Charlie start to ride his way, coming at a slow lope.

They had fried eggs and bacon for breakfast along with some canned peaches. Charlie said he'd had a good night's sleep and was feeling fit. Warner said his body was aching for sleep but all the coffee he'd poured into himself was still working and he felt as jittery as a tinker's wagon. Charlie said, "Whyn't you take yoreself a drank of whiskey? That'd settle you down."

Warner said, "Because we ain't got no whiskey is one reason."

Charlie nodded his head at the two big bottles of tequila. He said, "There's that Mexican poison. Do the same trick."

Warner said, grimly, "I've had all the tequila I want. Besides, that's to be saved for our guests."

Charlie said, "When you reckon they'll come, Mr. Grayson?"

Warner looked toward the river. "Soon," he said. "Soon, Charlie. The delay ain't doing either me or that fat Mexican one damn bit of good. Few more nights like that last one and I might get downright mean."

He helped Charlie get the horses untied from their lead ropes. Together they bunched them and shaped them up so Charlie could loose herd them. Then, at last, the coffee began to wear off and Warner could feel sleep racing toward him. He got in under the shade of the wagon, took his boots off, and was asleep almost as soon as he'd lain down.

# 9

Another night and day passed without any sign of the bandits and then another. Warner was starting to adjust to sleeping during the daytime and keeping a night vigil but he still didn't much care for it. Sleeping in the day made him feel guilty and he slept restlessly. Besides, it was starting to get hot during the afternoon, even under the shade of the wagon.

Each evening they took the horses to water at the river and, each time, Warner used the telescope sight to scan the low hills and valleys as far as the scope would let him see. By now they seemed to be drawing a larger and larger audience as they drove the horses to water. On the third morning a few *campesinos* even rode their sorry looking, underfed cayuses down to the Mexican side of the river and stared across at them. Warner was riding Wilson Young's black racehorse and he cantered the flashy horse back and forth for their envious gaze. Somebody, he thought, somewhere, has got to hear about all this horseflesh and get word to El Gordo. How much longer can he resist?

But another night and then another passed and all Warner saw were the stars and the waxing moon, a sight he wasn't particularly glad about.

He didn't want brightly lit nights; he wanted it to be as dark as the inside of a cow so that the only light the bandits would have to use would be the light of his campfire. He wanted them drawn to that like moths to a flame.

By the morning of the fifth day they had run out of bread and were forced to turn to the tinned biscuits. They could be eaten, but only after they'd been soaked in a cup of coffee for about half an hour. Charlie was of the opinion that they weren't biscuits at all. He said, "I figure these are old doorknobs that come off old falling down houses and somebody went around and gathered them up and shoved them in these here tins by mistake. Hell, they'd wear better than cast iron. Mr. Grayson, a man could make a boot heel out of one of these biscuits that would last him a lifetime. Only problem is you'd never get a cobbler's nail through 'em."

After a week Warner was starting to get discouraged and beginning to wonder if his plan had a chance. Maybe Wilson Young had been right, that he was wasting his time and that he should have got on with his regular work. He might well have lost his customers, but it was too late to worry about that now, he thought.

It was bothering Charlie. He said, "Mr. Grayson, I feel awful drawing wages for this. Hell, it ain't even work no more. This damn horse herd don't even have to be herded no more. They know when they're going to get grained and when they're supposed to go to water. And they know where the grass is and they stay right there. I swan, I believe they could look after themselves."

Warner said, "I ain't paying you to do hard work, Charlie. I'm paying you for the appearance of the thing. I wished you looked more like a kid. Maybe if they thought there was just one man here they'd come in. But, no, that ain't right. They walked in on me and Red and ain't nobody ever took Red for a kid. We just got to be patient."

Charlie shook his head. He said, "Wa'l, you are a determined man, Mr. Grayson. And I reckon you know what you're doing."

"I wonder," Warner said.

Another worry was that they were starting to run low on grain. In another day he was going to have to send Charlie back in with the wagon to pick up another load. And there was no way the trip could be made in less than twenty-four hours. That would leave him exposed on the prairie with no real way to carry out his plan.

He decided they'd have to stretch the grain a few more days. And maybe Laura Pico had some she could spare and that wouldn't be a very hard or long trip. It could be made during daylight hours.

They were also beginning to run short on fire- wood, a commodity that was even more important than the grain for the horses. The horses could afford to go on short rations for a few days, but he couldn't do without his beacon to beckon El Gordo and his gang of *bandidos*. A big night fire was common for cowhands doing night herding. It gave them a cheerful signal through the long night hours and also served as a homing light if one of them had to make a long chase of a determined stray. But they had used up all the downed wood from the nearest mesquite thicket and Charlie had had to resort to longer and longer forays to find enough wood to keep the fire ablaze all night long. He'd even resorted to tieing his lariat rope to live limbs, them having not thought to bring a saw or an axe, and using his horse's strength to break off big branches of green wood. Of course these could only be used when the fire was going good and even then all they did was mostly smoke all night long.

Now, on the ninth night, Warner lay under the wagon growing more and more impatient. He judged it to be about ten o'clock. When they had first been picketed the horses had neighed softly to each other during the early hours. But, once they'd fallen in with the routine, they very seldom stirred around much after they had, as Charlie said, "been put to bed." Warner had got up and reloaded the fire, unfortunately with some of the green wood that Charlie had been forced to bring in. It was making considerable smoke and the water that was being cooked out of it was sizzling and snapping. The three shotguns lay close to his side. Two of them were the kind favored by saloon keepers and peace officers. They were short barreled and consequently threw a wider pattern of shot, making a more effective gun for close work. He'd gotten them from Wilson Young who, he reckoned, could be considered both a saloon keeper and a peace officer in the sense that he had quit breaking it. The thought made him smile and he reminded himself to mention it to Wilson as a dig. He could say something like, "Yeah, I reckon you done more for law and order in Texas than all the sheriffs and marshalls rolled into one. Just by going into the cathouse and casino business." Wilson himself was always quick enough with a jab or a dig at the other fellow.

The third shotgun was Charlie's and it had a standard thirty-inch barrel on it, the kind a man used for duck or goose hunting. They were all loaded and he had a dozen extra shells ready to hand along with his revolver and the scoped .50 caliber Sharps.

He was lying there wondering what it would do to a man to get shot up close with the Sharps when he heard a quiet nicker from one of the horses on the picket line. It surprised him for a moment, but, after such a time together, horses tended to friend up and one of them might have been making a comment to his mate that had slipped his mind during the afternoon. The fire was blazing up and the green wood was snapping and popping and sending a stream of sparks and smoke skyward that Warner reckoned could be seen for twenty miles.

Then he heard another horse nicker, a little louder this time. It was strange, he thought. He strained his ears, but couldn't hear anything. However, just to be on the safe side, he eased one of the short-barreled shotguns into his hands. He felt like a fool doing it. The first three nights he'd kept one in hand the whole night long. Then, after a while, he'd grown content to have the guns ready at hand. He'd stirred at too many false sounds and hopes to get very excited about a couple of fool horses mumbling and grumbling around. Likely they were discussing the fact that the grain ration had been cut and were maybe trying to foment mutiny. Warner realized he was starting to think a little silly, but what else could you expect from a man who slept when everybody else was up and working and then lay under a wagon out on the bald ass prairie all night long. By rights he ought to be a raving lunatic.

There came another snort and then a neigh. He was almost certain it came from his horse because the Andalusian had a deep-chested voice that made him sound like he was about twice as big as he was. The sound immediately took Warner's attention because the Andalusian was one of the most attentive and alert horses he'd ever rode. Like all horses, especially blooded stock, he couldn't see much past his own shadow, but he had as good a nose and hearing as any horse Warner had ever encountered.

He looked up at the column of smoke and sparks that were rising in the air. They were blowing back over him, toward the north. That meant that the wind was from the south and that his horses would smell any horses coming from the river before they could wind his.

He looked carefully over the circle of firelight. It was twelve paces from his place under the wagon and about two more to the other side of the fire. Set off to the side, to his right, were the bottles of tequila and some pots and pans and the remains of a cured ham they'd been eating. Both bedrolls were in place with the one stuffed with potatoes and whatnot looking as if someone were curled up dead to the world. The other bedroll still looked as if the occupant had just got up to go and relieve himself or to see to some other piece of business. The idea was to make any visitors who'd been studying them believe that the two men they'd seen were accounted for even if one of them was somewhere out in the night.

The picket line that came off the wagon ran at a forty-five-degree angle back to the small knot of mesquite and post oak that the other end of the rope was tied to. Warner felt sure that, if any gunfire was returned, it would be directed his way and that none of his horses would be endangered.

After the little scrub of trees came the deep and rocky *barranca* that any visitors would have to circle if they wanted to come up on him from the back, or north side. Beyond that, some sixty yards farther, was the bigger grove of mesquite where Charlie was sleeping. He lay still, looking over his layout, trying to think if he'd missed anything—not that he felt like his quarry was finally coming, but as a way of controlling his own nerves.

The Andalusian nickered, and Warner could visualize him, his head raised, his ears pricked in the direction of the smell. Then, and the hairs on the back of his neck stiffened, he heard the faint sound of an answering whinny. It was difficult to tell how far off the sound was because noise carried differently at night when the air seemed to be heavy. But the sound set off a few snorts and nickers from several of the horses on the picket line. He could hear them waking up and shifting around, getting excited like all fool horses did.

But he wasn't ready to get excited yet, or hopeful. It could be a stray horse, it could be an honest rider out late and on his way home. It could be anything.

He let his attention go to the cooking gear that

was piled over to the side to look as if they'd just been used. There was a Dutch oven there, a big, cast-iron pot with a lid. He'd always wondered why it was called a Dutch oven but had never gotten around to asking. When they'd finally gotten desperate about the biscuits Charlie had tried to make some corn bread. They had corn-meal, but they didn't have any lard so they'd melted some of the ham fat and made use of that, using condensed milk in place of the real thing. They'd baked what Charlie called corn dodgers in the Dutch oven, setting it near the coals and then turning it every so often so that it would heat inside evenly. The corn bread hadn't turned out so bad. It was pretty flat and didn't rise because they didn't have any baking powder and it was kind of crumbly and didn't hold together so well. But it sure as hell had beat the biscuits which Charlie now swore were put out by a company that made false teeth in an attempt to build up business. There were a number of the dodgers still in the oven. He hoped the Mexicans, if it was them, would leave them alone and, instead, open one of the tins of biscuits and break off a few teeth to get the party started.

He suddenly gripped his shotgun tighter as he heard another whinny. This one sounded closer, much closer. It set off three or four of his horses but, strangely, the Andalusian held silent.

Warner tried to see past the fire, but soon gave

it up for a bad job. The fire was too bright. It made the encircling wall of darkness as impenetrable as if it were made out of brick.

He held his breath, listening hard. In the rigid stillness he could feel his own heart beating. It wasn't racing, but he could feel a sense of "getting ready" coursing through his body. He kept warning himself that it might be nothing, but it was the nearest thing to something in all the nights he'd kept vigil.

And then on the light wind he began to hear sounds that were different than the usual night noises. There came the faint creak of leather and what sounded like the low murmur of voices, of men talking. Then it seemed as if he could hear the sounds of horses traveling across the prairie. They weren't running or going fast, but it seemed as if he could feel and hear them through his body that was pressed against the ground.

Then, seeming sharply closer, a horse whinnied out in the night, followed by two or three more neighs. His horses answered back.

And now he was certain he could hear a party of men approaching his camp. He could distinctly hear the sound of saddle leather, the rattle of bits, the low talk they were making among themselves. He couldn't make out any of the words, but he knew that they weren't speaking English.

Straining to hear he had unconsciously scooted farther out from under the wagon toward the fire.

If they had ridden into the circle of light at that second he could have been seen if they'd had sharp eyes. He hastily crabbed backward into the darkness under the wagon. He lay, listening, his breath coming in little short bursts, his heart beginning to pound. If it wasn't El Gordo and his bunch it was somebody damn like them.

He heard the horsemen coming nearer and nearer. They sounded close enough to Warner to suddenly burst into the circle of firelight. But still they came on, walking, he could tell, and talking very low among themselves. His horses had grown quiet, but he could envision them with their heads up, their ears pricked, their nostrils flared, trying to identify these strangers. Now and then there came a soft nicker from the oncoming animals, but they were cut short as if a hand had suddenly clamped their mouths shut.

Then he heard the riders stop. They sounded as if they could be no more than twenty yards away. He heard one voice say something and then there was a general creaking of leather. They were dismounting. They intended to enter the camp on foot. It surprised and disappointed him because that had not been the way El Gordo, or Chumacho as he liked to be called, had done it before. But, of course, that had been much earlier in the day, barely at twilight. Maybe this bunch preferred to come in leading their horses so they might use them for cover.

He very slowly extended the first of the short-barreled shotguns out in front of him. It was still well concealed by the wagon. He was as taut as he had ever been in his life yet he suddenly felt an icy cool steal over him. It seemed he could see everything at a glance, hear every noise, even the slightest, even the smell of the campfire seemed heightened, more acrid. He put his finger inside the trigger guard of the shotgun and gently let it rest on the curved trigger. Both hammers were already cocked. If he extended his finger he could pull the double trigger and fire both barrels at once. But he knew, instinctively, that he didn't want to do that. The kick of the gun would be too great. Besides, the shots coming one right on top of the other would be more frightening and more effective. It would confuse them as to how many men were shooting at them.

A lone man stepped hesitantly into the circle of the firelight. Warner stared at him closely as the man looked around. Warner did not recognize him from before. The man was small and dressed in dirty white cotton clothes. He had a revolver, but he had not drawn it. It was shoved down in the waistband of his pants. He had his right hand on the butt, but his finger was not down inside the trigger guard. To Warner's eye the man looked more like a poor *campesino*, a farm or ranch worker, than he did a bandit. But then most bandits had been something else before they took up the gun in earnest. The man took a few cautious steps into the circle of light, looking around. He was not wearing his sombrero but had it hanging down his back, held by a chin cord. The man's eyes went to the bedroll that Warner had stuffed to make it look like a sleeping man. He took a step in its direction, but then stopped, his eyes going to the tequila and the food. Warner thought it was not too hard to guess that this was one of the least valuable members of the gang of bandits that El Gordo had sent in to see how safe the situation was.

That is if it was El Gordo lurking back just outside of the light.

As Warner watched, the man stepped quickly over to the bottles of tequila and picked up one that Warner had partially drawn the cork out of. He pulled the cork with his teeth, spit it away, and then took a long pull. Warner had also brought a dozen bottles of cheap whiskey and had about half a dozen set out, casually, as if the occupants of the camp wanted to have them quick to hand.

The man took a quick look over his shoulder, took another drink, and then set the bottle back down with the others. He took a few steps to the edge of the firelight and said something in Spanish out into the darkness. Warner didn't hear what he said, but he hoped he was giving the all clear and telling the others it was all right to come in. Warner could only hope and wish that the leader he was talking to was his old friend from the alkali plain.

A moment passed and then he heard a few words spoken in Spanish. Two other men came into the firelight. There was no mistaking them for peasants. They wore leather charro riding pants and the rowels of their big spurs dragged in the dust. The first man had worn *hurraches*, like the ones Warner had borrowed from Wilson Young's closet. It was as much that as his nervousness that had made Warner wonder if the man was really a bandit or just an unfortunate fallen in with bad company. But the two that had followed both wore holstered revolvers and one carried a rifle. Both of them had belts of cartridges crossing their chests. And one of them was wearing an American Western hat just as had several in the bunch that had jumped him and Red. One of the two that had just come to the fire said something to the little man in *hurraches* and he hurried back out into the dark. Then the one with the rifle yelled out, in Spanish, "*Está bien.*" (It's all right.)

Then the other noticed the tequila. He picked up the bottle that the first man had opened and had a long pull. He was about to hand it to the other man when the rest of the gang came in.

There were five more of them and Chumacho, El Gordo, was the third of the bunch to enter the circle of light. Warner smiled slowly and happily to himself. There he was, big ugly scar, big sombrero, big stomach, big gold tooth. Big target.

Warner waited, watching. Now there were seven all told inside the circle of light from the fire. The little man in white had not returned. Warner judged that he was standing just out in the darkness holding the horses until Chumacho could get the lay of the land and decide what to do. He stood, looking around. A leather quirt hung down from his wrist and he was wearing a felt sombrero that was decorated with silver conchos. There were also silver conchos down the outside of his flared charro riding pants. It was clear, from his dress, that he had been doing well since the last time Warner had seen him. His boots were shiny and new looking and he was wearing two ivory handled pistols in an expensive gun rig.

For the first time Chumacho seemed to notice the bedroll that appeared to contain a sleeping man. He yelled something at it in Spanish. The bedroll was at least ten yards from him on the other side of the fire. It was just to the right of where Warner lay.

Chumacho took a step toward the bedroll, drawing his right hand pistol as he did. He said, "Hey! 'R chou esleep? Chou *loco*? Chou have frens who hav' comes to sees chou. Chou geet up. Wh's the matter wid chou?"

Warner was itching to fire, but the rest of the

men were bunched up just behind El Gordo. He wanted them spread out a little more. But he also did not want Chumacho to come over to the dummy sleeping bag. He couldn't have that. It would put him too close for Warner to achieve the effect he wanted. He determined that if El Gordo took more than one step toward the bedroll he was going to fire and get as many of them as he could in the first volley.

Chumacho took one step toward the bedroll. He waved his gun. He said, "'R chou escairt? Chou escairt of Chumacho? Chou doan wan' to steeck chour head out of theese blankets? Chumacho es chou fren. Say, chou gots some nice horses por Chumacho, no? We take theese horses? Es hokay?" He laughed loudly and Warner could still hear that same laugh as the bandits had ridden away, leaving him to die.

But then Chumacho suddenly seemed to turn angry. He said, "Hey! Chou *pendejo*! Chou answer Chumacho! Meebe Chumacho pout a leetle boullet in chou *cajones*. No?" He cocked the pistol, but just then the man in the American-style Western hat tapped him on the shoulder and handed him a bottle of tequila. The others were busy boring out the corks of the remaining bottles with the points of their knives. Warner looked them over carefully. He was almost certain that the one in the Western hat and one more had been with Chumacho that bad other time. He thought he recognized one or two more, but he couldn't be sure. It made no difference. If they were with Chumacho that was condemnation enough for him.

They were beginning to spread out, some even edging up close to the fire in the chill of the night. Two of them were arguing over the ham, one holding it and the other trying to pull it away from him. Another one had opened a tin of the biscuits and had one in his hand, looking at it curiously. Warner wished he'd take a big, hard bite. It'd be the last time he'd have teeth to bite anything with.

Warner wanted them spread out a little more. At least three were covered by the other men and he didn't want to spend the night chasing bandits all over the prairie. Except for the little peon that had obviously been sent to hold the horses, the balance of the group were carrying enough guns to fight a war. To a man they were as mean looking as Warner expected they were. He'd been in their hands once and that was enough for any man. You didn't come out alive with the likes of these on the second try.

His mouth had gone dry. He wasn't nervous, but he was anxious for them to get in proper position where powder and shot would do the most good. But they were still grouped around the tequila and the supplies, just to the right of the fire. He knew, when he fired, that the man in peon's clothes would most likely flee, but he didn't much care. He wanted El Gordo and the few others he recognized.

Then Chumacho turned his back to Warner. He was talking to one of the other men, one of the hard cases that Warner reckoned to be part of his regular bunch. He overheard Chumacho say something about "*los caballos*," the horses, and he knew the man was talking about Warner's horses, the horses on the picket line. The *banditos* had been standing around, a little bewildered by the situation, but feeling they had no reason to be afraid because of their number. They were taking their time sizing up the situation. But it was the horses that had drawn their interest and it was the horses that Warner instinctively felt Chumacho was fixing to inspect. They'd either bring the horses into the firelight or they'd go into the dark to have a look at them. But Warner didn't expect them to tarry long. He had an idea they meant to make a quick search for any opposition and then cut the horses loose and drive them off.

Chumacho turned back in Warner's direction. He said something over his shoulder to the others, saying it hard as if it were an order. Warner hadn't understood the words, but the effect was to make every man drop what he was doing and start toward El Gordo.

For just a brief instant they were in sort of a ragged line with Chumacho at the head, nearest the wagon, walking, just coming around the campfire. Warner judged he was never going to have a better chance at a better distance. He didn't exactly sight the shotgun, but he aimed in the general area of Chumacho's big legs, just below his knees. He pulled one trigger and then the other and then dropped the shotgun he'd fired and grabbed up the other and fired one barrel after the other, the hammers already cocked. The shot was barely out the mouth of the second shotgun before the third was in his hands and firing.

The shots exploded *boom, boom, boom, boom, boom* as he walked them down the line of men, cutting them off at the knees. It was a second after he'd fired the last shot before the screaming began. The explosions of the shotguns were still ringing in his ears, deafening him. But he didn't need to hear, the evidence of his work was right before his eyes, well lit by the campfire.

As fast as he could he reloaded two of the shotguns, snapping open their breeches hard enough to eject the spent shells and ramming in new ones and then snapping the guns shut. One man staggered up out of the pile of screaming, writhing men, got to his feet and then his bleeding, shattered legs failed him and he fell into the fire, sending up a great shower of sparks. Somehow he jerked himself to his feet, his clothes on fire, and stumbled toward Warner and the wagon. Warner shot him dead center in the chest at a distance of no more than five yards. His whole middle seemed to turn red. The force of the blow knocked him backward as if he'd been struck by a giant fist.

Warner dropped the shotgun and drew his revolver. He hadn't wanted to kill the man, but he hadn't seen where he'd had any other choice, not with him charging toward the wagon as he had been. Some of the men down on the ground were firing, but it was wild gunfire, not aimed at anything or anyone. With the light of the campfire between him and them, for the main, he didn't believe they could have seen the muzzle flashes from his shotgun blasts. But he didn't like them shooting. They might hit one of his horses and the horses were his responsibility.

All of a sudden a man staggered to his feet and made as if to flee back the way he'd come. Warner let him take one step and then sighted carefully and shot the man between the shoulder blades. The bandit threw his hands into the air and pitched forward.

"*Baja*!" Warner yelled. It was the only way he knew to say "down" in Spanish though it didn't really mean that. But he wanted them to understand that the man that stood up was a dead man. He yelled, "*No alto*! *Muerta Baja sequero*!"

The bandits were in a long, ragged pile, some on their backs, some belly down. Most had fallen where they had been shot. The wave of shotgun pellets had cut them down like weeds under a scythe. To a man they were bloody from the waist down. Some of them had guns in their hands and were struggling to sit up. Warner dropped his pistol and grabbed up a shotgun and fired a shot just over their heads. The men attempting to rise immediately fell back to the ground.

Warner gave up on the Spanish and yelled, "Goddamit, throw out your guns! I'll kill the next man I see with a gun in his hand! Do it now!"

He had not expected all of them to understand, but a few had dropped their guns. Only one man seemed to be able to make out where Warner's voice was coming from. He was lying just to the fire side of Chumacho. He was on his back, but he rolled over on his belly, a revolver in his hand, and tried to search into the darkness for where the shots were coming from. But Warner could see that the campfire was blinding him. Warner yelled, "*Baja*! *Baja*, damnit!"

The man came to his knees and leveled his pistol, searching around for the sound of the voice. Warner switched back to his revolver. He sighted carefully on the man's chest. He didn't want to shoot him; he wanted as many of them alive as possible. But this man seemed determined to give him no choice. The man suddenly fired and Warner heard the sound of the bullet strike the side of the wagon a few feet over his head. He carefully squeezed off a shot and the man jerked backwards and then fell over on his side.

Then, suddenly, and to Warner's absolute surprise the man in the *hurraches* and dirty white pants and shirt came racing into the circle of light, waving the big old Navy Colt pistol he was carrying. He charged straight toward the wagon, trying to aim the pistol as he ran. Warner could only surmise that, from the darkness, he'd been able to see the muzzle flashes and locate the source of the fire. Now in some fool, idiotic act of stupidity he was going to save his comrades, if they could be called that. Warner watched in astonishment as the man came running around the fire and headed straight for the wagon. He was either crazy, Warner thought, or he was trying to get steady work with the bandit leader. But with that gun in his hand Warner couldn't afford to let him get too close. He shot him twice. The first bullet was low, catching him in the abdomen. It stopped him, but it didn't knock him down. Warner raised his sights and shot him just below the neck. The force of the bullet almost flipped the little man over. Warner reckoned the slug had taken him in the collarbone judging from the *thunk* it had made.

It was not going the way he'd planned it. Eight men had been in the band and he'd had to kill four. And, for all he knew, of the four still on the ground, one or more might be dead or dying. He had been trying to get a good look at Chumacho, but there'd been so much activity from the others that he hadn't had time to study the man. He had very carefully fired low on the bandit leader, not wanting to ruin his knees or to shoot him so far up the thighs that he might sever a main blood vein where the man might bleed to death.

Now that things seemed to have quieted down, except for the groans from the remaining four, he turned his attention to Chumacho. The fat bandit was lying on his back. He was rolling his head from side to side as if in pain, but he was making no attempt to rise. Warner could see most of his legs. The brunt of the shot seemed to have caught him between the knees and ankles. His new boots were now a bloody mess. Warner could see a few spots of blood above his knees, but it didn't appear to be anything serious. He wanted Chumacho to be able to walk.

The remaining three were spaced out a little with the last man being near the supplies. He'd gotten his hand on a bottle of tequila and was having a drink. Warner judged him to be all right. The bandit in the Western hat was lying just below Chumacho on his belly. He had his head up, searching the night. The fourth man didn't seem to be moving.

Warner said, "Chumacho! Chumacho!"

He saw the bandit leader stir. Chumacho had

lost his fancy hat in the shooting and now he tried to crane his head around to look in the direction of the voice. He said, "Who es chou?"

Warner said loudly, "Never mind who I am. You and the rest of your men throw away your guns. Pitch them clean away from you."

Chumacho said, "What fors chou choot us? We doan do you no'zing. We es no mean fellows."

Warner said, "Goddamit, I ain't going to tell you again! Get rid of every gun you got. I'm about to come in amongst you and if I see a man with a gun that man is dead."

There was no movement from the others but Chumacho said, "How comes chou choot us in the feets? Chou crazy?"

For answer he aimed his revolver carefully at the tip of Chumacho's left boot that was sticking up in the air. It was a hard shot with a handgun and he planned to err on the side of missing. He gently squeezed the trigger and saw the very tip of the bandit's boot fly off. Chumacho let out a frightened scream.

Warner said, "Tell them other men of yours to throw out their guns. Throw them toward the fire. The next shot is going to take your whole foot off."

Chumacho said, "I doan un'nerstan' all chou talk. I doan speak so beery much English."

Warner cocked the hammer of his revolver. It

made a startlingly loud noise in the stillness of the night, made even more quiet by the contrast with the booming the shotguns had made.

Chumacho said hastily. "Hokay, hokay. No shoot no mores." He yelled out rapid orders in Spanish and tossed his two handguns in the direction of the fire. Warner counted seven guns thrown out. Since there had been other men who might have dropped their weapons he was not reckoning that all the guns had been accounted for. But it was the best he could do for the moment. It was time to come out from under the wagon and move things along a bit.

He took a moment to make sure his revolver held six cartridges and then he came slowly out from under the wagon, holding one of the short-barreled shotguns. He walked carefully toward the line of men, coming at them obliquely so he could see the slightest movement any of them made. He was holding the shotgun at the ready, his finger inside the trigger guard. Three sets of eyes turned to look at him. Only the third man in the tangled line didn't move. He lay in a crumpled heap, on his side, his legs drawn up. Warner motioned with the shotgun toward Chumacho. He said, "Get up. Get on your feet."

The fat Mexican looked at him. He said, "Es chou *loco*? I am chot. I can not walk."

Warner pointed the shotgun at Chumacho's feet. He said, "I'm about to blow both your fucking feet off and then you damn sure won't be able to walk. Now *get up!*"

Chumacho struggled to a sitting position. He was staring at Warner all the while. He said, "Say, *señor*, I know chou. Chou es the gringo I doan keel. Chees! Hey, Chumacho do chou one beeg favor. Chure fren he die because he want to fight. But Chumacho let you go. Why fors chou want to hurt Chumacho?"

Warner didn't say anything. He was damned if he was going to waste any words on the man. He took two quick steps to Chumacho's side and kicked him hard in the ribs with the toe of his boot. The Mexican let out a cry and clutched his side, gasping as the breath left him. Warner said, "I ain't going to tell you again. Get up on your goddam feet!"

He wanted them separated so he could watch them better. He didn't know exactly what time it was, but he calculated it to be quite a few hours until dawn.

Slowly, as if the effort were too much, Chumacho got to his feet. He stood in front of Warner, wavering slightly. But Warner suspected the man wasn't hurt as bad as he let on. His high boots had taken most of the shot and his knees appeared to be unhurt. Warner waved the shotgun to his right, toward the wagon, dim in the shadows. He said, "Move four steps to your left. *Escarda*! Move!"

Shuffling grudgingly, Chumacho slowly made his way a few yards from where the other three lay. He started to stop but Warner waved him on a few more steps. All the while he was studying Chumacho for any concealed weapons. He saw a knife hanging in a scabbard from Chumacho's belt.

Out of the corner of his eye he was watching the other three. They were not moving. Only the second man in line, the one on his belly, the one Warner remembered from the other time, was watching, but he seemed to be eyeing his *jefe* more than Warner.

Warner said to Chumacho, "Now lay down. On your back."

Chumacho said, "Why chou do theese things to chou good fren, Chumacho? I save chou life. I no keel you. I let chou go."

*"Get down, goddamit!"*

The fat bandit sat down slowly, having to catch himself with his hands. He was watching Warner with his malevolent little pig eyes, but his gold tooth was gleaming in a false smile. He said, "My fren, chou have made the mistake. We only comes for a leetle water." He lifted a hand off the ground to make a drinking motion. *"Agua."*

"Lay flat!" Warner said. "And spread your arms out. I'm tired of talking to you. Keep your mouth shut or I'll blow you to ribbons."

Chumacho slowly eased himself onto his back

255

and spread-eagled his arms. Warner said, "You move so much as a finger and that will be all she wrote."

He turned to the next man, one of the two men who'd pounded him in the stomach after they'd poured a gallon of water down him. He didn't say a word, just motioned with the shotgun and stared at the man, letting the man know that he remembered.

The bandit got up on his hands and knees and began crawling. When he was three feet from Chumacho, Warner said, "*Alto!*" ("Stop!") Then he made a motion with the shotgun. He pointed it at Chumacho. He said, "*Mismo. El mismo.*" ("The same.") The thin-faced and hard-looking man turned slowly and lay on his back. He was about to put out his arms when Warner caught a movement out of the corner of his left eye. He whirled, pulling the trigger of the shotgun as he came around. The man who'd been curled into a ball had suddenly began to unwind. Warner shot him dead center just as the man was able to get out the revolver he'd hidden in his shirt, but before he could bring it to bear. The blast of the shotgun pellets took the man mostly on his right side as he raised his shoulder to fire. At such a short range the blow of the full load of pellets flipped him over so that he lay away from Warner on his stomach. The revolver he'd been holding had gone flying somewhere out into the dark.

Warner instantly swung the shotgun back on the thin-faced man and Chumacho. Chumacho hadn't moved, but the thin-faced man had sat up. Under the shotgun he lay back and spread his arms out. Warner looked at the fourth man in line. This one got quickly to his feet and, stepping carefully around his dead comrade, made his way slowly down the line, his eyes on Warner. Warner motioned with the shotgun for him to stop and lie down like the others. He did so, keeping his hands wide of his body. Warner judged him not to be so very old, but he wasn't a kid, either. Warner didn't remember him, but he was hard enough looking to fit in with the bunch.

Warner stepped back from where the three lay and propped his shotgun on the saddle at the head of one of the bedrolls. He drew his revolver. They were too close together now to use the scattergun and, in case one of them got to cutting up, he didn't want to lose all three with one shot. The revolver was better.

He got over next to the fire, which was getting dangerously low, and got out his watch. To his astonishment it was almost one o'clock. It seemed like only moments had passed since he'd heard the first sounds of their coming.

He put back his head and yelled, "Charlie! Charlie! *Charlie!*"

After a second he heard a distant, "Mr. Grayson?"
*"Charlie. Come in! It's safe. Come in!"*

The answer came faint, "Yessir. Right now . . ."

Warner squatted down in front of his three prisoners, his revolver pointed casually in their direction. Chumacho raised his head slightly. He said, "*Señor, por favor, poquita agua.*" ("A little water.")

Warner said, "In a minute. Pretty soon I'm going to give you all the water you want, just like you did me." He got up and picked up one of the bottles of tequila. It was lying on its side, but almost half remained. He took it over and handed it to Chumacho. He said, "Try this. You like it better than water. You can sit up."

Chumacho took the bottle eagerly and had a long pull. When he was finished Warner motioned him to pass it on and then lie back down. By the time the last bandit was finished with it the bottle was empty. Warner said, "Never mind, *caballeros*, there is plenty more where that came from."

Chumacho said, "The tequila es beery nice, *señor* fren, but a leetle water . . ."

Warner laughed. He said, "Well, *señor* fren, it is not time for water yet. But soon. You better learn to like being thirsty. You are going to get enough practice."

Chumacho raised his head. He said, "What es that chou tell me? Are chou taking us to the hoosegow?"

"To jail?" Warner smiled slightly. He said, "You

258

might call it that. It's nearly as hard to get out of."

He had once been full of hate and fury at these men. Now he didn't feel much of anything. He had set out to do a job and, once it was over, it would be forgotten.

Chumacho said, "Say, *señor*, chou are a *bandido*. Chure. Chou are a *bandido*. Chou keel us an now chou rob us. Chou weel geet in a *mucho* troubles. Chou better let us go."

At that moment Warner heard the sound of a running horse and Charlie came skidding into the circle of campfire. He swung off his horse and looked around. He said, wonder in his voice, "Lord, have mercy! I never heered so much shootin' in all my borned days. And no wonder! Look at all them dead folks!" He turned to Warner. He said, "Be you all right, Mr. Grayson?"

Warner didn't answer him. He said, "You always run a horse across the prairie at night like that? Good way to lose a horse."

Charlie hung his head. He said, "I'm right sorry, Mr. Grayson. I got all excited, what with the shooting and all. And worrying like I was. I couldn't make heads or tails of what was going on. First it was them shotguns, then handguns, then shotguns again. I got took up in it."

Warner said, "Well, that's all right. But we've got a lot of work to do. I think we got some stout cord in the wagon somewheres. Get it. I want you to tie these three gentlemen's hands good and

259

tight for them so they'll be more comfortable, or at least so I'll be more comfortable."

Charlie came back with a big hank of quarter-inch cotton cord. While Warner stood over each of them with revolver in hand Charlie first turned out their pockets looking for money or concealed weapons and then bound their hands tightly in front of them. When they were done Warner had Charlie scour the area for all the firearms he could find and pile them in the empty bedroll and then roll it up and tie it with a cord. He counted six rifles and ten pistols that Charlie was able to find. Finally he had him put the last of the mesquite wood on the fire. Some of it was green and it took a while for it to blaze back up again.

The excitement had worn off for Charlie and now he was a little sickened by the sight of all the bodies. Warner had planned to have the boy drag all the corpses out of the immediate vicinity of the camp, but he thought it might be a little hard on Charlie. Instead, Warner had him stand guard over the three bandits while he went about the laborious business of dragging the five dead bandits well away from the camp and throwing them into the *barranca*.

When he was finished he came back into camp and said to Charlie, "These here bandits came with at least eight horses. I think there's more. But their horse holder got to feeling heroic and, as a consequence, he's resting in the *barranca* right now. Get on your horse and take you some lead lines and make a quick swing around and see how many you can catch up. Don't be too long about it because we've still got a lot of getting ready to do."

Charlie rode out and Warner got a canteen out of the wagon and had a long drink of water. Fighting, he decided, was thirsty work. All of the bandits called for water but he ignored them.

He retrieved the ham where the Mexicans had dropped it when he'd started shooting and took his canteen of water and washed it off. Then he set it on the grill as near to the roaring fire as he could. Some of them Mexicans, he thought, might have been rabid. He figured it was a good idea to singe the poison out of the ham.

He turned it once while he waited for Charlie and then, when it was cool enough, wrapped it back in the oil paper it had been wrapped in and put it with the rest of the supplies. Chumacho called to him. He said, "Chou take us to theese *calaboosa* in Del Rio, no? Say, chou let us go I geeve chou pleenty *oro*, gold. *Mucho rico*."

Warner just smiled and didn't answer. After the initial excitement he had been as calm as if the whole business had been everyday work. He had made a plan, it had worked, and now he was going to finish it up.

Charlie came in with three horses on lead. One of them he could see was carrying Chumacho's saddle. It was big and decorated with silver. Chumacho's horse was also in better shape than the others. The other two horses were ridden down and underfed and showed all the signs of poor care and hard usage. Warner throught that his prisoners made damn poor bandits not having any better sense than to take care of their means of escape. Catch Wilson Young letting his get-away horse not be in peak condition? Not likely.

Thinking of Wilson Young made him smile. He would have liked for Wilson to have been there to see how much and how often he had hesitated.

Charlie was unsaddling the horses and taking off their saddlebags. As he drug the saddlebag off what they took to be Chumacho's horse Charlie said, "This is pretty heavy, Mr. Grayson. What you reckon is in it?"

Warner lifted a flap. He could see a horde of silver and gold pesos inside. He said briefly, "Money."

Chumacho yelled, "Say, chou better leave my moneys alone! Chou *bandidos*!"

Warner said, "Unsaddle and unbridle all these horses and put their gear with the supplies. Then tie them to the picket line. How many others out there?"

Charlie said, "I counted eight or nine, from what I could see. You want me to go back and try and fetch them? Ought to be easier at dawn. They ain't goin' nowhere. They all trailing their reins and, everytime they try to walk, they step on the end of their bridles and nearly jerk their heads off. Most of 'em are just standing around. They won't be no trouble to catch."

Warner said, "We'll wait until morning. But I don't want to lose them. These are my stock, in payment for what this sonofabitch stole from me before. No, right now I want you to take the two mules and my Andalusian down to the river and give them a good watering."

"Now? You don't want to wait until dawn?"

Warner shook his head. "No. I'll be long gone before dawn. Give them a good watering. They've got a long ways to go through some rough country."

Charlie looked at him a long moment. He said, "You ain't thinkin' of going where I think you're going, be you?"

Warner said, "Charlie, just do what you're hired to do. It'll take you two hours nearly to get down there and back. You better take the mules and the Andalusian on lead. I don't want them running off."

"Yessir," Charlie said. But he looked down at the ground and didn't move.

Warner said, "What else? You want to eat first?"

"Nosir. I—" He was still looking down at the ground. He said, "You told me what them bandits done to you. And I ain't saying you ain't got a right to be mighty angry. I just—I just—"

Warner said, an edge in his voice, "Get moving, Charlie. And make it as quick as you can. I need all the time I can get before the dawn and the sun."

"Yessir," Charlie said. He moved off, leading the three horses that had belonged to the bandits, taking them back to the picket line where he'd tie them and taking the mules and the Andalusian.

Warner watched him. He knew what the boy was thinking, but he didn't care.

# 10

While Charlie was gone, Warner cut himself several slices of the ham with the big butcher knife and then wrapped that, along with some of the corn bread, in a piece of paper and stowed it under the wagon seat. He put two cans of tomatoes and two of apricot in a sack that had once held coffee and placed the sack under the seat with the meat and bread. Then he got up in the bed of the wagon and took the lid off the big barrel that had been full of town water. It appeared to still be about half full. They had three two-and-a-half gallon canteens and Warner made sure all three were full. He put one under the seat of the wagon and put the other two with the supplies. He didn't reckon Charlie would need more water than that while he was gone, but, if he did, he could always go down to the Rio Grande and dig some up. They'd brought a big bucket and he made sure that was in the wagon. After that he unloaded what little was left in the bed. He wasn't planning on taking a bedroll because he didn't plan to spend any time sleeping on the trip he would be taking. He figured it to be pretty close to forty miles round-trip. Well, he knew he and the Andalusian could do the distance. The mules would have to. Hell, he'd driven mules as much as sixty miles in one stretch. A mule was hard to walk down. They were stubborn and they were damn fools, but they were tough.

Finally he turned his attention to the three *bandidos*. He walked down the line jerking off their boots. Chumacho tried to resist but it did him no good, even as long as his boot tops were. Warner tugged all the harder, skidding the fat bandit along on his back on the rough ground.

When he had all their boots off he went along and carefully inspected their legs and feet. They weren't hurt nearly as bad as he had thought at first. Mostly it had been the force of the blast and the shock of the attack that had put them down. They had bled enough to make them think they were dying, but most of the bleeding had stopped. No, he had merely peppered them good, not seriously disabled them. Probably they would all get infected and die of gangrene, but that wouldn't matter, he thought. They'd die of thirst before that.

The third man in line intrigued him. He had a hard face, but he seemed calm about what was happening to him, not wildly nervous and scared as Chumacho was or watching for his chance out of hate-filled eyes as the thin-faced man in the Western hat was.

Warner walked down to the third man in line and squatted beside him. The man turned his head and returned his gaze with quiet eyes. Warner asked him if he spoke English. The man shook his head. He said, "*No, no habla.*"

Warner thought a moment and then, in as much Spanish as he could manage asked if this was the man's first raid with Chumacho. The man shook his head. He held up his bound hands and extended two fingers. He said, "*El segundo.*" ("The second.")

That meant, Warner thought, that the man had had to be along when Chumacho had jumped him and Red. So far as he knew there'd been no raids since that one. Except this present one. Warner tapped himself on the chest. He said, "Saavy me?"

The man nodded. He raised his hands and tugged at a lock of his hair. He said, "*Tiene un amigo con roja este.*"

Warner nodded. The man was talking about Red's hair. Warner got up. The man had just convicted himself out of his own mouth. Warner was about to walk away when the man said, "*Momento, por favor.*"

He said, trying to make the Spanish simple for Warner, "*Yo no marcho por caliente mesa. Es no bueno. Yo vamanos. Chumacho no migusto.*"

Warner stared at the man. If he was telling the truth he was trying to tell Warner that he had not been in favor of leaving him on the alkali plain and that he had left. Thinking back it did seem as if the bandits had been a man short. But he really hadn't been in much condition to notice. Still, there was something about the man.

He walked down to where Chumacho was lying. He noticed that the bandit was wearing silk socks. Chumacho was fairly rolling in it and Warner had a pretty good idea where it had come from. He wondered how much money was in Chumacho's saddlebags. He doubted it would be anywhere near enough. He'd reckoned they'd robbed him of three thousand dollars in horse-flesh and supplies and weapons and money. And then there was the amount he'd laid out on this little expedition. He knew he wasn't going to break even on the money, but he calculated to more than get ahead on the vengeance end.

He knelt down by Chumacho's head. He said, conversationally, "Listen, Chumacho, you stole some horses a few weeks ago from a ranch over there." He pointed east toward the Pico ranch. "They were different horses than you had ever seen. You stole six, but you lost one. You have seen me riding it down by the river when you watched us come down to water all our horses."

Chumacho was shaking his head violently. He said, "*Yo* no steal no horses. Chumacho is no *pinche* horse thief. No, no, *señor*."

Warner acted as if he hadn't heard him. He said, "They were different horses, Spanish horses. You killed the man who owned the ranch. He came out shooting at you."

Chumacho was looking sullen. He said, "Chumacho doan keel nobodies an' he doan steel no horses."

Warner said mildly, "Hell, you stole my horses. Don't tell me you don't steel horses."

"Chour fren want to fight. He keel *mi hermano*."

Warner wanted to laugh. He said, "He killed your brother? Bullshit, Chumacho. But I don't want to talk about that. I want to know what you did with those five horses you got back across the border with. You sold them. Who did you sell them to?"

Chumacho shook his head. He said, "I doan un'erstan'. I doan sell no horses."

Warner sighed. He said, "Well, you are going to tell me sooner or later. You can save yourself some mighty big hurt if you tell me now."

Chumacho shook his head. He said, "You *loco*. I doan sell no horses."

Warner got up. He said, "Have it your own way."

He walked over and got a saddle out of the pile where Charlie had dumped them and brought it back over and laid it lengthwise on top of Chumacho's legs. The bandit said, "Hey! Whot chou do?"

Warner went over to the fire and jerked out a three-foot-long stick of wood that was burning on one end. He came over to Chumacho and knelt down, putting his right knee on the seat of the saddle so Chumacho couldn't move his legs.

Then, holding the burning branch in his left hand, he lowered the fire down toward Chumacho's feet. He said, "Well, old 'fren,' you roasted my feet for me one time. I reckon I can do the same for you."

As he brought the fire close to Chumacho's feet the fat bandit suddenly reared up. Pivoting with his shoulders Warner smashed the bandit in his fat face with a hard backhand. Chumacho went flat on his back with blood spurting from his nose and mouth.

Warner said calmly, "Now, you want to tell me who you sold those horses to? Or you want me to roast you all the way up to your knees?"

Chumacho was snuffling and moaning. He said, "I doan know. *Yo no se.*"

Warner said, "Well, maybe you don't know, but I think you do. Though, I swear, I hate to ruin these here fancy silk stockings of yours. But I don't see no way around it 'less you want to tell me right quick what you did with them horses."

Chumacho said, "I doan steel no horses!"

Warner said, "If you're worried about being hung for a horse thief you can forget about it. I ain't going to take you to jail. Now where are them horses?"

"I doan 'member," Chumacho said. He had his bound hands up to his face, feeling his smashed nose. He said, "What chou care for dem fonny horses? They *loco* them horses."

Warner said, "Last time. Where?"

Chumacho said, with a whine in his voice, "I doan know."

Warner put the blazing end of the stick to the soles of both of Chumacho's feet. He could smell the silk burning. Chumacho tried to heave up, tried to jerk his legs around to get them away from the searing pain. But Warner had his legs pinned with the saddle and his weight. As Chumacho reared up Warner backhanded him again. He went down hard, his head almost bouncing off the ground. He said, "Oooh! Ooooh! Yeeeeooow! No, no, no!"

The thin-faced man next in line tried to rear up. Warner thrust the flame in his face and he fell backward. The last man in line didn't even rise up. Warner had the feeling he knew what was in store for all of them.

He turned his attention back to Chumacho. He said, looking at Chumacho, "This time will be *muy malo*." ("Very bad.") Chumacho was sweating, staring up at the dark sky, his face bloody and battered. He said, "*Yo no se*." ("I don't know.")

"Fine," Warner said. He pressed the glowing end of the stick across the soles of both of Chumacho's feet. The bandit jerked and bucked. Out of his mouth came a wail that didn't quite sound human to Warner's ears. He yelled, "*Yeeeeeoooooowwwwwww!*"

Warner pulled the stick away. He looked at Chumacho. The Mexican had his mouth open and was gasping and moaning at the same time. Warner said, "I'll roast you alive. Who did you sell those horses to? Where are they?"

A voice suddenly said, "Theese man you want es named Don Fuego Hernando."

Warner looked up in surprise. It was the man at the end of the line, the man who had said he could not speak English, the man that Warner had subconsciously felt was different from the rest. He didn't look like a peon turned bandit as the others did. Warner immediately got up and walked to his side. He said, "You speak English?"

"Yes."

"Why did you lie to me?"

The man shrugged as well as he could lying flat on his back. He said, "I thought it would do no harm and that I might hear something when you were talking with the young man you have sent to the river. Something that might help me."

"Why are you telling me what I want to know?"

The man pulled a face. He said, "Because I do not theenk Chumacho is to tell you. He es more afraid of Don Fuego than he es of you. And I theenk that you test first one of us and then the next. I did not want you to burn my feet. I saw them do it to you. You were *muy bravo* of it. I do not theenk I could be so courage."

Warner knelt down by his shoulder. He said, "Where'd you learn all that English?"

The man said, "Since I was small I work with the cattle on the Texas *rancheros*. I speak English almost as soon as I speak Espanish."

"You're not still a *vaquero* in Texas, are you?"

The man shook his head slowly. He said, "No. When Don Fuego comes, maybe two, three year ago I am to work for him. He is the only one in Mexico that can pay the *dinero* for the first-class *vaquero*. Of course that is why I am working so long in Texas. There is much more money, but the English is *muy importa*."

Warner studied the man's face. He was considerably more intelligent looking than the others. He said, somewhat amazed, "Chumacho is not going to tell me because he is more afraid of this Don Fuego? And I got him tied up and laying on his back with a gun on him?"

The man nodded silently. "Yes," he said. "But then Chumacho is very estupid. He does not know what you are going to do with us. He theenks he will get away, but I don't theenk so. You are too careful. I have watched you."

"But you know what I'm going to do with you?"

"Oh, yes," the man said. There was a note of sadness in his voice. "I do not blame you, *señor.* I would do *mismo.* (The same.) If I were you. I do not know how you survived the devil's mesa, but

273

I don't think we will. I have seen it although I had left when they were taking you there."

"And Chumacho couldn't stop you because you work for Don Fuego, is that it?"

"Yes. Chumacho is very *loco* and veery estupid, but he es very escairt of Don Fuego."

Warner said, "Just who the hell is this Don Fuego?"

The man shifted his eyes and made a face by pulling down the corner of his mouth. He said, "He is Espanish, from *España*. He is *muy rico*, (very rich,) but I theenk he does som'zing very bad in *España* and he can no stay there no more. So I theenk he comes to Mexico. I theenk these horses he es tol' of make heem, how you say, seeck for the, the—"

"Homesick."

"Yes," the man said. He put out his tongue and tried to lick his lips. He said, "Me mouth es *muy* dry. Es hard for the speak."

Warner let it go. He wasn't ready to offer the man any water. He said, "So he wants the Andalusian horses."

"Yes!" the man said. "That is the name of how they are called. Anda—Andal—"

"Andalusian."

The man said, "That is a rare word. It is *muy difficil* for the mouth."

Warner said, "So he sends Chumacho to steal the horses?"

The man nodded. "Yes. But chust the Espanish horses. Chumacho es doing the other for heemself. He es a very crazy man, very cruel."

Warner said, "A lot of people were surprised that horse thieves had come into Texas again. It had been three or four years since it had happened. It had become too dangerous for the thieves. But Chumacho comes for the Andalusian horses. Is that the way it started, Don Fuego paid him to steal the six Andalusians?" He spoke slowly and carefully because he knew the man didn't speak English that well. But it did make sense, this sudden outbreak of horse stealing again.

The man thought for a second over what Warner had said. Then he nodded slowly. He said, "Yes, I theenk so. Chumacho comes for the Espanish horses, but he is greedy so he wants to get more. To get as many as he can. He comes back after he has taken the Andalusians though he has lost one. The one you have. It would be very rare to hear how you find that horse. Don Fuego was very angry that Chumacho lose that horse. I theenk he is going to choot him."

Warner said, "And then word got back to Don Fuego that one of the rare horses has been seen along the river, seen many times."

The man nodded. He said, "Yes. Many reports came to Don Fuego. I knew it was a trap though I did not theenk it could be you. I did not theenk anyone could leeve on the hot mesa. I tell Don Fuego, but he doan care. He tell Chumacho to go get hees horse. An' he send me weeth Chumacho."

Warner said, "Just like he did the first time."

The man nodded. He said, "Yes. He theenks I can control Chumacho. Make heem get these horses and come back to the *hacienda* weeth them. But Chumacho es crazy. He es getting drunk, muy *borocho*, he es shooting hees own peoples. He es a cruel man."

"But he is scared of Don Fuego?"

The man smiled grimly. He said, "Chumacho es choust a leetle bit cruel. Like a leetle child weeth a bug. Don Fuego es *muy* cruel. Besides, Chumacho is a peasant and Don Fuego is a Espanish Don. He es very angry weeth me I doan stop Chumacho from all the else he does."

Warner said, "What's your name?"

"Carlos. I am called Carlos."

Warner said, "So, Carlos, you only go with Chumacho when Don Fuego sent you for the Andalusian horses?"

Carlos nodded. He said, "Chess, but Chumacho also go by heemself to steal odder horses. He brag how easy et is and the stupid *campesines*, the peasants, some of them go weeth him. When they doan come back he tells people that they stays en Texas, but he lies. They are killed."

Warner said, "Where does Don Fuego live? Where is his *hacienda*?"

"Et es *norte* of the river. *Proximal* of the small village of El Milagro. I theenk maybe et es twenty miles from the river? These peoples in El Milagro know."

"And you say he is a hard man?"

Carlos nodded vigorously. "Oh, chess. *Muy duro*. Very hard."

"Will he sell me the horses back?"

"Oh, no, *señor*." He shook his head from side to side. "That would be a thing so rare it would not happen."

"But he knows they were stolen."

Carlos shrugged. He said, "That is of no matter to Don Fuego."

Warner suddenly got up and walked toward the wagon. Chumacho was lying with his eyes shut whimpering and moaning and twisting his feet around. The thin-faced man followed him with hard eyes. As he passed Warner said to him, "I bet you'd like to get a knife in me, wouldn't you?"

The man made no sign that he'd heard or understood.

As he was getting a canteen out of the wagon Warner thought that at least the sudden outbreak of horse stealing raids had been explained. It had started up because a man named Pico had imported some Spanish horses near where an exiled Spanish Don had chosen to live. It had taken some odd coincidences to make it happen, but, he thought, at least it wasn't the beginning of a fresh outbreak as many had worried. As soon as he'd settled Chumacho, the stealing should come to an end until another fool like the fat man came along.

He walked back toward Carlos. Chumacho saw the canteen in his hand and called out, weakly, "*Agua, agua.* Water, *por favor poquita agua.*"

Warner ignored him and walked to Carlos and knelt down again by his shoulder. He handed him the big canteen. Even though the man's hands were bound at the wrist he could hold the canteen. But it was difficult for him to rise to a sitting position so he could drink. Warner reached out and took a handful of his vest and helped him up. Carlos rushed to get the canteen to his mouth, spilling a little water in his haste.

Warner said, "You're gonna wish you had that pretty soon."

The man took the canteen from his mouth and sighed. He said, "*Yo savvy.* I know." He took another drink and then another one and then Warner took the canteen back. From down the line Chumacho was calling out, "*Agua, agua, agua. Por favor*!"

Carlos said, "I theenk he wants some water."

Warner said, "Yeah, I bet he does." He pushed Carlos back flat on the ground. He said, "Tell me, do you know which two men held me while Chumacho put my feet to the fire?"

Carlos nodded. He said, "The one who lays to my left and the one you killed with the shotgun."

"Which one was that?"

"The one who lay near me, who had the *pistole* hiding in his chirt. You blow him up with the shotgun. Heem and theese one who lies next to me are Chumacho's *amigos*. They go weeth heem always. They are not like the estupid *campesino* who Chumacho sends into the *peligrosa* (the danger), like the one tonight. He was *loco* to come back. He comes with all the chooting, waving hees leetle gun." Carlos shook his head. "Those peons are so poor they have no brains."

"Were you there when they beat me in the stomach so I vomited away all the water they had given me?"

Carlos shook his head. "No. When they say et will be foony to leeve chou on the *caliente mesa* I am for my horse and to be gone. Is that why you gave me the water? Chou are going to make me lose it?"

"No. I gave you the water because you are telling me what I want to know."

Carlos smiled slightly. He said, "Chou could have saved chure water. You choust wave the fire stick at my feets an' I tell you *todas*, evertheeng. I doan want to hurt no more than es of the necessity. I am not afraid of Don Fuego because I know I will never see heem again."

"What makes you so sure what I'm going to do with you three?"

"Because," Carlos said, "of the way you chot

279

us. You chot us in the feet and legs. You deed not choot to keel us, you only keeled when you had to. You choot us so it make it hard for us to walk. Like Chumacho burn chu feet to make it hard for chu to walk. Is the same, no?"

Warner shrugged. He said, "You're a pretty bright boy."

"An' they take you to die on the hot mesa. I have seen that you are a hard man, a very hard man. I theenk you set up theese trap only for to make us walk on the hot mesa. I theenk you don't want to choot to keel because you want Chumacho and hees mens to suffer as you did." He turned and looked directly into Warner's eyes. He said, "If I geet the chance I am going to make you keel me."

Warner said, "Do you know how much Don Fuego paid Chumacho for the horses?"

Carlos pulled a face. He said, "I am not so very sure. I theenk it was two thousand pesos. *Dos mil.* He es very angry Chumacho lose the other horse, the one you have. I theenk maybe he tell him he geeve him another two thousand pesos if he geet the last horse."

Warner did some calculating. Two thousand pesos. A peso was worth about twelve cents American. That meant he'd paid Chumacho a little less than forty dollars for each of the five horses he'd brought in. And he was going to give him another two thousand for the last one that would make six. It didn't make much sense, but it didn't matter to Warner. Probably the man had meant to give him four or five thousand pesos in the first place and he'd gotten angry when Chumacho had carelessly lost one. He probably thought, him being the only Spanish nobility around, that nobody else should have an Andalusian horse. Well, Warner thought, he had a shock coming because there was somebody else around that had one and wasn't about to give it up.

Carlos said, "I tell Chumacho theese is one beeg trap, but he don't listen. He is stupid." Then he turned his head to the side. "But I come weeth him so that makes me estupid *tambien*."

Warner said, "He must have wanted that other horse pretty bad. Don Fuego."

"Oh, chess. En *España*, he say, only *el grande caballeros* have the Andalusian. Et es the law. Only the king can say who have the Andalusian."

"Do you believe that?"

Carlos smiled slightly and shook his head. He said, "No, I doan theenk so. I theenk sometimes Don Fuego is *poco loco*." He suddenly raised his hands to his hair. "Don Fuego *es mismo* chur friend."

"My friend they killed?"

"Yes. The one with *rojo* hair. Red?"

"Yes, red. And Don Fuego has red hair? He is Spanish and he has red hair?"

Carlos smiled. He said, "Espanish es very different from Mexican. He es not so very dark and he has *azure ojos*."

"Red haired and blue eyed?"

"Yes. And he speaks very good English. He speaks English like a *caballero*."

"But he's mean?"

Carlos nodded slightly. "I theenk you ask all these question because you go to get these rare horses back. I theenk then you find out how mean he is. He is of a rare hardness."

Warner stood up. He said grimly, "Well, we'll see."

Before he could walk away Carlos said, "You owe me nothing, *señor*. As I said I would have told you what you wanted to know because I did not want to be hurt. I would ask the favor that you shoot me. I do not want to die on the hot mesa." He turned his head toward Chumacho and the thin-faced man. "Not in the company of these *cabarones*." He looked back toward Warner. "It would be a kindness, but I want you to comprehend that I do not ask it because I have talked with you. I ask it as a favor."

Warner looked at him grimly. He said, "I can't help you."

"But it was not me who took you to the hot mesa. Or burned your feet."

"You didn't try and stop it, did you?"

"It was not possible. Chumacho is of such a

nature that he is not to hear the words of another. It is an impossibility for him to hear."

Warner said, "Chumacho stole a great amount of stock on these raids across the river. And he killed and hurt quite a few people."

"I have killed or hurt no one."

"But you were with him, weren't you? You are laying there now with shotgun pellets in your legs and feet and your hands tied because you were with him. Is that not the truth?"

Carlos looked away, taking his eyes from Warner. He shrugged in resignation. He said, "It is no *importa*. I do not like to suffer. That is all."

Warner said, "Does anybody?"

Carlos didn't reply and Warner walked away. Chumacho was still moaning and calling for water. Warner was very sorry that the man he'd had to blow half in two had been one of the ones who had helped hold his feet to the fire. He'd also probably been one of the several who'd taken turns hitting him in the abdomen and the stomach. Well, he thought, two out of three wasn't all that bad.

It wasn't long before Charlie was back with the two mules and the Andalusian. Warner asked him if he'd had any trouble. Charlie said, "No, sir. Easy as pie. That there Anda . . . Andalush . . . that there different horse is just as sweet as pie. Boy is he a treat to handle."

Warner said, "Well, you better hook up the

mules. I need to get out of here as quick as I can. It's near half-past two now."

"Yessir," Charlie said, but he looked down at his feet.

Warner said, "Something bothering you?"

"No, sir. Nosir."

"Then get those mules hooked up to the wagon. I want everything unloaded out of the wagon except the barrel of water and the bucket. I'll need that to water the stock on the way back. I've left you two canteens and I'm taking one."

"Yessir."

While Charlie was hitching up the mule team to the wagon Warner saddled and bridled the Andalusian. Then he led him around into the firelight in front of Chumacho. The fire was starting to die down but there was still plenty of light to admire the horse by. Chumacho had his eyes closed. Warner kicked him in the thigh. Chumacho gave a start and looked up. Warner said, indicating the horse, "This what you come for, El Gordo?"

Chumacho said, half-blubbering, "I doan want chu horse. Some bad mans send me. He makes Chumacho. Some *agua*. A leetle water, *por favor*."

Warner said, "If the horse pisses I'll catch some for you. That'd be about a square deal, wouldn't it?"

"*Agua*. For a favor."

Warner said grimly, "I'm going to do you

a favor, Chumacho. Same kind you done me."

"Bout I doan keel you. I am nice to chu. I am chou fren. Why you be so bad to Chumacho."

Warner said, "Your feet hurt?"

Chumacho made a face and rolled his head from side to side. He said, "I am on the fire. They are red-hot."

Warner found a bottle of tequila and handed it to him. He said, "Here, drink up. You told me it would make my feet hurt less. Swallow it down." He glanced down the line of men and saw Carlos looking at him. He said, "You want some tequila, Carlos?"

Carlos smiled slightly and said, "I doan theenk so."

Warner waited while Chumacho drank almost a third of the bottle. Then he took it away from him and offered it to the thin-faced man. The man sat up stiffly, needing no help from Warner. He took the bottle and held it to his mouth, sucking it down until it was empty. Then he pitched it away and lay back down without a word or look at Warner.

Carlos said softly, "Estupid."

Warner stepped to his feet. He said, "Maybe they don't know where they're going."

"Es steel estupid. Soon they will trade all the tequila in the world for one drop of water. They have been *borocho*. They know these next morning how chou want water."

Warner smiled thinly. He said, "Well, they gave me a bunch of tequila right before they was kind enough to let me go. I figured I ought to return the favor."

Carlos was looking at him steadily. He said, "I want to ask you one theeng."

"Don't cost nothing."

Carlos considered his words for a moment. He said, "From the questions you ask me about Don Fuego I know you are to try and geet the rare horses back. No?"

Warner shrugged. He said, "I might. Why?"

"Perhaps I could be of service to you. Thess horses are beery well guarded. They are the prize of Don Fuego and he has many *vaqueros*. Maybe *diez*. (Ten.)"

Warner smiled slightly. He said, "You wouldn't be scheming to save your life would you?"

Carlos said, "Of course." He half smiled. "I am not *loco*. I could be of help to you."

"Yeah," Warner said dryly. "But would you? Now you say you would, but what about when it was just me and you in Mexico. Might be a different story then. What if this hadn't been a trap. What if Chumacho and the rest of you had caught me off guard? What would you—"

Charlie came up just then. He said, "The wagon's hitched, Mr. Grayson. And I got it loaded like you said."

Warner turned away from Carlos and walked

over to the wagon, still leading the Andalusian. He said, "Only thing, the picket rope is tied to the wagon. And we ain't got nothing else on this end to hitch it to."

Charlie said, "Don't matter. I can cut the horses loose and then just loose herd them the rest of the night. Them bandits' horses might come on in by they ownselves."

"You ain't had much sleep."

"Don't need none."

"Well, guess it's time to load our passengers. You might have to help me, Charlie. I don't think they are going to want to go."

Warner took a step toward where the three were lying and realized Charlie hadn't moved. He said, "Didn't you hear me, Charlie? We got to load these bandits aboard."

Charlie said, "Mr. Grayson . . ."

"What?"

Charlie cleared his throat self-consciously. He said, "I know this ain't none of my affair . . ."

"You are right. It ain't."

"Yes, sir. I know. But I look up to you, Mr. Grayson, and I hate to see you do this. I know they put a load of sufferin' on you, but what you're a-gonna do ain't like you."

Warner said evenly, "Charlie, were you there? Were you out in the middle of that alkali flat crawling on your knees? Were you so thirsty your tongue was swole up as big as a Irish potato? Did you lay out there and wish you had a gun so you could quit hurting? Did you hurt for better than a day and a night? Did you?"

Charlie looked down. He said, "No, sir. And I know I can't know how you felt. I'm just sayin' that doing the same thing to them ain't like you, Mr. Grayson. It ain't the Christian thing to do."

Warner said harshly, "Maybe not, but it's the Old Testament way. An eye for an eye, a tooth for a tooth."

Charlie said, "I know they got to be punished. And I know you ain't gonna take them to jail so they can be hung. But it would be a kindness if you just put one right between their eyes."

Warner laughed, without humor. He said, "Funny, one of them has already made the request. When they killed Red I was sorry for him. But later, when they left me out in that badlands, I was sorry for me. I figured Red got off light. Finding this horse was a miracle. This horse saved me. We'll let fate decide if they should get off. Maybe they'll find a horse just like I did. Out there in the middle of an alkali flat."

Charlie said, "Aw, Mr. Grayson, you know they ain't going to find no horse. They gonna die slow and awful. They—"

Warner said evenly, "That's enough, Charlie. I let you have your say. Now I've got to get moving."

He put Carlos in at the front of the wagon, laying him down across the width of the bed with his shoulders propped up on one side and his feet hanging over the sideboard of the other.

The thin-faced man walked, without struggle or argument, and lay down in the bed of the wagon where Warner indicated, lengthwise with his feet hanging off the tailgate.

But Chumacho claimed he couldn't walk, that his feet were too painful. Warner got another flaming stick and hurried him, hopping on first one foot and then the other, over to the wagon. Warner had him lie down in the bed next to the thin-faced man.

When they were loaded he mounted the Andalusian and told Charlie to loose tie the reins to the brake handle and put a lead rope on the near mule. He said, "I guess you better untie that picket rope first."

Then it was all done and Charlie was handing him up the end of a ten-foot lead rope. He didn't figure to need it once he got the mules lined out, but he would need it to get them started. Charlie said, "Well, good luck, Mr. Grayson. When you reckon to be back?"

Warner said, "Sometime tomorrow afternoon. I figure six or seven hours each way. You ought not to have any trouble."

Charlie said, "What about these, these bodies that are just barely in the *barranca*?"

Warner said, "First light, get a rope on them and drag them on down farther. It's pretty deep in some places. But turn out their pockets for whatever money they might have. This fat bandit owes me pretty nearly twenty-five hundred dollars, best I can figure."

Charlie said, "As them bandit horses come in I'll save their saddles and what else they be carrying."

Warner paused for a second. "I appreciate the way you feel, Charlie. It don't happen to be the same way I feel. And it was me got done the wrong."

"Yes, sir, Mr. Grayson," Charlie said. "I reckon I understand."

Warner jerked on the rope to get the mules started. He said, "Take care of things, Charlie. I'll be back quick as I can."

Warner calculated it was fifteen miles to the beginning of the alkali plain. His direction was northeast and he wanted to hit it somewhere around the middle of the north-south edge, then drive east into the barren land for another five or six miles. The mules could make six or seven miles an hour if he kept them stepping along and he figured he had about four hours, maybe three and a half, of good dark left. The dark was important because he wanted to do them the same way they'd done him; drop them at a spot where they'd have no idea in which direction lay water and gentler country. They had forced him to choose to travel as due south as he could because that was the only certain direction he knew would take him out of the alkali country. It had also proved to be the longest route. He wanted his prisoners to have the same pleasure, to be able to enjoy as much of the dead country as he had.

So he kept the mules moving along at a pretty good pace. As soon as he had them lined out and they had accepted the pace he wanted he was able to wind the lead rope around his saddle horn and ride along beside the wagon. In the dark it was difficult to see the men's faces, but it wasn't difficult to hear Chumacho moaning and whining.

They traveled across the flat prairie, the wagon jolting now and again as its iron-bound wheels hit a rock or a rough stretch of ground. The moon was down and what stars there were came and went behind high, floating clouds. Clumps of bushes and trees would suddenly rear up out of the prairie, coming into view almost too late for the mules to swerve around them. From the wagon came soft curses from the thin-faced man as the jolting of the hard wagon bed banged him around. Carlos said nothing, but seemed to keep his eyes fixed on Warner.

Once, as they hit a level stretch of soft ground where the wheels of the wagon made a soft whispering sound in the night, Carlos said, in English, "Will you do it for sure?"

"Yes," Warner said.

Carlos said, "I have not been your enemy."

Warner said, "You are in the employ of the man who caused all this trouble. The bandits were afraid to come across the river for many years. It was too dangerous for the reward they could hope for. But Don Fuego made it worth their time. Chumacho would have never come into Texas without a push."

Carlos was quiet a moment. Then he said, sighing, "I can not make the argue with you. I want to make you believe that I could help with Don Fuego. I want to say what I can to save my life."

Warner said, "I can't disagree with you there. I'd do the same if I was in your boots. But I can't trust you. I don't want Don Fuego in front of me and you behind me. Here, you will tell me anything. But I think it will be different in Mexico."

Carlos said, in his soft voice, "I speak the *verdad*. The truth. I would not betray you."

"You'd betray Don Fuego?"

"No."

"Then how would you help me?"

"The horses are stolen. *Claro* it would be the right theeng to geet them back to the *patron* who has owned them."

Warner laughed. He said, "That's why you came along to get the one that was missing, the one that I'm riding."

Carlos said, "Are the *otro*, the other five horses your horses?"

"I think of them as belonging to me."

Carlos was silent for a moment. Then he said, "Are we beery far from the badlands?"

"You'll know when we get there."

"I am going to make you shoot me. I do not want to die of thirst crawling on the ground like a snake. *Mi esposa* will be sad, I theenk."

Warner laughed. He said, "Now you've got a wife. What will you try next to save your neck?"

"What will come in my mind. And I will theenk hard."

Warner broke off the conversation by touching the Andalusian with his spurs and moving back up to the head of the mule team. They rolled on through the soft, chill tempered night. It was an illusion. In twelve hours, even though it was not yet March, the sun would be beaming down with a relentless, energy sapping power. However thirsty the three men were during the night that thirst would be magnified a hundred times under the sun. Chumacho and the thin-faced man were still drinking tequila. He could tell from the babbling, slurred way that the fat man was talking that he was getting really drunk. Well, Warner thought, he was going to sober up in hell, the one on earth to begin with and the real one in a couple of days.

He knew almost the instant they entered the alkali plains. One second they were traveling through grass, sparse though it was, and the next instant he could feel the hooves of his horse breaking through the salt crust of the dead alkali flats. It was too dark to see, but he knew without sight that nothing was growing, nothing could grow, nothing could live. Even the Andalusian sensed it. He snorted and began picking his feet high as if he didn't want to touch the barren ground. And the mules almost came to a stop. Warner had to tug on the lead rope to get them back up to a good pace. He turned the wagon as due east as he could reckon by his last sighting of the north star that had since slipped below the horizon. He calculated that he had little more than three-quarters of an hour of darkness left. He wanted the three men to be totally disoriented when he let them out to fight for their lives, a fight he knew they couldn't win and that he didn't want them to win.

He stopped the wagon by taking hold of the head harness of the near mule and pulling him to a stop. The other mule was obliged to stop as well. The sun was well clear of the horizon and already starting to get warm. He had just looked at his watch and he knew it was half-past seven. He calculated they were a good five or six miles inside the badlands. He watched his prisoners looking around. In every direction they looked the land was lifeless, dead. Rocks grew and sand grew and salty patches of dead earth grew. The land was so full of gypsum and brine that it was nearly white in places. Just looking sent a pang of remembrance through Warner that was almost as real as the pain in his feet had been. He said, his voice hard, "Get down."

They stared at him. All three were sitting up, Chumacho and the thin-faced man with their feet sticking out the tailgate, Carlos with his back to the sideboard of the wagon.

Warner had expected trouble and he had prepared for it. He had taken his lariat down from where it was tied to the horn of his saddle and shaken out a small loop. He was not as expert with a rope as cowhands were who used them every day, but then he didn't need to be for the job he had in hand. He walked the Andalusian a few steps forward, made one whirl of the loop just below his shoulder, and cast it over the feet of Chumacho. Before the fat Mexican could react he'd jerked the loop closed and turned the Andalusian and rode away from the wagon. Behind him he heard the thump and the yell as Chumacho hit the ground. He whirled the horse around while Chumacho was still down, the wind knocked out of him, and rode back and freed his loop. He had drug Chumacho twenty or thirty feet away from the wagon. He sat his horse, slowly coiling his rope, and said, "I said get down. The next man I'll drag a mile. Carlos, if that thin-faced, mean looking bastard don't understand what I'm saying you'd better tell him in Spanish. Tell him I haven't forgotten that he helped hold my feet to the fire and that he hit me in the stomach to empty me of water."

But there was no need for Carlos to speak. The thin-faced man got out of the end of the wagon and limped partways over to where Chumacho was slowly trying to sit up. The man turned and faced Warner, his arms crossed. Warner thought: *He is thinking of rushing me to get a bullet, but he still isn't sure that I am hard enough to leave them here.*

He turned and looked at Carlos. Carlos shrugged and slowly crawled out of the back of the wagon. He took a few halting, limping steps and stopped. He too turned to face Warner. Behind them Chumacho had begun to vomit, the discharge running down his shirtfront. But he was vomiting up tequila and bile, not the precious water they'd beaten out of Warner. When Warner had been lying in Wilson Young's bed envisioning his revenge he had seen himself punching Chumacho in his fat belly, hitting him again and again until the man had vomited up his guts. But he no longer had a thirst for that touch.

What would now happen to them would be enough. He turned his horse and rode back to the wagon and took the lead rope in hand. He cast one look back at them. They were standing as he had left them. He doubted if their wounds were serious enough to cause them much trouble. It would be the land and the sun that killed them. Two of them had been truly evil men who should have died a long time past either by the gun or the knife. Now they would die because their very own nature had brought them to a place where nature could kill them. He pulled on the lead rope and started the mules moving, turning them toward the south so as to mislead the men on which direction was the fastest way out. He had meant to wish them a sarcastic "*bueno suerte*" ("good luck"). But, at that moment, he found it to be pointless. He touched spurs to the Andalusian and pulled the mules into a trot, heading falsely south. After a couple of miles he'd swing back to the west.

He held to the south for what he reckoned to be twenty minutes. Then he stopped and looked back. There was nothing to be seen except bleak, cruel land that would never allow man or beast, much less welcome them. The men had disappeared below the horizon. Warner stepped down from the Andalusian, loosened his cinch, and tied his reins to the tailgate of the wagon. Then he went around, got in the buckboard seat, untied the reins, and slapped the mules on the back. "Go along," he said. They obediently struck a walk.

He drove for another half an hour, slowly turning west. He was trying not to think, trying not to be bothered by his thoughts. He said, aloud, "That damn Charlie ought to have kept his mouth shut. It ain't none of his affair. He never went through what I did."

Five minutes later he said, "That lying, fucking Carlos. He ain't got no wife. If they'd have got the best of me that sonofabitch would have strung me up by my thumbs and had the skin off me over a slow fire."

Then he said, "Damnit! Goddamit to hell! They don't deserve it!" But he pulled the mules to a sudden halt and tied the reins to the brake handle. They might wander but they wouldn't get far. He reached under the seat and got the big canteen and jumped to the ground. He went back to the Andalusian and slung the strap of the canteen over the saddle horn and then tightened the girth of the saddle. He untied the reins from the tailgate. The Andalusian turned to look at him with his big liquid eyes. Warner said, "What the hell do you know about anything?"

He mounted and wheeled the horse and put him in that fast lope of his and headed back the way he'd come.

# 11

He found them pretty much as he'd left them. Chumacho was still on the ground, his head between his legs. The thin-faced man stood nearby. Carlos had separated himself from the other two, but none of them appeared to have made a move to save themselves. They hadn't even bothered to untie each other's bound wrists.

Carlos saw him coming first. He was squatting in the sand and he rose slowly. The thin-faced man had been looking away and now he turned to face Warner as he rode up. Chumacho raised his head and opened his mouth but no sound came out that Warner could hear. He reckoned Chumacho's mouth and tongue were too dry to work. He stopped fifteen yards short of them and slowly dismounted. He walked around the Andalusian and stopped. He stood there, staring at them. He would let it be their choice and he would not give them much time to make it.

It was the thin-faced man who understood first. He bent down and found a jagged rock. He straightened, holding it in both hands. He looked at Warner, locking his eyes, holding the rock out so there could be no mistaking his intentions. Then he started a limping, stumbling charge at Warner. Warner watched him in grudging admiration. He said, "You're a mean sonofabitch, but *usted es muy macho hombre*."

He let the man get to within five yards of him and then he pulled his revolver and carefully shot the man in the forehead. The thin-faced man's momentum carried him a step farther and then he stopped and fell over backward, the jagged rock flying off to the side.

Chumacho just sat. His head was up and he was working his mouth. Warner walked slowly toward him, holding the revolver by his side. He stopped six or seven paces from the fat bandit. He said, "I ain't sure you deserve this."

Chumacho said, his voice a croak, "I chu fren."

"Yeah," Warner said. "I guess I must be yours." He leveled the revolver and shot the bandit just above the nose. Chumacho instantly fell over on his back, his arms going out akimbo.

Warner turned and started back toward the Andalusian. The horse was standing quietly. Carlos stood fifteen yards away, watching. He made no effort to move. Warner got to the horse and mounted. He rode slowly over to Carlos, looking up toward the sky. Overhead, half a dozen buzzards circled lazily, riding air currents, waiting. Warner looked back toward where Chumacho and the thin-faced man lay. Chumacho looked like a pile of old clothes. The thin-faced man seemed much smaller than he had when he'd charged with the rock, asking for the bullet.

Warner stopped the Andalusian five yards from Carlos. The man stood, watching, his face showing nothing. Warner pointed to the west. He said, "Good country is six or seven miles that way. I don't know how far it is to help or if anyone will help you. I don't know how bad you are hurt or if you can walk very far. If you do not get the pellets out of your legs and feet the wounds will become infected and your flesh will putrify and you will die very badly." He held up the canteen. "Do you want this or the bullet? You asked for the bullet before. Do you still want it?"

Carlos said, "Will you give me a knife to cut the leetle bullets out of my flesh?"

Warner slowly shook his head. "You ask too much. I am still amazed that I came back for those." He gestured toward the two bodies. "I owed them a great deal of suffering before they died, but they would have surely died. Now I don't even understand why I am offering you this water. Perhaps it is because I am an easy man."

Carlos shook his head. He said softly, "No, you are not of that nature. You are a very hard man. I do not theenk I want trouble weeth you again."

Warner said, "Make up your mind. The canteen or the bullet. No knife. But I was here once before . . ." He smiled without humor. "There is a good supply of sharp rocks if one has the *cajones* to dig into ones flesh with them. If the little holes where the pellets went in have closed up I am told it is a good idea to make them bleed again."

Carlos said casually, "There is still the way of the help I could geeve with Don Fuego. I could go with you."

Warner laughed dryly. "You've had my answer on that."

Carlos shrugged. He said, "Then I tell you for nos'ing that he is a very dangerous man. Who can say which one of us will be *muerte* first."

Warner was growing impatient. He said, "Which do you want? The water or the bullet?"

Carlos nodded his head at the canteen. He said, "I theenk I have chust a leetle chance with the water."

"Fine by me," Warner said. He pitched the canteen to the man's feet. He said, "Carlos, you are no less a bandit than Chumacho or the other one. If you get out of Texas alive do not return. If I see you again I will kill you on sight. Make certain of that. If it had not been for you and this Don Fuego a lot of people would still be alive." He jerked his head at the two dead men. "They are ignorant peons. They didn't know any better. But you speak as a man who has learned enough of life to know what is permissible and what isn't. The same goes for this Don Fuego. You are the two culprits."

"Then why do you give me the water?"

Warner said, "For the same reason I gave them

the bullet instead of leaving them to suffer. I don't think you will live, not even with the water. But I can know for myself that I gave it to you. I did it for myself, just as I killed those two for myself. They thought I was being kind to them. At least the thin-faced man did. Chumacho was too sick to know what was happening."

"Ah," Carlos said. "I understand. You are a man of religion, of conscience."

"I'm whatever I am." He wheeled the Andalusian around. He said, "You don't have much more time before the infection."

Then he pointed the horse to the southeast and rode off at a good clip. He did not look back. He had done what it was within him to do.

The mules had not strayed far by the time he found the wagon. He got down from the Andalusian and tied him to the wagon, then got back in the buckboard seat. He drove the team on until about eleven o'clock. There was a little grove of post oak trees and he got down and tethered the team to one of the trees. Then he sprinkled out some grain for the two mules and then took the bits out of the Andalusian's mouth and put down some grain on the sparse grass. After that was done he wrestled the water barrel to the end of the wagon and tipped it over and poured a bucketful. He set it next to the Andalusian so he could drink when he was ready. Then he climbed back on the wagon seat, got the corn bread and ham out, and made himself a lunch. His mouth was a little dry and he was obliged to climb into the bed of the wagon and dip up some water out of the barrel and have a drink before he could eat. Just being on the alkali plain had made him thirsty. He knew it was all in his mind but that didn't make him any less dry.

After he'd eaten what he was obliged to call a meal he sat for a while, letting the livestock rest and letting himself come down off the fine edge he'd been on for what seemed years. He deliberately did not think about what he had done with Chumacho or the thin-faced man or Carlos. That was past, it was over, and he was not a man to come back later and question himself over matters that had been settled. Once a horse trade was made the deal was done and you rode what you traded for. It was a simple philosophy, but one that he found worked for him. He tried to live so that he never had to look back in regret. He knew that there were many times he had taken a wrong turning, but if the return road was closed and could not be reopened, then it was best to ride ahead without a look over the shoulder.

He put more water in the bucket and waited while the mules drank, then he put the gear away, climbed up in the wagon seat, took the reins, and slapped the mules on the back. "Get along," he said.

It was close to four in the afternoon before he came in sight of the camp. He saw the herd of horses and saw Charlie loose herding them in a slow circle. Then Charlie saw him. He raised his hat and waved and then put spurs to his horse and rode out to meet Warner. He said, pulling up his horse to walk alongside the wagon, "Mr. Grayson, mighty glad to see you, sir."

Warner smiled slightly. He said, "Hell, Charlie, I ain't been gone that long. You act like I been to Dallas or someplace."

Charlie said, "Well, yessir. Reckon that's right. Still, when you go up yonder to that place . . ." He let it trail off.

Warner said gruffly, "I know what you mean."

He didn't say much about the trip until after they'd had an early supper. With the extra horses thrown into the herd there wasn't room enough on the picket line so they'd decided they'd let them run loose. What little grass was left was near their camp and, in any case, the horses weren't going far.

Warner said, "Well, Charlie, you'll be glad to know I done what you called the Christian thing, though I don't reckon as many Christians would call it that."

Charlie said, "I'm right glad to hear that, Mr. Grayson. I don't reckon it is in your nature to bring suffering to another man."

Warner said, "These weren't just other men, Charlie."

"I know, sir. They had punishment coming and I knowed you didn't have time to haul them to jail, not with what you got to do."

Warner looked at him. He said, "How do you know what I got to do?"

Charlie was wiping his hands on his jeans. He said, "Well, I never took you for one left loose ends hanging. And I don't reckon that's so now. I reckon them Spanish horses be on your mind."

Warner said, "Charlie, it is a comfort to me to know that you know what I'm thinking. That way, if I forget, I can ask you and you can set me back on the road."

"Yessir," Charlie said.

"Yessir, what?"

"Just yessir. To whatever you mean."

Warner nodded. He said, "That's a hell of an attitude, Charlie. You'll go far with that kind of thinking. But, now, tell you what—I know it ain't good dark yet, but you get what sleep you can for the next few hours and I'll go on herd duty until about eleven o'clock or so. Then you'll have to take it the balance of the night. I want to get off as early as I can and I figure to need as much sleep as I can get. I don't calculate to get much once I cross over into Mexico."

Charlie said, "I can take it all night, Mr. Grayson."

"Ain't no need. If I can get a good five or six

hours tonight I'll be fine. You was up most of last night so you ought to be about ready for some shut-eye yourself."

While Charlie bedded down Warner selected one of the range horses they'd borrowed from Wilson Young. He was an old, range-wise pony who knew all about night herding. With him doing most of the work Warner was able to nod off and on as the horse circled the mostly sleeping horses. He was glad to see that the Andalusian was getting some good rest. He had the Spanish horse tied near the camp and the animal had his head down and was balanced on three legs, one hip cocked, sleeping the way horses slept. Next morning he'd get fed a good bit of grain, if there was much left, and watered and groomed. He was, Warner reckoned, as strong and as durable as any horse he'd ever rode. Every time he was on the back of the animal he grew more pleased with him. It was going to be a chore to give him back to Laura Pico. But give him back he must because he sure couldn't think of any way to buy him.

The booty from the Mexicans had been disappointing. While he'd been gone Charlie had gotten it in and collected and accounted. All told, the money, both in Mexican and American currency, hadn't come to much more than four hundred dollars. The saddles and other riding tack, except for Chumacho's silver-embossed saddle, had been mostly junk, not worth carting away. Charlie had collected a dozen pistols, but of the lot only about half were of much value. He'd counted on recouping most of his losses from the horses. They'd been rode down and underfed, but they had appeared to be good stock needing only some rest and good care. Unfortunately, about half of them, the better stock, bore the brands of nearby ranches. They'd been stolen and Warner was obliged to return them. He'd get some thanks from the ranchers who'd lost them and their return might go a measure toward rebuilding any good will he might have lost by not showing up to do the job the ranchers had come to depend upon. But they wouldn't help him recover the money and stock that Chumacho had robbed him of. This entire lot wasn't worth much more than half of what he'd lost, not to mention the trouble he'd been put to.

Of course there was the fee that Laura Pico would be obliged to pay him if he was successful in recovering her five lost Andalusians. But he calculated he'd better recover the horses before he started counting his reward. All around, near as he could figure, that damn Chumacho, and by association, this damn Don Fuego had cost him money and given him more trouble than he'd been looking for.

He called Charlie a little after eleven o'clock and then crawled into his bedroll. There was a nice crispness in the air and the sky was so clear that the stars seemed embedded in black velvet just out of his reach. He took off his boots and his gun belt, loosened his jeans, and then lay down. Only when he began to relax did he realize how tired he was. He could feel his body settling into itself, grateful not to be doing anything except resting. He'd meant to lie a few minutes and think out his plans for the next day but he was asleep before the first thought could take root.

Charlie let him sleep until seven the next morning. At first he was annoyed and then he was grateful. He was going into a strange situation in a strange country against unknown foes and he was going to need to be at his best. His body had obviously needed the sleep or else he'd have awoke as soon as the sun had hit his face. The sleep had been good and he thanked Charlie for his thoughtfulness.

Charlie said, "Mr. Grayson, you jest looked so wore out last night, I seen you had to have some rest and I knowed you wadn't going to agree, not while you was awake, anyway. You been drivin' yourself mighty hard. I been watching and, while I admire you, it's like my momma says, a body can stand jest so much."

Warner looked at him with a half smile. He said, "Charlie, if I don't get killed over in Mexico, me and you are going to be working together for a good long while. Are you going to talk this much all the time?"

A stricken look had come over Charlie's face. He said, "Was I gettin' mouthy? Daddy says I'm given to it."

Warner laughed. He said, "Charlie, take a joke once in a while. I was kidding you. If you talked too much I'd've let you know."

Charlie said, "Well, it's kind of hard to tell with you, Mr. Grayson. You been mighty serious here of late. I don't mean that you ain't a pleasure to be around. Nosir, I never meant that. I . . . well, I meant what I said."

They were finishing up breakfast, bacon and eggs and the last of the corn bread. Warner was making an especially big breakfast because he wasn't sure how often he'd get to eat in the next few days. He said, "Well, I've been on some serious business, Charlie, and it ain't over yet."

Charlie said hesitantly, "I was a little worried you might have been talking about last night, about what I said."

"You mean about doing them bandits a kindness with a bullet?"

Charlie looked at his tin plate. He said, "Yessir. I reckon I was speaking out of school. Like you told me, I never went through what you did. I might have felt the same way."

Warner said, "Charlie, I'm glad you spoke up. Mind you, I don't like you making a habit of it, but I'm feeling a good deal better this morning than I might have been if I hadn't heard what you said. A man can carry this vengeance business too far." But then his thoughts turned to Carlos and he wondered if he'd carried it far enough. He might have left an enemy alive, one that he might later regret having left on his feet. But it was no time to worry about such matters. He had to get moving. He said, "Charlie, I'm going to ride that Andalusian, but I want you to pick me out another horse that can double as a packhorse and a saddle horse. We got something like that around here?"

Charlie said, "Oh, shore. Any of them good range horses from Mr. Young's place will do. I take it you don't want that black of his, that racehorse?"

"I don't reckon he'll do as a pack animal. Little skittish. I want something solid and dependable. I wish I had two of that Andalusian."

They both instinctively looked to where the Andalusian was standing, bending his neck every now and again to take a bit of grain and then raising his head while he chewed it.

Charlie said, "Damned if he don't look shiny as a new penny the way that sun is hitting him."

Warner said, "I also need you to rig me up some kind of pack. It don't have to be much because I ain't got much to carry, just what grub I can eat cold, though you might put me a frying pan in and a slab of bacon if we got any left just in case I can build a fire. You reckon you can figure something out?"

Charlie thought a minute. Then he said, "I reckon I could take a piece of that ground cloth and make a thing like a big canvas saddlebag. Rig it on the horse with some of that soft rope."

"And I want to take that long shotgun of yours. I know we brought some buckshot and this time I intend to use it. Put me in at least two boxes."

"What kind of rifle you going to carry? I got my carbine you can take though I ain't got no whole bunch of cartridges."

Warner looked across toward Mexico and squinted his eyes. He said, "See if that big Sharps with the scope that Wilson Young loaned me will fit in my saddle boot. If it won't, tie it on behind or in whatever kind of pack you rig up. Wilson Young said I might need to use it if I needed to even out the odds long distance. Well, this time I might. Many cartridges for the thing?"

Charlie said, "Lord, yes! They's a leather sack plumb full. Must weigh twenty pounds. I bet they's a hunnert, hunnert and fifty rounds in that thing. Mr. Grayson, I never seen such bullets. That thing a cannon or a gun?"

Warner smiled and got up, stretching. He began rolling his bedroll in his yellow slicker. In that country a slicker was more a decoration than anything else, but men who traveled the rough land carried them because, as one had said, "It's handy if you ever need to get buried in something."

Charlie said worriedly, "Mr. Grayson, I hate to see you goin' over there into Mexico on your own like you are. Reckon I couldn't tag along just to watch your back?"

Warner glanced around. He said, "You reckon these horses are smart enough to drive themselves home?"

Charlie said, "We could drive them down to Mrs. Pico's an' pen 'em up."

"Yeah," Warner said. "I'm sure Mrs. Pico would love to feed twenty horses. No, Charlie, I'm obliged for the offer, but I reckon I better see this through myself."

"You know much about this feller supposed to have them horses?"

Warner smiled slightly. "One of them *vaqueros* I give a ride out to the alkali flat claimed to be Don Fuego's head *vaquero*. Said the man was a pretty hard case. Even offered to go along and give me a hand with the matter. But then I reckon he was trying to strike a bargain for his life. For all I know, when the man finds out he's holding stolen horses he'll give them up. I'm going to offer to pay him back what he laid out. So take some of them gold pesos that fat bandit had in his saddlebags and throw them in with my gear. Two thousand pesos' worth. I got some American money on me in case he wants to trade hard."

Charlie said, "Mr. Grayson, I heered just a little of that talk you was having with that one bandit.

313

The one didn't look like he ought to be a bandit. Don't sound like this feller in Mexico is going to be all that easy to deal with."

"We'll see," Warner said. He put a saddle blanket on the Andalusian and smoothed it out before throwing the saddle on his back. "I'll do what I have to."

"Where'd you say you was headed?"

"I didn't say, Charlie. But if you got to know, this man is supposed to have a pretty big *hacienda* north of El Milagro. I figure to go to El Milagro and get directions from there."

"That puts you a pretty good distance into Mexico. More'n twenty miles."

"Then the faster I get started the faster I can get back. And I can't get started if you keep asking me questions instead of getting me a pack rigged up."

Charlie ducked to his work. He said, "Yessir. I'm getting right smart after it. Ought to work out fine."

As it was he was late in getting away. Not that it mattered; he wouldn't be seeing Don Fuego Hernando that night and maybe not even the next day. He believed what Carlos had said about the man and the Don was one hombre he intended on scouting out as well as he could. Mounted on the Andalusian he said, "Now you know what to do, Charlie?"

"Yessir. I'm to drive the whole kit and caboodle

314

to Mrs. Pico's and drop off her horses. Then I'm to take the rest of the horses and the mules and the wagon and go on to Mr. Wilson Young's ranch on the other side of the river."

"What are you supposed to do at Mrs. Pico's?"

"Nuthin'."

"What if she asks you?"

Charlie said, "I'm supposed to tell her I don't know nuthin'. That I ain't seen nuthin', I ain't heard nuthin', and I don't expect I ever will. Then I'm to go on to Mr. Wilson Young's and wait."

"How long?"

"Till you get there."

Warner said, "That's fine, Charlie. I wish I could tell you how long that might be, but I don't know myself. Might be three days, might be a week. Might be longer."

"I'll be there."

Warner said, "Tell Wilson Young I found me some folks that hesitated."

"Sir?"

Warner smiled. "Don't worry about it. Mr. Young will know what I mean. Well, I better get kicking. Look after my property, Charlie."

"Just like it was mine."

Warner pulled up the slack on the packhorse and then touched his spurs lightly to the Andalusian. He said, "Take it easy. I don't know how we stand on wages, but pay yourself up-to-date out of that money we took off the bandits."

Charlie said, "You take it right easy too, Mr. Grayson. I'm anxious for you to get back and us to take up our regular work."

Warner smiled and nodded and put the Andalusian into a slow lope down toward the Rio Grande.

Two miles from the river the country began to rise. After another half mile Warner was into some low hills with higher ones to come. In the distance he could see the crags of the *sierras*, the big northern mountains, but they were a hundred miles away, visible only because of their size and the clear air. He was already in rough country, but he was glad not to have to challenge the *sierras*. He'd ridden through mountains and he was always hard-pressed to understand why God had felt it necessary to plague man with such a useless article.

He didn't know exactly where El Milagro was but he wasn't much worried. He would hold a southeastern course and, sooner or later, he'd strike a track or a trail or some kind of road and he'd turn east on that and, soon enough, he'd come to a village. It might not be El Milagro, but his destination would be close. There was little useable land in northern Mexico and the population put it to as much use as it could stand. He didn't reckon he'd have much trouble finding Don Fuego's *hacienda*. Such an area wasn't likely to be overrun with rich landowners or big ranches and, probably, most anybody could direct him.

Warner rode until he calculated it was a little after noon, then pulled up in a little valley between a couple of hills. The mesquite was starting to mix in with mountain pine and he shaded up under some fair-size trees and fixed himself some lunch, such as it was. There was grass for the horses, so he tied them together with the lead rope and left them to graze while he opened himself a can of pork and beans and a can of peaches. He ate both cold, drinking water out of the big canteen he'd brought and doing without bread. He wasn't worried about water for the horses. He knew the country was cut and crisscrossed with streams that started way south in the high mountains and ran downhill to empty into the Rio Grande. He had some time in northern Mexico, but nothing like the experience of Wilson Young. Wilson or Chulo would be a help with the Don, but Warner was still determined to resolve the entire matter by himself.

Of course it could be said that his job had ended with the finish of Chumacho and his gang, but he'd more or less promised Laura Pico to have a try for her horses and he intended on doing just that. Besides, it was clear that the Don was the true cause of the trouble and Warner reckoned that fact needed to be called strongly to the Don's attention so he didn't get any similar ideas in the future. And there was the fact that Warner had grown very fond of the Andalusian Laura had lent him and he hated to see such good horses not receiving the best of care. For all he knew the Don might be doing just that, but the horses didn't belong to Don Fuego and it could be said with certainty that no one was going to take better care of them than Laura Pico.

And there was the matter of his finder's fee for returning the horses to her. Yes, he decided, he had plenty of reasons to consider this side trip part of the original job he'd cut out for himself.

Warner finally located El Milagro late in the afternoon by following a road that was really nothing more than a wagon track, though it was likely that the trail had seen more ox carts than it had horse-drawn wagons.

The little village was in the middle of a broad, surprisingly green valley that lay between little runs of rising hills on all sides. He saw the town a good way off, rounding out of a valley and around a little hill. There it was, a scattering of big and little adobe buildings sitting brown in the middle of cultivated corn and bean fields with orchards of limes and sparse pastures where herds of sheep and goats were tended. He rode straight into the town. There wasn't anything that could really be called a street, just a space between the buildings that were scattered in a sort of way that suggested the town had grown as need arose. Warner knew it was the kind of Mexican village whose main function was to serve the needs of the farmers and the herdsmen who populated the hills and valleys for miles around. At a glance he saw several stores that probably sold the simplest of staples. He saw two cantinas and a butcher shop with fresh beef carcasses hanging in front that attracted both customers and flies. As he passed he saw the butcher come out and hack off a large hunk of meat for a little stooped peon woman. He didn't reckon that the majority of the people could afford to raise cattle. It took money to buy cattle and to feed them. Goats and sheep were much cheaper and easier to care for. But a family had to eat beef sometimes so they traded a goat or a pig or got together a little money and ate *carne* either as stew or in enchiladas or some other way that would make it last.

The biggest building in town was the Catholic church. There was a big bell in its tower and Warner marveled at the labor it must have taken to get such a heavy object up so high. That was a peon for you, Warner thought, he'd spend more labor getting an iron bell forty feet in the air than he would in making a corn crop or feeding his goats. But it was no affair of his, not so long as they stayed on their side of the border and left his horses alone.

He drew very little attention, riding along. This close to the border the town was used to gringos. He'd bet half the goods and products sold in the stores came from the United States. And probably by ox cart.

Warner drew up in front of the more prosperous of the cantinas and dismounted, tying his horses to a handy post. He tied them tight, making knots that would take a thief a moment or two to get undone.

The door to the cantina was wide open as he entered. The bar was a long affair of planks polished down from years of use by drinkers of rum and tequila and pulque. The place had Mexican beer and he ordered a mug and asked the barkeep if there was a cafe in town. The bartender shook his head but said, in half English and half Spanish, that his wife sometimes cooked for strangers. He said that she was making a pot of *guisado*, or stew, that would be ready in an hour or so and, meanwhile the *señor* could drink *cerveza* and make himself comfortable.

The place was nearly deserted. He didn't imagine there was much money in such a poor town to spend on afternoon drinking. He sat down at a table to wait. The beer was warm, but not too bad, and the proprietor, at his request, brought him a large jug of water. He didn't know if he was going to ever get over the thirst that seemed to always be with him. He knew it wasn't a real thirst, just part of the scars he'd come away from the alkali flat with.

When he seemed less of a stranger to the barkeep Warner asked after the *hacienda* of Don Fuego Hernando. The bartender said, with some pride as if having such a rich man near them was a source of considerable civic capital, that the place was easy to find, that it was only a little better than ten or twelve kilometers away, and that Don Fuego himself had been in this, his very own, cantina. He said that there was a small road that ran south out of town and that it was only a matter of following that and keeping a sharp eye and the *hacienda* could not be missed. The barkeep said, "*En diez kilómetros es* a leetle turn to the *derecho*, the right. Et es chust a little trail but it will take you between some hills and then there es the *hacienda. Es muy grande, el hacienda de* Don Fuego Hernando."

Which, as best as Warner could understand it, meant there was a little trail ran off to the east about six miles out on the road south out of town. Then, apparently, the little trail led straight back through the rough hills and crags to the rich ranch of Don Fuego Hernando.

The proprietor's wife brought Warner a bowl of spicy stew with a stack of soft, warm, buttered tortillas. He ate the stew, drinking water to offset the heat of the spices, but was mainly grateful for the soft tortillas. He was sitting where he could see through the door to where his horses stood tied. It was nearing six o'clock and he wanted to get started for Fuego's *hacienda* while it was still light enough to see.

When he'd finished his stew he bought four dozen tortillas and two dozen tamales, wrapped in corn shucks, from the barkeep's wife. Then he paid his score, giving the man a dollar when the whole affair couldn't have come to much more than fifty cents. But he was feeling good. He was on his way to finishing some business that had begun too long ago and had interfered with his life enough.

Outside, he untied both horses, regretting having done such a fine job with the knots, and then mounted his horse and headed south out of town leading the packhorse. Hardly a head turned as the people of the town moved about their own business. It was one of the things he liked about Mexico, nobody was much concerned about any affairs outside of their own. They were too busy trying to scratch out a living to see or hear or take interest in the affairs of others.

He hurried along. He wanted to find a place to camp for the night before darkness set in. And he also wanted to be as close to the turn for the *hacienda* as he could get so as to make an early visit the next day.

He rode for what he calculated was three-quarters of an hour and then judged it was time to begin looking for a nest for the night. He turned off the little track into a draw between two big hills, then wound his way back into the hard country that was covered with pine and cedar and mesquite. A half mile back into the country he saw what looked to be the mouth of a big cave halfway up the side of a sloping hill. There was a narrow creek running down the side of the mountain, looking as if it came from somewhere near the cave mouth. He rode along the edge of the hill until he found where the creek pooled up, then dismounted and let both horses drink while he looked carefully around. He didn't see a soul or any sign that a soul had recently been in the area. Certainly he was on no farmer's land or ranch. But in backcountry Mexico you could not be too careful. A man who was not a bandit and had never thought of becoming one could suddenly change, as if by magic, into a *bandido* once he had a gun in his hand or too much temptation came his way. And two fine horses and the gear and trappings of a gringo were a great temptation.

When his horses were through drinking he took the reins of the Andalusian in one hand and the lead rope of the packhorse in the other and started climbing the gentle slope of the hill.

The cave was wide and shallow and still pretty well lit from the lowering sun that looked right into its mouth. The floor was rocky, but flat enough and there were no bats. Warner was always nervous about caves because he didn't like bats. They scared him the way they flew in all different directions. A man couldn't tell what they were liable to do. But this cave was too shallow and too light for bats. He led the horses inside. The water that fed the creek had leaked out of the limestone walls on one side of the cave. It came in tiny streams, but collected at the bottom and then ran on down. Fortunately, only one side of the cave was wet. The other side was higher and dry. The cave was big enough to hold both himself and his horses. He got his big bowie knife out of the pack saddle and went out of the cave and cut and hacked down enough brush from pine and cedar and mesquite saplings to make a brush fence that would hold the horses in. It would also keep the casual passerby from having a look inside.

It took him four trips to gather and drag enough brush to make a good fence across the mouth of the cave. When he was finished Warner took the bridle off the Andalusian and unsaddled him and put his tack up on the rock shelf where he intended to sleep. Charlie had done a fine job of securing the pack to the horse and it took him some time to get it loose from the animal. When he had it in hand he lugged it, with some effort, up to the shelf. The Sharps rifle had fitted into the saddle boot, though not like it looked as if it belonged there. Charlie had broken down the shotgun and put it in the pack. Warner took the rifle first and made sure it was loaded and then sighted through the scope, across the valley, to make sure the scope hadn't gotten banged around and was no longer sighted in correctly. Then he assembled the shotgun, took two buckshot shells out of a box, and loaded the big gun. He laid the two firearms side by side.

It had come good dark now, and, even though there was a moon outside, it was very dark in the cave. But it made no difference. Warner wasn't going to build a fire. He didn't want to call attention to himself and he doubted that a fire would draw unless he built it right next to the mouth of the cave. Anyway, all he planned to do was eat a cold supper and then get some sleep. He wanted to make an early start because he did not intend on approaching Don Fuego until he'd made a thorough scout of the country roundabouts.

It was too early for sleep and he wasn't hungry, having eaten just a few hours before. So, for something to do, he stood in the door of the cave, looking over his brush fence and watching the country, his gaze traveling from as far as he could see in one direction across the hills and valley to the end of his vision in the other. He figured he couldn't be more than three or four miles from Don Fuego's *hacienda* and he wanted to see how close his neighbors were. He watched for better than an hour and only saw one light and that was back toward El Milagro. Of course there could have been any number of huts and houses hidden down in the valleys and blocked from his gaze by the jagged hills. But he rather thought that most of the surrounding countryside belonged to the Don or was under his control. It was good land for Mexico, but it still wouldn't feed many cattle or horses per acre. And he knew that the farther south he went, the worse it was going to get.

Finally he tired of the game and got out a can of beans, opened it with his big knife, and ate the beans cold out of the can with a big spoon. At least, with the tortillas, he had bread, though he knew they wouldn't stay fresh more than a couple of days. The cantina owner's wife had wrapped the tamales tightly in oil paper and he was hopeful they would keep for several days, especially if he didn't open them until he had to.

He laid out his bedroll, put his saddle in place for a pillow and lay down, all his guns close to hand. He could just barely make out the horses licking the wall where the water dripped out of the limestone. He reckoned that was the first time either of them had ever watered off a rock wall.

He deliberately did not try and think what he was going to do the next day. It would be foolish, in his mind, to plan for an action when he'd never seen the ground or situation, much less his adversary. He was still tired from all the nights of watching for the bandits and was asleep almost as soon as he closed his eyes.

He awoke well before dawn, but he made no attempt to leave the cave until the first light began to appear on the hills. Then he took both horses down the slope of the hill and watered them. After that he stayed with them while they grazed on the grass that lined the little creek. He wished he had some grain for them and thought that he should have tried to buy some shelled corn in El Milagro, but it was too late for that. Besides, both horses were still plenty strong from all the good feed they'd had for the last two weeks. They could get along for a few days on grass and whatever else they could find.

Finally he took them both back up the hill and put them in the cave. He'd decided to build a little fire. There was some dried mesquite handy and mesquite didn't make much smoke. He got a small blaze going on a rock ledge just outside the cave entrance and then went into the cave and sliced a skilletful of bacon and made a small pot of coffee. He waited until the blaze had turned into coals and then set the skillet and coffeepot right on the embers. Within minutes the bacon began frying and Warner knelt by the side of the fire, moving the bacon around and turning it over with the point of his knife. When it was almost done he spread half a dozen tortillas on top of the bacon to warm them up. Then, when it was all done, he poured himself a cup of coffee and began making bacon sandwiches by wrapping a slice of bacon in a warm tortilla and eating it like a taco. He decided it was the best way to eat bacon he'd ever discovered.

Without warning his mind went fleeting back to the last sight he'd had of Carlos, standing there in the badlands with his bloody feet and legs, looking after him with that wistful expression on his face. The thought made him angry. Hell, he'd treated the sonofabitch better than he'd been treated by a damn sight. And he doubted that Carlos would have served him as well if the situation had been reversed. Carlos would have never come back and brought him a canteen of water and pointed out the fastest route out of the alkali country. Offering to help him get the Andalusians back. Well, that had been some joke. Warner thought that if a man was going to beg for his life he ought to come out and do it rather than dressing it up with feathers and ribbons and bows. Not likely Carlos would have helped with this Don Fuego, not unless he meant he'd help him, Warner, to get killed. Well, he reckoned old Carlos was having himself a pretty hard time along about now. Which, maybe, was just what he deserved.

He finished his breakfast, doused the fire with what was left of the coffee, and did what he could to clean out the skillet with a tortilla, deciding that bacon grease was as good as butter.

Warner went in the cave and packed his gear and loaded the packhorse. The only change he made was to break down the Sharps rifle and put the shotgun in his saddle boot. Then he saddled the Andalusian and pushed aside the brush fence and led both horses back down the hill. He mounted the Andalusian, took the packhorse on lead, and cut through the little washes and wide places between hills until he struck the road running south. He turned left and went along, hoping to not meet anyone. He had deliberately waited until around nine or nine-thirty before he took the road. He had reasoned that would lessen the chances of meeting any *campesinos* traveling either to or from town.

Within a mile he struck what could only be the road back to Fuego's *hacienda*. Now he moved slowly, riding off the road and in what cover he could find. The trail seemed to lead right down the middle of two sets of high hills running east and west. When he'd left the main road the hills had been at least a quarter of a mile apart, but the farther west he went, toward the *hacienda*, the closer they seemed to come together. And they were high hills, some of them five and six hundred feet in altitude.

Then he came around a curve in the trail and he was looking straight down what he would have called a box canyon. The hills on either side finally joined in a kind of ragged *U* a quarter mile or better from where he was sitting his horse. He backed his outfit up so that he was in the cover of some small pine trees while he studied what he could see at the distance. He had no doubt it was the *hacienda* of Don Fuego. He could make out one big, rambling structure that he figured to be the headquarters ranch house. It was made of stuccoed or whitewashed adobe and topped with the red Mexican tiles that looked like six-inch pipe that had been cut in two. That was on his left and the house appeared to be backed up flush against the big hill on that side. It seemed to have been done deliberately because he could see where the hill face had been worked away until it was almost vertical. It made the house look as if it were growing out of the hill. Warner figured that it had been done for defensive purposes so that the place couldn't be attacked from the back.

To his right he could see a scattering of buildings, some that appeared to be built of adobe—though not whitewashed—and some of sawn lumber. He could see a good many corrals and some big enclosures that were built with adobe bricks but not roofed. Between the main house and the other buildings he calculated that the distance was at least two hundred yards. It was clear that the Don didn't like to live too near the hired help. Which brought up another question that had been puzzling him since Carlos had told him about this Don Fuego. If he was such a big shot nobleman, what in hell was he doing living in such a backwater place as El Milagro? Maybe, Warner thought, he was the type that didn't care for company or maybe he wasn't as high and mighty as he let on.

One thing that Warner had noticed as he'd gotten into the rising country was that most of the hills seemed to be topped with huge boulders, some as big as two wagons put together. The same was true of the hills that surrounded the *ranchero*, though none of them threatened the *hacienda* Fuego. The boulders all looked like they'd been in place for a long time and were likely to remain so unless an earthquake came along. He didn't know of any wind strong enough to move them and, certainly, they couldn't be budged by the hand of man.

But they did give him an idea. He turned the Andalusian and rode back the way he'd come, pulling the packhorse along.

When he got back to the main road he cut over to his right, to the foot of the row of hills that bordered the ranch. Then he rode along the edge, cutting in and out of thickets and going around boulders. He went until he judged he was somewhere even with the *ranchero*. He dismounted and went to the packhorse and got out the barrel of the Sharps, the part of the rifle that held the scope. Then he tied the packhorse in a pine thicket and took the Andalusian by the reins and began scrambling up the hill. It was much rougher going than it had been climbing the gentle slope to the cave and, less than halfway to the top, he stopped and tied the Andalusian to a handy bush. It would give him another free hand and make it easier to scramble up.

But even then it was rough going. When Warner arrived at the top he was about half out of breath and had to sit for a moment and breathe. He was leaning up against a big rock that was in a cluster with a bunch of others. Some of them were six and seven feet high. There was an opening between the rocks and he slipped in. It was like being in a big, rock-walled room though there were some hellacious cracks in the walls where the rocks didn't touch. But it would, he thought, just about suit his purposes.

A plan was already beginning to form in his mind, a plan based on the fact that he didn't believe Don Fuego was going to cooperate and either sell or give him those Andalusian horses. Not willingly at least.

He wiggled through a crack between two rocks and got to the edge of the mountain where he would have an overview of the *ranchero*. He saw at once that he was about two hundred yards short of the main house, but that was all right for his purposes. He got the scope up to his eye and began to study the place in great detail.

Of course the first thing he'd noticed was that the natural *U* the hills made created as fine a big catch pen as a man could want if he was holding a cattle gather. And Warner figured that Fuego had cattle scattered all over the poor country for half a dozen miles. But all he had to do was drive them through the mouth created by the line of hills and then break them up into smaller groups and pen them in corrals.

Of which there were a number, most of them built of split rails and some big enough to hold a hundred head of cattle.

But he was mainly interested in the buildings. There appeared to be two barns, both of them built of sawn lumber and roofed with mud thatch. Then there were several small adobe buildings topped with the tile. They had windows and looked to be homes for the married *vaqueros*. Then there was a long adobe-walled, tile-roofed building that Warner figured was the Mexican equivalent of a bunkhouse. But the structure that interested him the most was a long and narrow, tile-roofed adobe building that looked an awful lot like a stable. It had a large wooden door in one end, but it ran at a different angle than the other buildings that faced the *hacienda*. A wall, about five feet high, projected from its back and made a square corral. Through his scope Warner could just catch sight, every now and then, of a head or flash of color of horses that looked exactly like the one he was riding. Well, at least he knew where they were, but he reckoned the odds of sneaking them out of there as pretty close to certain death.

No, he was just going to have to convince Mr. Don Fuego Hernando to give him back those horses, be a good citizen and do the right thing.

He saw a few *vaqueros* going about their chores, but it was so close to noon he reckoned that the most of them were getting ready for lunch.

After he had looked as long as he thought necessary he got up and made his way back down the hill to where the Andalusian was. He unsaddled the horse, took the bridle off, and then struggled back up the hill with the animal. He could have ridden up, but judged it would have been too hard on the horse. Once at the top he pushed the animal into the enclosure of rocks and used his lariat to tie the horse to some greasewood bushes that were growing nearby. He wasn't much worried about the horse wandering away, but he didn't want to leave him down near the road where he might be discovered and made off with.

Halfway down the hill he picked up the saddle and bridle and carried them down to where he'd left the packhorse. In getting the rifle barrel out of the pack he'd noticed a plug of chewing tobacco. Charlie chewed tobacco and Warner figured it had somehow gotten mixed in with his gear when Charlie was packing up. Warner himself didn't chew tobacco, but he figured to put this plug to use. He stuck it into his pocket and led the packhorse over into a thicket of pine and mesquite. He got some tamales out of the pack and unslung the canteen and then settled down to make himself a meal while the packhorse grazed. One thing he did want to find was a nearby stream where he could water both horses. He didn't know how long his business was going to last, but it might take more than a day.

But, then, he wasn't in any big hurry.

# 12

It had taken a considerable amount of time and persuasion for Warner to induce the old *mozo*, the house servant, to call the Don to the door. He had deliberately waited until three o'clock, the middle of the siesta hour, to approach the house. He had come riding the bay, the former pack-horse. Naturally he hadn't wanted Don Fuego to see him on the Andalusian who was safely hidden above the Don's very own house. He was wearing the revolver Wilson had loaned him and Charlie's long-range shotgun was in his saddle boot.

The Don had come out in an unfriendly mood. But Warner had assumed that would have been the case no matter what time he'd arrived. Since no one had invited him to step down from his horse he had stayed mounted. It only served to emphasize the Don's small stature. He had come out wearing a white silk shirt and a gray chamois vest and blue trousers of some kind of material that Warner would have sworn were velvet except he'd never seen a man wear velvet trousers before. Even the tips of the Don's boots were ornamented with beaten gold. He was as much of a dandy as Warner had ever seen.

Warner had come straight to the point. He'd

said, "I have reason to believe that you have five Andalusian horses here."

Don Fuego had taken two steps toward him, his face going angry. He did indeed, Warner noticed, have red hair and blue eyes. Now his sharp blue eyes were snapping with anger. It was difficult to tell from the back of his horse, but Warner didn't believe the man could have been more than five feet six inches in height. He'd said, "What concern is that of yours, *señor*? And by what right do you come here to disturb me in the middle of the day?"

"Now," Warner said, leaning his arms on the pommel of his saddle, "it concerns me because those Andalusian stallions are stolen. They ain't your horses, *señor*. They were stolen in Texas."

Fuego took another step forward. Warner noted that he wasn't wearing a side arm, but he might have a derringer or some other small gun hidden under his vest or shirt. Warner straightened up so that his hand was near the butt of his revolver. Fuego was now so angry there were spots of color on his cheeks. He said, "Do you call me a thief, *señor*?"

Warner said, "I know you've got some stolen horses. You may not know them as stolen. But if you do that makes you a thief, yes."

Fuego said, "What makes you think I have such horses?"

Warner pointed without taking his eyes off

Fuego back toward what he thought were the stables. He said, "Why don't we go look in there and see what we find."

Fuego said, "I think you are trespassing on my property, *señor*."

Warner said, "Yes, and you sent the bandit Chumacho to trespass on some people's property in Texas and steal their horses. Andalusians. You paid him two thousand pesos for five of the horses. The sixth one got away only you heard that it had lately been seen and you promised him or paid him another two thousand pesos to go and get that one."

Fuego's eyes were blazing. He said, "I know of no bandit Chumacho."

"How about your head *vaquero*, Carlos? You sent him along both times. Is that not so, *Señor* Fuego?"

Fuego said tightly, "What do you know of my man Carlos?"

Warner said easily, "I know you ain't going to be getting a lot more work out of him. Now, I am willing to pay you back the two thousand pesos you gave Chumacho for the five Andalusian stallions. I will take them back to their rightful owner and the affair will be over."

Fuego raised his arm and snapped his fingers. He said, "Get off my land, *hombre*. And be quick about it. I have a dozen *vaqueros* here and some of them are *pistoleros*."

Warner looked over his shoulder. He could see four or five men wandering out in front of the building he took to be the bunkhouse. He turned back to Fuego and said, "They may be *pistoleros*, but they are at least a hundred yards away. And I am right here. And I am a *pistolero* also." He looked at Fuego significantly.

"Are you a law officer?"

"Of course."

"You have no authority here. You are in Mexico, *señor*."

"Listen," Warner said harshly, "you sent Chumacho over to steal them Andalusians. Well, in the bargain he managed to steal a lot of other horses and to kill and hurt quite a few people. Then you sent him back. Only he ain't going to kill or hurt anybody anymore. Now, I'm here for those horses. You can give them to me now or you can give me them later. But, I promise you, you will surrender those horses to me. You understand?"

Fuego drew himself up. He tilted his head back in a haughty manner. He said, "The Andalusian is for men of noble houses. They are not for peasants."

Warner said, "Well, if you're so noble what the hell you doing hiding out in this place?"

Fuego said severely, "That is none of your affair."

"You speak very good English. Where did you learn it?"

339

Fuego said, "I am married to a woman of your country."

Warner nodded toward the house. "She in there?"

"That also is none of your affair."

Warner said, "Well, if she is I recommend you get her under a bed or something."

The red spots appeared on Fuego's cheeks again. He said, his voice grating, "You do not speak of my wife! Now get off my land before I set my men on you."

Warner smiled slightly. After what seemed forever he finally had before him the man who had put him afoot and waterless on that alkali prairie. He was in no rush to take his satisfaction. He intended to prolong it as long as he could. He said, "I'm beginning to get the idea you ain't going to invite me in."

"Begone! Begone!" Fuego was almost hysterical with rage. "I will call on my *pistoleros* to shoot you!"

Warner leaned toward him. He said, "Don . . . or George or Roy or whatever your name is, I reckon I'd be a little careful of my mouth. You are the one closest to the business end of a pistol."

Fuego stepped back, toward his door. Just inside, the *mozo* was peering out. Fuego said, "You leave."

Warner said, "I'm fining you two thousand pesos for horse stealing. If you'd returned the horses to me I'd have given you back the money you paid for them. A mighty cheap price I might add. But now I'm not only *not* going to give you your money back, I'm going to fine you two thousand pesos a day for each and every day, beginning now, that it takes me to get those horses back."

Fuego's face was flushed with rage. He suddenly turned and dashed into his house. Warner backed his horse, watching as the *mozo* closed the big door. Then he wheeled his horse. The *vaqueros* were walking toward him, but he didn't see any with a drawn gun. He put spurs to his horse and rode out the road between the hills. After a half mile he stopped and looked back. No one was following him. He reckoned that Don Fuego felt pretty secure in his fortress with all his *pistoleros*. He reckoned that such a regal fellow didn't feel he had anything to fear from one single gringo.

Warner smiled as he reached the end of the line of hills and turned back toward the place where he'd hidden his pack. He needed to find two things: a place to water his horses and an easier trail up the side of the hill.

He found the water first. It was about a half mile from the row of hills, back toward the main road. It was a stream flowing from someplace back in the high ground. He watered the horse he was riding and then went searching down the row of hills until he found a trail that wound gently up toward the crown. It appeared to have been made by goats. He followed it to the top, careful not to show himself above the crest and rode until he found the cluster of rocks where he'd left the Andalusian. He turned the old cow horse in with the Andalusian and stripped the saddle off the animal and took the bridle off. Then he took the lariat off the Andalusian and secured the packhorse. After that he put the bridle on the Andalusian and mounted him bareback. He rode the Andalusian down the path and took him to water, getting off and waiting for about an hour while the Andalusian grazed. There was some grass on top of the hill, but it was pretty poor stuff. Finally, he mounted the Andalusian again and rode to where he'd left his supplies hidden. He slung the pack that Charlie had rigged up over the startled Andalusian's back. The horse turned around and looked at it and then looked at Warner. Warner said, "Yes, you're going to have to work for a change. And don't act like that pack weighs a ton. It don't." He led the horse over by a big rock so he could step up and board the horse, straddling the pack. The action reminded him, grimly, of how he'd mounted the horse out on the alkali plain.

He headed the Andalusian along the foot of the hills until he found the goat trail and then pointed him upward. Half an hour later he had both horses settled in the rock cluster. The first thing he did was take the plug of tobacco he'd found, bite off a piece, work up some tobacco juice, and then spit a big glob on his fingers. With one hand he grabbed the Andalusian by the mane and rubbed the inside of the horse's nostrils with the fingers soaked with the tobacco juice. The Andalusian jumped back and snorted. Warner kept a tight grip on him. He worked up some more juice, spit on his fingers, and gave the inside of the Andalusian's nostrils another swab. When the horse kept trying to cut up Warner said, around the cud, "Damnit, it's for a good purpose. You get wind of them horses down there and you are likely to let off your big mouth and give our position away and that will bring bullets flying. Want to get shot, you damned fool? Then hold still. This tobacco juice may not be so pleasant but it's going to keep you from smelling and getting us all in trouble."

When he was through with the Andalusian he did the same with the packhorse who liked it even less than the Andalusian had. Warner said, "I calculate neither one of you has ever used tobacco in any form in your life. Well, that's good. And if you'll lay off the strong drink as well you'll be the better for it."

After he'd doctored up the horses so they couldn't smell as well as they might have he took his big bowie knife and hacked up as much green brush as he could find and gather and threw it into the rock corral. It might not give the horses much to eat but it would give them something to worry and play with. They didn't know it but they were in for a long wait.

Finally, with dark not far off, he knocked off gathering brush and sat down to make himself a supper out of tamales and beans and a can of peaches. As he ate he reflected that he had neglected to tell Fuego what kind of sign to make when he was ready to give up the horses. He didn't dwell on the thought long. That was Fuego's lookout and he'd have to be imaginative enough to think up some way of getting word to him, Warner, that he was ready to be reasonable about the matter.

After he'd eaten, and with dark fast approaching he reassembled the Sharps rifle and got out the leather sack of shells. Charlie had been right, there was a power of them. Well, he thought, that was just as well because Fuego might turn out to be a very stubborn man. He added two boxes of the twelve-gauge buckshot shells to the leather bag and then laid the two guns side by side. He intended to take a short sleep before going to work and he calculated he could get in a good five or six hours before it was time to begin. He laid out his bedroll and made himself comfortable as the sun completely left the sky and the moon began its rise. It was a little early for him to be sleeping, but he made himself relax by thinking of how near the end of the trail he was and, soon enough, he'd dropped off.

He awoke at two A.M. and sat up immediately. First he pulled on his boots and put on his hat. Then he strapped on his gun belt, took a handful of the tortillas that were starting to get a little stale, stuffed them into a shirt pocket, and then bent for the rest of his load. He slung the big canteen over one shoulder and the strap of the leather bag containing the cartridges and shells over the other. Then, with the big Sharps rifle in one hand and the shotgun in the other, he threaded his way south along the crown of the hill some two hundred fifty yards. It put him right over the roof of Fuego's *hacienda*. He got down on his belly and crawled up to a place that looked directly down on the little cul-de-sac Fuego's *ranchero* made between the two rows of hills. It was a good firing point. As an added protection he pushed several melon-size rocks over to the edge, leaving himself a firing port between them. He doubted they were necessary. It was at least five or six hundred feet down to the roof of Fuego's house and no return fire could come from there because of the angle. The only shot that could be made at him from long distance would have to come from the buildings across the dusty span that lay between them and the main house. From there up to where he was, was better than five hundred yards. He doubted that Fuego's *pistoleros* had anything other than Winchester carbines, and damn few of them. And a carbine was no good at much over three hundred yards. Any bullets fired his way would be spent by the time they arrived. The only way they could get at him would be to get to the base of the hill and charge up it. And that was what the shotgun was for.

He took the big Sharps and sighted on the door of what he thought of as the bunkhouse. It seemed he could damn near see the latch handle. The moon was full and still high. It was, he thought, what was called a "hunter's moon." It made him smile grimly to himself. He was a hunter, all right. He was hunting horse thieves and low-down murdering bastards.

He was no longer angry. In fact, the rage and hate had left him long ago, even before he had caught Chumacho and his bunch. When he had taken Chumacho and the other two men to the alkali plain he wasn't full of hate or vengeance. He was simply going about a job he'd long ago promised himself he'd do. And now, this night, the same thing applied. He'd traced the trouble back to its source and now he intended to eliminate the source so it couldn't cause any more trouble. Warner was an uncomplicated man in that respect. He didn't cloud his judgment with a variety of emotions; he didn't see the sense in it. He just went about his business and worked until the job was done.

Now he lifted the breech of the Sharps rifle and slipped in one of the huge cartridges. He hoped the shells were still good. Some of the copper casings were starting to turn green, but that didn't mean anything. A cartridge casing could do that in a week. Besides, he'd gotten the shells from Wilson Young and that was good enough for him. He sighted down on the top of Fuego's house, smiling grimly at the picture that came to his mind of the confusion that would result when that first shell came crashing through the roof and buried itself in the floor. He did hope that the man didn't have a woman in there. But, if he did, surely he'd have sense enough to get her someplace safe because there would be more than one hole in Don Fuego's roof before the night was out.

He held the stock of the big gun tightly to his shoulder to lessen the shock of the recoil and fired. The *boom* rolled and thundered through the hills like a clap of lightning. Through the scope he'd seen the red tile go flying. He'd fired at the rear right quadrant of the house, intending on systematically working it over.

The echo of the shot was still sounding when he flipped up the breech lock, ejecting the spent casing, and inserted another cartridge. He fired again, about four feet to the left of where his first shot had gone. The same thunderous noise exploded in the quiet night. Even with his naked eye he could see how the tiles had shattered. Working quickly he reloaded and fired again. Part of his mind was on the house, but he had an eye on the bunkhouse door across the way. It was well that Fuego's men learned a lesson early and quick. He would have to kill less that way.

On his fourth shot he saw dim lights in the windows of the bunkhouse. He held his fire on the roof and sighted on the bunkhouse door. In a moment he saw it opened cautiously, partly. Then it was pulled back and a man stood there. He fired. He didn't see the man's face, just his chest as the big slug hit him and knocked him backward like the slam of a tornado. He flipped up the breech and inserted another shell and fired just as the door was being shut. He heard a scream, even at the distance. He expected splinters had flown all over the room as the heavy bullet had torn its way through the wooden door.

He quickly reloaded and fired through one of the windows. The lights went out, but not before he put another bullet through the second window. He was, as Wilson Young would have said, evening up the odds, but he was also trying to discourage the men from thinking they had any chance of getting at him.

As he swung back to the roof he saw several figures in women's clothes come fleeing out a side entrance and head for the bush at the end of the *U*. He wondered if Fuego was one of them. He was small enough to wear women's clothes, and probably a big enough coward to hide in them. But Warner wasn't going to fire into a party of women just on the off chance that Fuego might be one of them.

He was about to fire another shot into the roof when he saw a figure edging its way out from the porch roof that he had noted, that afternoon, ran all the way across the front of the big house, obviously to shade the windows from the afternoon sun. He put the scope on the figure backing his way into the clear and looking up toward the top of the hill. It was the old *mozo* and Warner reckoned he was scared to death. He wouldn't have been surprised to find out that Fuego had forced him to go out and take a look at where the firing was coming from at the point of a pistol. But, whatever the reason, he couldn't allow the old man to look his fill. He sighted at the edge of the tiles just a few feet to the right of the old man and fired. The tile exploded, sending splinters of glazed clay in every direction. He heard the old man yowl and saw him scuttle for the house.

He went back to methodically firing shots into the roof of the house, varying the interval between rounds and varying his point of aim. Then, just as he had straightened up and was swinging his right arm to keep it from stiffening up from the pounding it was taking from the kick of the Sharps, he saw a man suddenly come running from the building he thought of as the stable. He seemed to be heading for one of the little huts. Warner had half an idea he was trying to get home, get to his wife, but he still couldn't allow anyone the freedom of the common ground. He had to make them believe that so long as they stayed in the buildings, and didn't shoot back, that they'd be all right. It took him ten seconds to reload the Sharps and the man was halfway across the dusty ground from the stable to the hut he was obviously heading for. Warner sighted in on him, picking him up in the cross hairs. With the naked eye the man had just been a shadowy figure, now, looking through the scope, his face and clothes jumped out as if he were standing only a few feet from Warner. It was going to be a difficult shot because the man was running sideways to him. He led the man two feet and fired. As the butt of the rifle slammed into Warner's shoulder the bullet slammed into the man. It seemed as if he suddenly stopped running forward and jumped sideways, landing on his shoulder, and then rolling over and over. Warner put the scope on him. He had hit the man in the point of the shoulder. The shoulder had simply exploded. *Damn,* Warner thought, *this thing will thread a needle.*

Throughout the rest of the night he fired

sporadically into the roof of the house, occasionally firing a shot through the window of the bunkhouse just to let the occupants know he hadn't forgotten them. Then, just before dawn, as he was resting his head on his arm on top of one of the rocks there came a sudden burst of firing out of the windows of the bunkhouse. It was in his general direction, but he knew it was harmless. Nevertheless it put him on the alert. The firing was intended as a cover of some kind and he halfway expected to see some sort of charge toward the hill. He wasn't anxious about himself, but he was fearful that someone might somehow circle around and get to the crown of the hill and discover his horses. He was watching back toward the northwest when he suddenly saw the big door of one of the barns open and two riders come out, spurring and whipping their mounts furiously. They were coming straight at him, and, for a second, he thought they intended to try and ride up the hill. But then they began bearing away to the left, heading down the long chute away from the ranch.

The first shot was fairly easy because the rider was nearly facing him. He fired just as the man began to turn his horse to the left and the rider flipped off, almost going under the hooves of the animal running just behind.

Warner reloaded as rapidly as he could. The second shot was going to be much harder because the man was a good six hundred yards away by the time he could get reloaded and swivel around. He knelt on one knee, resting his left elbow on his thigh, and sighted on the back of the fleeing rider. He didn't know if the man was trying to save himself or was going for help. It made no difference. All he knew was that he couldn't let him get away. But he also knew, with a sinking heart that, because of the angle, if he hit the man he would probably also hit the rider's horse. He fired. Almost instantly horse and rider went down in a tangle with the rider flopping forward on his face, skidding, and then rolling to a stop. The horse kicked out a hind leg, tried to raise his head, and then lay still. The rider slowly got to all fours, crawled a few feet, and then lay back down.

Warner estimated that he had killed at least four of Fuego's men and possibly more. He knew some of them had to have been damaged by flying splinters of wood or even splinters of lead. The gunshots from the bunkhouse had ceased.

But then, at dawn, a gunshot suddenly whistled over his head. He looked down at the house. Someone, and he doubted it was Fuego, had poked a carbine through one of the big holes in the roof and was firing up at him. He aimed at a spot just under the gun barrel and fired. He was rewarded with a loud yell and the rifle disappeared.

He fired off and on until dawn, now beginning to husband his ammunition. He didn't know how stubborn Fuego was going to be so he wanted enough ammunition to last for several nights if need be. He calculated he'd fired forty rounds so far, but he'd expected to use more at first in order to get Fuego's full attention. Of course he had his own problems. His horses were going to need water sometime during the day and the trip to and from the creek would take at least an hour. It could be that sometime during that hour, some man or men that worked for Fuego could summon the courage or be driven to make a scout or a rush at his position. There was nothing Warner could do about that. The horses had to have water and he had to trust that no one would pick that particular time to get brave.

He got to thinking, later, that the bunkhouse must have a back door to it or someway to get out that he couldn't see. There was no other way to explain why the two men would have come riding out of the barn at the hour of the morning they had. He hadn't started firing until around two A.M. and they wouldn't have been in the barn then. It meant they'd slipped over there sometime during the dark hours and he'd missed them. Not that it made much difference. He didn't really care what they tried. If they tried to ride out they were dead; if they slipped over to the other hill and tried to climb up its face they were dead. He didn't give any thought to what he'd do if Fuego waved a white flag. He'd wait until that happened and then assess the situation as best he could figure it. But he doubted the little banty rooster of a man was anywhere near ready to surrender. So long as he had *vaqueros'* lives to sacrifice, he was going to be stubborn.

He was stretching his back and eating tortillas when he saw a man suddenly break out from under the porch roof of the *hacienda* and race toward the bunkhouse. It wasn't the old *mozo* and it wasn't Fuego. But he looked more like a servant than he did a *vaquero*. The move had caught Warner off guard and he grabbed up the first gun he could lay his hands on. It was the shotgun and the man had already covered fifty yards by the time he could get the gun to his shoulder. The distance was really out of the shotgun's range, but he was using buckshot and he had gravity on his side. He fired a barrel, leading the man by ten yards. It took at least three seconds for the shot to catch the man. When it hit him he suddenly jumped up in the air, spun around, and started racing back toward the *hacienda*. Warner let him have the other barrel just before he got to the porch overhang and the man jumped up in the air again and then staggered a bit and went down to all fours and crawled the last few yards. Warner doubted he was hurt very bad but he did reckon the shot had stung like the blazes.

A few minutes later he heard the sound of someone shouting—it sounded like they were under the porch overhang—across to the bunkhouse. He couldn't understand the words, but whoever was yelling sounded angry and Warner guessed it was Fuego telling his men in the bunkhouse to do something about this matter. He fired two shots into the porch roof and the yelling stopped. Then, for good measure, he put a bullet through the bunkhouse window to make sure they understood it was better for their health that they stayed put.

When it was good light he could see the damage he'd done to the roof of Fuego's house. Even though the roof was huge there were areas where the tiles were splintered and broken, exposing the wood beneath them. And in some cases, where he'd put two or three shots close together, they'd torn away the wooden lining and he could see into the house. He wondered what the occupants were thinking, what they were doing. He expected Fuego was hidden under the bed with a couple of extra mattresses piled on for good effect. From picturing the house, any house, from the inside, he couldn't think of a place that a person would be safe from such an attack from such a powerful gun.

He kept up a sporadic fire until about one in the afternoon. He didn't know if the Mexicans would keep the custom of the siesta under siege, but he intended to give them the chance. He hid the rifle and the shotgun in some brush and then hurried back and got the horses and took them as quickly as he could down to water. They wanted to graze and he let them have a few moments to eat as much grass as they could while he filled his canteen. Then he hurried back. He put the horses away and then approached his firing position with care. It was clear no one had been there.

He lay down behind his rocks and cautiously looked the situation over. All appeared as before. He loaded the big Sharps and put a shot into the house just to make sure that Don Fuego didn't get a very long afternoon nap.

The afternoon was very quiet. Occasionally there would be shouting between the bunkhouse and the *hacienda*, but a shot from the Sharps into either place usually put a quick end to the conversation. Late in the afternoon he could hear someone shouting up through one of the holes in the roof. It sounded like someone was yelling, "*Hombre! Hombre!*" as if to get his attention. But if that was the case Warner considered that Don Fuego should have been more careful to get his name so that he could address him properly rather that shouting, "Fellow! Hey, fellow!"

It was a long day. As it waned he put a succession of shots into the house, the bunkhouse, and the hut from which a few shots had been fired. Then he quickly went down to the rock corral, as he now called it, although the rocks were high enough to keep the horses from being hit by any stray shots, and looked over what he had left for supper. He was out of tortillas and tamales and down to two cans of beans and one can each of peaches and tomatoes. The matter, he thought, was going to have to get resolved pretty quickly even if it meant riddling the bunkhouse until he was sure all of Fuego's gun hands were dead. He had held off doing that, but if a conclusion had to be reached quickly that was the most likely to work.

Before he went back to his guns he cut some more brush and threw it over for the horses to gnaw at. They were another consideration. Except for a little grass by morning they would have had nothing to eat except the leaves off some mesquite trees and different kinds of weed and brush.

He wasn't worried about sleep as night started to come on again. He'd spent too many nights on herd duty where he'd learned to doze in thirty-second and one-minute snatches.

He held off eating until around seven to make the food last longer. Then he got out his knife and opened the can of beans and the tomatoes. The peaches, he figured, would go better for breakfast.

He fired all night long, but not in any set pattern. He might go an hour without a shot and then fire five in quick succession. If he wasn't going to sleep he didn't want anyone else sleeping either. He smiled to himself picturing what must be going on inside the *hacienda*. He imagined it was a shattered mess. Surely such a big, expensive house would be full of big, expensive furniture. He was willing to bet that there wasn't an object in the *hacienda* bigger than, say, a chair, that he hadn't hit. And, before it was all over, he intended to put a hole through every square yard of it. He didn't know what it cost to build a big *hacienda* in the backwoods of northern Mexico, but he bet it was considerable more than the price of five Spanish horses.

He was just thinking that it must be close to four in the morning when he heard the sound from behind him. It wasn't a big sound, but it was an unnatural noise that wasn't part of the night. There was a screen of brush just behind him and he took the shotgun by the breech and slid backward and to the side, working his way toward the end of the brush. The noise could have been made by a deer or a goat or some other animal but it had sounded like the noise a heavier animal might make, like a man in boots.

He got to the end of the screen of brush and peered around the corner. It took him a moment, looking through the small trees and bushes that populated the hillside, but he finally spotted them. There were two of them. They were about fifty yards down the slope, quartering their way toward the top, walking crouched over, but with their heads up, searching for his position on the crown of the hill. He slid the shotgun into position and covered the hammers with his left hand while he softly cocked them with his right. He made certain there were just the two of them by looking as far down and on both sides of the slope as he could. Then he watched them come on. They'd been about thirty yards away when he'd first spotted them and he let them climb the slope, awkward in their high-heeled boots. When the leader was about fifteen yards away he fired the first barrel. The blast knocked the man flat. He shot the second, who was about five yards behind the first, as he turned to run. The power of the shot at such a close range knocked the man over on his head and sent him tumbling and bouncing down the slope some three hundred feet before he hit a pine sapling and stopped. Warner watched him for a long time, seeing if he moved. He saw the man twitch and decided to play it safe. He hated to waste a cartridge, but he didn't want the man having another chance at him. The moon was down and it was dimly dark, but he could still make out the man's form through the cross hairs of the Sharps's scope. He fired once and saw the man almost lift off the ground and then settle back.

He turned and went back up to the ridge and

yelled down at the *hacienda*: "Fuego, that's two more dead! Soon it will be just you and me."

But it scared him that they had been able to get so close to him. What they'd done, he figured, was to slip out the back of the bunkhouse and make their way to the side of the hill across the way. They'd climbed up it, probably after the moon had disappeared, gone down and made their way around the rim of the *U*, and then come up his side of the hill looking for him. They would have had a fair idea of where he was, but it would have looked different once they got to the side he was on. That was what had caused them to come up the hill so short of his position. But what really scared him was that they might have overshot him and come up where his horses were. If they had he could have ended up afoot.

It made Warner decide to change his position. Taking the bag of shells, which was now considerably lighter, and with his canteen slung over his shoulder, he cradled both guns in his arms and worked his way down the ridge until he was within ten yards of his rock corral. He needn't have worried about return shots endangering his animals. Their rifles simply wouldn't carry far enough. Besides, he noted as he lay down, the new position now gave him a different firing angle which should produce some interesting results. He could see the whitewashed side of the *hacienda* and four big windows that were clearly hitable. Now he'd be able to send some glass flying around and also have slugs coming in where they might go under a bed. He smiled at how Don Fuego was going to react to this new development. Sighting carefully he fired through first one window and then another. He imagined glass was a pretty precious commodity in such a backwoods community.

But he was going to have to start being stingy with his shots. He calculated he had no more than fifty cartridges left. He did not know what he was going to do when he ran out of shells. He'd think of something when that happened. Perhaps make a big brush ball and set it on fire and roll it down on the *hacienda*. There were enough holes in the roof that some of the fire would get through. All he knew was that he wasn't leaving without the five Andalusian horses. Don Fuego was going to have to be broke of the habit of sucking eggs and stealing other people's property.

About dawn he dozed, heavily. He awoke half an hour later with the premonition, even before he opened his eyes, that something was happening, something out of the ordinary. He raised his head warily and looked down on the ranch common ground. A rider was entering the place where the rows of hills began to narrow. He was riding straight for the ranch headquarters. Warner stared at him, uncertain if some peon had carelessly wandered into his siege or if it was a trick of some kind. The man was riding bareback and appeared to be using a rope as both bridle and bit. He was wearing some kind of hide on his feet that appeared bound on with strips of leather. There was something vaguely familiar about the man. He put the scope on him, trying to see his face, but it was obscured by the big, ragged straw sombrero he was wearing. Warner aimed about ten yards in front of the horse and fired a shot into the dirt. The horse shied and stopped, but the man lifted his sombrero and smiled up at Warner. Through the scope Warner was amazed to see that it was Carlos. Carlos? The man should have been dead or a hundred miles away. And here he came riding into a situation that could easily get him killed. As he watched, Carlos kicked the horse back into motion and rode sedately on. Warner couldn't tell if he was heading for the *hacienda* or for one of the other buildings. He tracked him with the rifle, his finger inside the trigger guard. Then he veered off a little to his right and began heading for the stables. Warner took his eye from the scope and yelled, as loud as he could, *"Carlos!"*

The reply came back faintly. "Es hokay!"

Warner could see he was definitely heading for the stables, but he had no idea what his intentions were. His only choices were to wait and see what happened or to shoot him. He didn't want to shoot the man even though he'd warned him he'd kill him the next time he laid eyes on him. But he had the feeling, and it was nothing more, that he should play along, that Carlos was trying to do him a favor.

And then he heard a shout. He'd been so involved with watching Carlos that he'd forgotten all about the *hacienda*. He looked left and was startled to see Don Fuego running out in the open. He had a pistol in his hand and was shouting at Carlos. Warner quickly whipped the Sharps around and took a snap shot, fearing that Fuego was about to use the pistol on Carlos. The bullet plowed into the dirt right at Fuego's feet. All in one motion he stopped, jumped in the air, whirled around, and started running back toward the *hacienda*, dropping his pistol as he ran. Warner didn't have time to reload the Sharps so he grabbed the shotgun and fired both barrels as rapidly as he could. He knew he couldn't do the man much damage, but, about a second after each shot, Fuego would jump in the air and slap at his shoulder and chest and, on the second shot, his cheek. Warner said, aloud, "Maybe I put the bastard's eye out."

He saw Carlos look up at him, doff his sombrero, and then jump off his horse and run over and get the pistol Fuego had dropped. He stuck it in his waistband and went back to the horse and, with considerable agility for a man who'd had the feet and legs shot out from under him only three or four days past, jumped back up on the horse's back and pointed him toward the stable. As he rode he shouted something in Spanish toward the bunkhouse. Carlos had told Warner he was the head *vaquero* so he guessed he was telling his remaining men what he was going to do.

Warner watched while he opened the big door to the stables without dismounting. Then he watched as Carlos rode inside. A long time seemed to pass and then he saw the first of the Andalusians appear. He counted them as they came trotting out of the stable. The fifth one came out with Carlos right behind. He immediately cut up to their right side, bunched them, and started them up the flat valley away from the *ranchero*.

Suddenly afraid of what Fuego might do, Warner began firing as rapidly as he could into the roof tiles at the front of the house, even firing a few shots into the porch overhang.

But there were no shots and no one appeared. Carlos just sedately drove the Andalusians straight on away from the *hacienda*, toward the road at the end of the rows of hills.

Warner grabbed his gear and guns and ran in with the horses. As quickly as he could he threw the pack on the bay horse and secured it in place with the rig of ropes Charlie had devised. Then he bridled and saddled the Andalusian, all the time taking quick looks back toward the *hacienda* and the bunkhouse. Not a soul was in sight. The common ground remained as empty as it had since Warner had fired at Fuego.

He led the horses out to a clear space, mounted the Andalusian, took the packhorse on lead, and then rode along the crown of the hill, alternately watching Carlos driving the five other Andalusians and looking back to make sure there was no pursuit.

After a quarter of a mile he struck a place where the hill shallowed out enough so that he felt it was safe to point the horses toward the bottom. He stayed aboard the Andalusian, content that the slope wasn't too steep for him to carry a load down. Once at the bottom he cut sharply left along the foot of the hill and put the animals into a fast trot. He rounded the end of the hill line just as Carlos was emerging with the other horses. They met where the trail to the ranch intersected the road to El Milagro. They both stopped. Warner had the shotgun in his saddle boot and was holding the Sharps sideways across the pommel of his saddle. Warner said, "Well, I'll be a sonofabitch!"

Carlos smiled. He said, "See, I tell chou I can help you weet these horses."

Warner said, "I ain't gonna ask you how you got here or what that is you've got on your feet. Let's get these horses moving and get out of this part of the country before we stop to talk."

They drove the horses down the road to El Milagro and then cut west around the town before picking up the road on the other side. They rode until the hills began to diminish and the land became easier going. Finally, they pulled their horses up at a grassy patch near a small creek. They got down. Warner took a drink out of his canteen and then offered it to Carlos. The *vaquero* smiled and shook his head. He said, "No, you doan have to geeve me water no more. The last water you geeve me save my life."

Warner looked down at Carlos's feet. They seemed to be bound in sheepskin because he could see the fleece on the inside. He said, "Well, I reckon you're glad you didn't choose the bullet. Though I'm not even sure I would have given it to you even if you'd asked. Now you want to explain to me how the hell you come to be where you was and how come you're still alive?"

Carlos told him that he had walked out of the badlands by dark. He said, "Et was *muy difficil.* Me feet an' me legs es hurting beery bad. But I walk and I walk and I walk. And I dreenk plenty of the water. Then, that night, I see theese fire, theese campfire. And I find an old Mexican man who es herding sheep toward Mexico. He es a beery nice ol' man. An Indio. He geets all the leetle bullets out of my feet and out of my legs and he puts on sum medicines he makes heemself. Theese Indios knows about theese

366

thing. Theen he rubs on some oil es from the wool. Et got theese foony name. I doan know. An' theen he wraps my feet en theese skeens. And he gives me to eat and I lay down and sleep. Next morning I am much better."

"What the hell made you come riding into that damn fight? You could have got your ass blown clean off. You see the size of this rifle?"

Carlos smiled. He said, "Chess. I hear that sucker when I am still sum miles away." He whistled. "You shoot de chit out of Don Fuego's *hacienda*."

"But even if I didn't shoot you what made you think Fuego wouldn't?"

Carlos shrugged. He said, "Because my *vaqueros* would have keel heem first. You keel many of my *vaqueros*?"

"A few," Warner said. "Maybe seven."

Carlos said, "Well, es no trouble to geet more. Pleenty hongry peoples."

Warner looked at him. He said, "Why did you do this? Man, I left you to die. Why help me?"

Carlos shook his head. "No, you din't. You know the badlands weel not keel me when I have the water. Why did I come? I come to save Don Fuego. I know you going to geet them horses no matter what. I chust hope I geet there before you keel everybody."

Warner said, "You were worried about Don Fuego?"

Carlos looked at him like he'd lost his mind. "Heem? That *pendejo*? Cheet no. But he geet keeled es no mas *trabajo*, no work, for many *vaqueros*. Fuego *es muy importa por* the *dinero*, the money. For nothing else."

"I don't understand," Warner said. "What's a rich *caballero* like him doing living where he is?"

Carlos laughed. He said, "He es a fool, that es why. He keel an important man in *España* so they send him to Mexico City. Theen he keel a couple of important mens in Mexico City so they send heem away. Hees *padre* geeves me *dinero* to watch heem. He *es loco*."

Warner said, "You wouldn't want to go to work on a Texas ranch, would you? A horse ranch?"

"For chou?" Carlos gave him a startled look. He said, "Chou are a dangerous man, a beery dangerous man. I around you maybe four days an' how many mens chou keel? Ten, twelve, fourteen?"

Warner smiled slightly. He said, "You can go back to work for Fuego?"

"Hah!" Carlos threw back his head and laughed. "He weel beg me to help heem. The *vaqueros* doan work for heem, they work for me. An' I weel tell heem I save heem from a very hard and determined man. That es the truth too. An' he weel know et. Maybe I make heem geeve me some moneys for making you go away." Carlos laughed.

Warner put out his hand and they shook. "Well, maybe we'll run across one another some time." He turned and put a foot in the stirrup of his saddle and said, "You take it easy, Carlos."

He bunched the five Andalusians and started them out. After a few hundred yards he looked back. Carlos was still standing, watching. He raised his hand in a little salute. Carlos took off his sombrero and waved back. Then Warner turned his attention back to the five horses he was driving.

They came out of the hills and hit the flat prairie leading to the river. He was pointing the horses northeast, toward Laura Pico's ranch. He was tired and dirty and almost dead from lack of sleep but he intended to drive the horses until they were in a corral on her ranch. He calculated it was at least twenty miles, but he didn't much care. It was not quite noon and, even though he intended to take it easy and let the horses graze along the way, he figured he could make it in six hours, maybe seven. But, one way or another, he was going to have a bath and a good dinner and sleep in a bed this night with all six of the horses secure in a corral. He was too worn out to feel much elation about what he'd done or that the job was finished. Maybe, he thought, that would come later.

But even as tired as he was he couldn't help smiling about one incident of his meeting with

Carlos. As they had been talking about the miraculous way Carlos had shown up, Warner had looked curiously at the horse Carlos was riding. He was a good-looking six- or seven-year-old chestnut. Warner had said, "Where'd you get the horse?"

Carlos had said, looking heavenward, "Ah, the good God send me theese *caballo*."

Warner had pointed at the horse's flank. He'd said, "Well, God may have fixed it for the horse to be there, but it was Jim Rollins you need to thank. That horse is carrying a Rocking R brand. He's off of Jim Rollins's ranch."

A smile had slowly worked its way over Carlos's face. He said, "Chou mean—"

Warner had said, "Yes, you're still a horse thief. But don't worry about it. Keep the horse. Next time I see Jim Rollins I'll pay him for it."

Carlos had said, "Well, chou be chure you geeve him a hundred dollars. I doan like to ride no cheep horses."

# 13

Warner was sitting at the big table in Laura Pico's kitchen drinking a tumbler of whiskey with a glass of water on the side. All he was wearing was a pair of pants that had once belonged to Laura's dead husband. They were way too big for him in the waist and he had them clutched up with his belt. Laura's maid had washed the filthy clothes he'd arrived in and they were now drying on a line outside. The previous evening he had seen to the horses' care, taken a bath, shaved, ate some cold ham and biscuits, and then collapsed in Laura's bed. She'd wanted him to tell her what had happened, but he had firmly gone to sleep and slept for almost fourteen hours straight. Then he had gotten up, eaten a big breakfast of ham and half a dozen fried eggs and some biscuits. Finally he had told Laura, in broad outline, what had transpired since he'd left her ranch. Unfortunately for him, Charlie had preceded him and his lurid account had only whetted Laura's appetite.

She was sitting across from him drinking a glass of white wine. They had just finished a lunch of stew and fresh baked bread. Toward the end of the meal she had said, "Are you ever going to stop eating? My God, where are you putting it all?"

He'd pushed his plate away and called for whiskey and set himself for what he knew was going to be a long talk. She said, "You won't give me a straight answer if that fat bastard really suffered. You keep talking around it."

"My gawd, Laura," he said, "A hell of a lot has happened since then. A lot of caps got busted, a lot of gunsmoke went up in the air. Am I supposed to remember every little detail?"

She said, "Well, considering it was him you were so angry at, yes, I'd think you'd remember pretty clearly about him."

He threw up his hands. He said, "Fine! The man wandered around on the alkali for three days, screaming and begging for mercy until his voice finally give out. Then the buzzards ate him. Alive. Goddam, you are one bloodthirsty female."

"Charlie said you went back and shot him. Charlie said you went back and put a bullet between the eyes of all three that were still alive. Charlie said you were going to leave them out on the flat to suffer like you did, but that you changed your mind and went back and gave them a merciful death."

"Well, Charlie wasn't there, was he?"

"No, but he said that's what you came back and told him. Said you said something about doing the 'Christian' thing. Said you said 'whatever that was.'"

He took a sip of brandy. "How do you know I

didn't tell Charlie that to make him feel better?"

"Well, did you? I'd hate to think you let that fat bastard off easy."

"Laura, I think you can rest easy knowing he suffered like hell. I shot his legs and feet all to hell and then I roasted the soles of his feet and then he died on the alkali plain. Now I am tired of talking about all this and wish you'd give it a rest. I've been nearly two weeks on this, two weeks away from my regular work, and I'm ready to forget about it."

She said, "You can't forget about it. You're famous."

He looked at her. "Are you crazy?"

"You single-handedly killed eight bandits and you don't think that makes you famous? You laid a trap that even I thought was silly and it worked. Of course you're famous. Word is all over the county."

Warner pulled a sour look. "Well, now, that is just dandy. Goddamit! This is just what I need."

She said, "You still haven't told me exactly how you got my horses back. You sort of skimmed over it."

"There's nothing much to tell."

"Try."

He wagged his head in exasperation. "Laura," he said, "you've got your horses back. Why do you need to know how?"

"Tell me."

"Fine. I found out from one of the bandits who had your horses. He was a rich rancher in Mexico. I went over to see him and he didn't want to give me the horses back because he'd hired the fat bandit, Chumacho, to steal them. And after going to all that trouble he didn't want to give up the horses, said the Andalusian was supposed to only be ridden by noblemen or Dons or some such manure. Anyway, we argued about it and then another man came along and helped me convince him and that was that."

"You just argued?"

"Yes."

"It was four days ago that Charlie came through here and said you had gone to Mexico. Am I supposed to believe you argued for four days?"

He said sarcastically, "There was some time spent getting there and coming back. Or did you reckon me and them horses just sprouted wings and flew?"

She said, "You are undoubtedly the coldest sonofabitch I have ever met in my life."

He said, "I thought that was supposed to be your game? I thought that's what you was famous for."

She said, "Well, I have met my match. Is there a chance this Don will try and steal my horses again?"

He shook his head. "The bandit population has kind of gone down. I reckon they are a little discouraged. You ready to talk about my fee yet?"

"Your fee?"

"Yes. For retrieving your horses. You didn't figure I done that for my health, did you?"

She said, "I don't remember any talk about a fee."

He gave her a look. "We sat here and talked just as plain as day about a fee. Horses are my business. Anything I do with a horse or horses is meant to show a profit. I told you the fee would be based on the trouble I was put to. It was considerable."

She cut her eyes at him. She said, "I sort of thought you had already taken your fee?"

He gave her a disbelieving look. "In bed?" He laughed. "Hell, I'll make you a deal. I won't charge you if you don't charge me. We'll call it a warsh. How's that?"

She said, "You can't insult me. I expect that from you now. You are certainly no gentleman. Now . . . what did you have in mind in the way of a fee?"

He said casually, "Oh, I reckon I'll settle for that horse I've been riding."

She jumped up. "Paseta? You're crazy as hell!"

He yawned. "All right. Then I'll take money. Customary fee for recovering livestock is twenty-five percent. By your own mouth them horses are worth two thousand apiece. That's twelve thousand dollars. Twenty-five percent of that is three thousand. You can make me out a check."

She sat back down. She said, "Maybe I've got a better idea. I've been thinking about it ever since you rode in last evening. Why don't you stay here and help me run this operation? You're supposed to know more about horses than anyone else. We could turn out the perfect cow horse."

He laughed and said, "Laura, *you're* crazy as hell. First of all, I don't work for people. I work for myself. I got my own ranch. And if I was looking for a partner it damn sure wouldn't be you. You're just about one whip short of being bossy. But the main reason is you ain't going to accomplish a damn thing. Those Andalusian horses make as good a traveling animal as I ever sat on, but they ain't got no more cow sense than you do and that is absolutely essential in a cow horse."

She said, "They'd get it from the mares we use, the range horses. Cow sense is built into them."

He said, "Yes, there is a chance that some of the colts they throw will have a smattering, but that ain't enough. A horse can be slow and he can be clumsy, but if he's got cow sense he can work on a ranch. But I don't care how fast or how nimble or how strong or how much endurance a pony has got—if he ain't got cow sense he ain't shucks."

She said, "You just don't want to work with me."

"Of course I don't. But if you're going to breed those Andalusians then you ought to breed them the way they're pointed. Breed them to a Morgan cross or an American saddlebred. You'd bring the price down where the ordinary man could afford one and you'd have nearly as good a traveling horse as the Andalusian himself. If you'd given me that horse for my fee I was going to breed him to some Morgan mares I've got and produce what I said, a hell of a good road horse and I'll sell them right and left."

Laura was wearing a dress for a change, a short-skirted frilly yellow frock. He hadn't been able to keep from noticing what a comely woman she was. And the memory of what was under her frock was strong in his throat.

She said, "So you liked Paseta?"

"I think *that* horse done his job, yes. I don't know when I've ever rode a more responsive, nimbler animal in my life. But I don't think about liking or disliking horses. I save that for people. You like or dislike people, not horses. If a horse does his work and doesn't give me any trouble I will feed him and water him and take care of him. If he don't I either sell or trade him. You can't do that with people. It's against the law."

She made a pouting face. "You make me so damn mad I could just smack you." She got up and came around the table and put her hand on his cheek and then on the back of his neck. Her breasts were right in front of his eyes. She said, "All right, take the damn horse. You've probably ruined him for anyone else anyway."

He laughed. He said, "You mean you ain't got three thousand dollars, don't you?"

She grabbed him by the hair and shook him. "Are you going to take me to bed or not? Or do I have to wear this damn dress all day? You wouldn't wake up last night and I did everything to you I could think of."

He got up slowly. He said, "I was tired. You want me to take the rest of those Andalusians to my ranch outside of Corpus Christi and breed up some traveling horses to the Morgans and quarter horse mares I got?"

She was pressing up against him, kissing him on the neck and ear. She said, "Of course. But I'm going with them."

"Good," he said. "You'll be able to look after the place while I'm going about my business."

She said, "I'm not kidding."

"Neither am I," he said. "Neither am I." He picked her up and started down the hall toward her big bedroom in the back.


He and Wilson Young were sitting on the porch of Wilson's ranch house just across the river in Mexico. It was midmorning and Warner was drinking some lemonade Evita had fixed for him. Wilson was drinking brandy. They were sitting in wicker chairs, watching Charlie assembling the outfit. Warner had arrived the day before and they'd had plenty of time to visit. Now it was time to leave. He'd returned the big Sharps rifle and the two shotguns along with three hundred dollars in cash. Wilson had protested, but Warner had said he was in pretty good shape for money. He had insisted on writing out Wilson a bill of sale for the running horse he was holding for him on his ranch in Corpus. Wilson had been very curious about how he'd managed to get the Andalusian horse away from Laura Pico but Warner had just shrugged and said she'd preferred it to giving up reward money. Wilson had wondered if there hadn't been more to it than that. Warner had told him it was none of his business. Wilson had just smiled and said he hoped Warner didn't let Mrs. Pico's name slip around Lupita since she was pretty well taken with the young hero.

He had told Wilson as little about the recovery of the horses as he could. But while he could lie to Laura Pico he didn't have much luck with Wilson, especially after his friend had seen how few cartridges remained in the leather bag. He had whistled and said, "Whew! I bet your shoulder looks like somebody's been stomping on it. You fired way over a hundred cartridges. That must have been some siege you laid on that *caballero*. I bet he was sick of the sight of you.

You still going to claim you didn't get no actual count on the number you left fast asleep?"

Warner had said he didn't know for certain and really didn't care. "Look, I had a job. I was angry at first, then I wasn't, but the job still had to get done. Some folks tried to get in the way of me doing that job and I dealt with them as I had to. That's all there is to it. All there'll ever be to it."

Now they were sitting comfortably, having one last drink together before Warner pulled out. Wilson said, "Warner?"

"What?"

"You recall asking me several times what it felt like to be Wilson Young?"

"Yes. So what?"

Wilson said softly, "Well, now you'll be able to find out for yourself."

Warner frowned. "What the hell are you talking about?"

"About you, about the bandit killer. About the man who went up against odds of twenty to one and come out the winner. About the hero who saved this part of the country from hordes of bloodthirsty *bandidos*."

Warner couldn't help but think of what Laura Pico had said. He said, "Where are you getting this bullshit?"

"From everywhere. If you haven't heard it it's because you ain't been around nobody."

Warner pulled a face. He said, "Aw, cut it out, Wilson. It ain't funny."

Wilson said steadily, "I ain't kidding, kid. You'll find out what it's like to be Warner Grayson."

Warner gave him a strange look, then stood up. He yelled, "Charlie! Hurry up! We got to get to making tracks."

He picked up his glass of lemonade and looked around to say good-bye to Evita. She wasn't in sight. He said, to Wilson, "I'll get your horse to you as quick as I get home."

Wilson rose and said, "No rush. I still think you sold him to me too cheap."

"Hell, Wilson, I reckon I ought to know. I'm in the horse business."

Wilson smiled slowly. He said, "You're also in the gun business."

He ignored the remark and put out his hand. They shook and Warner thanked his friend for all his help. "I'll be seeing you. You take it slow."

He was walking away when he heard Wilson call his name. He stopped and looked back. "What?"

Wilson said, "Remember I told you I practiced every day?"

"Yeah?"

"You was surprised."

"Yeah."

"Was I you I'd do the same. Stay in practice, Warner. Your life ain't never going to be the same again."

He gave Wilson a long look, started to say something, changed his mind, and walked toward where Charlie was waiting. Before he mounted the Andalusian he called out to Wilson. "What can I do about it?"

Wilson said, "Nothing. It's too late. Just remember not to hesitate."

He nodded his head and mounted the Spanish horse and then rode out with Charlie following with the wagon.

# About the Author

Giles Tippette is a Texan by birth and by choice. A full-time writer since 1966, he has also been a rodeo cowboy, a Mexican gold mine owner, a diamond courier, a mercenary pilot, a private investigator, a reporter for *Sports Illustrated*, and was scouted by the St. Louis Cardinals (but claims he couldn't hit the curveball). In addition to his books, he writes articles for various magazines, including *Time*, *Newsweek*, *Sports Illustrated* and *Texas Monthly*. He lives with his wife, Betsyanne, in Corpus Christi, Texas.

**Center Point Large Print**
600 Brooks Road / PO Box 1
Thorndike, ME 04986-0001 USA

(207) 568-3717

US & Canada:
1 800 929-9108
www.centerpointlargeprint.com